I'll See You Again!

I'll See You Again!

Myron S. Augsburger

HERALD PRESS
Scottdale, Pennsylvania
Kitchener, Ontario

Library of Congress Cataloging-in-Publication Data

Augsburger, Myron S.
    I'll see you again!

    1. Manz, Felix, 1500-1527—Fiction.   2. Anabaptists—
Switzerland—Fiction.   I. Title.
PS3551.U387I45   1989   813'.54   88-31997
ISBN 0-8361-3489-3

The paper used in this publication meets the minimum requirements of
American National Standard for Information Sciences—Permanence of
Paper for Printed Library Materials, ANSI Z39.48-1984.

To Caitlin

Contents

Author's Preface

This is a historical novel on one of the lesser-known but important figures of the sixteenth-century Reformation of the church. The left wing of the Reformation was called "Anabaptist," a term meaning rebaptizers. The name stems from the actions of this group in instituting an adult, believer's baptism where before there had been only infant baptism. But beyond the question of baptism was the larger issue of personal faith in Christ as Lord. And while baptism itself was important, it was, for these believers, only a "sign" of this new, personal faith in Christ.

The early leaders of the group were Conrad Grebel and Felix Manz, who were joined by George Blaurock, Michael Sattler, and many others. Harold Bender describes their vision as having three essential elements: the discovery of the Christian life as discipleship, the recognition that the church is a voluntary fellowship of the reborn, and the conviction of love as a lifestyle.

Felix Manz was one of the colorful figures of the movement, although he only lived about three years after his conversion. In 1527 he was the first martyr in Zurich at the hands of the Protestants, yet he helped to shape the basic beliefs of the free-church movement.

While the first three chapters are largely fiction, the remaining chapters are supported by careful historical research. I have tried to make the account as historically correct as possible. I have worked from the premise that Paul Peachey is correct in saying that Felix Manz was one year older than Zwingli (*Die soziale Herkunft der Schweizer Täufer in der Reformationszeit*). This allowed me to make some assumptions about involvements in the early chapters, assumptions which Ekkehard Krajewski only suggests as questions in his work, *Leben und Sterben des Züricher Täuferführers Felix Mantz*, Kassel, 1957. It also permits me appropriately to emphasize the interrelationship of the early Anabaptists with the humanism which was enriching the culture of the day. Also, while there was actually a Trini Hottinger living in Zollikon, there is no evidence of a friendship between her and Felix of the type I have created in this story.

Beyond the first three chapters and this romance, the historical character of the life and work of Felix Manz is based on the best sources available. These include, among many secondary sources, the significant primary source *Quellen zur Geschichte der Täufer in der Schweiz*, Vol. 2, by Heinold Fast, Zurich, 1973; and *The Sources of Swiss Anabaptism*, edited by Leland Harder, Herald Press, 1985, abbreviated here as *SSA*.

I want to express my appreciation to Pam Harmon of the Washington Community Fellowship for typing the early drafts of this manuscript, and to Melissa Aberle and Barbara Connell of the same Fellowship for reading the manuscript and making helpful editorial suggestions. I want to thank Leonard Gross of the Mennonite Historical Library, Goshen, Indiana, for reading an early draft and making helpful suggestions. But above all, I would like to give special recognition to the significant work of my daughter, Marcia A. Kincannon, for editing, stylistic improvements, and for the creative enrichment of the story by her descriptive expansions at many places in the narrative—a creative contribution without which the reading would be far less interesting.

This book is an authentic expression of the little-understood history of the free-church movement of the sixteenth century known as Anabaptist, the root of the faith of the Mennonite, Hutterite, Amish, Brethren, and Baptist churches.

It is my sincere hope and prayer that those who read this story will be as inspired by the faith in Christ which transformed the life of Felix Manz as I have been in the research and writing of his story.

—Myron S. Augsburger
Washington, D.C.

Chapter 1

Life by the Limmat

He sat with his hands clasped around folded legs, chin on his knees. The water of the Limmat was black-green and fast-moving. Felix Manz threw back his head and sighed. Light brown hair waved and brushed his broad shoulders. He unclasped his long fingers, placing his hands on the ground behind him as he leaned back, gazing into the blue sky. One didn't often have to make a decision that would directly affect the rest of his life, he thought.

Several years before, when Felix enlisted as a soldier, he had had no inclination that the military might become his career. Being a soldier was not an unpopular occupation for a Swiss citizen. Now, however, he wanted to study, to develop his mind rather than his muscles. But just the day before, Felix had been confronted and asked to join the Swiss guard.

Yesterday, as he passed through the marketplace, returning from his early walk, he had met the papal legate from Rome. He was in Zurich to secure soldiers whose assignment would be to protect the pope. The role would no doubt be an honorable position, not dangerous in the way that military work could be, and paying well. Money, or the lack of it, had always made decisions for him, thought Felix with resentment. Now, once again, his wish to pursue university training depended on receiving a stipend. This, he knew, was almost impossible without a sponsor. One was never allowed to break free of one's background.

Felix thought back to the application he had been required to render for military service, recalling the space that asked for the description of his parentage. "Mother: concubine...." There was never enough room to write about the sacrificial spirit and loving attention with which his mother had shaped his life and the life of his younger brother, Heinrich. Never enough room to write about the support and encouragement his father had given him.

The young man by the dock sat motionless; only his barrel chest moved in and out with his breathing. His stare moved beyond the busy workers to scan the horizon. The spires of the city cathedral, the Grossmünster, jutted up from the cityscape. How familiar the architecture was to him. East of the Grossmünster was his mother's home, where as a child he had roamed the narrow cobblestone streets. He had played by the fountain in the open court of the great church, and sang in the boys' choir for the worship service. He had always known of his mother's situation and had always felt the pull between shame and pride. His mother, Anna, had taught him to overcome his insecurity, to strive for his dreams, to achieve, in spite of the prejudices of their society.

For years she had worked at the Great Church, cleaning and doing hard labor. Her hands told of it. Felix hated to see her drag herself home each night, exhausted, a weak smile on her face, her blond hair limply hanging across one eye. But he knew that although the work at the Grossmünster was difficult with little reward, it was the only way Anna Manz, as she called herself even though it was not and could not be her legal name, was able to be near the father of her sons.

Hanz Mans, Felix's father, was the chief choirmaster in the Grossmünster and, as a good Catholic minister, was enjoined by the church to live a celibate life. But Hans Manz had fallen in love. And, as Felix had learned, by paying an annual fee of four gulden to Bishop Hugo of Constance, Hans Manz along with hundreds of other priests could have a concubine. It was the only way to satisfy both his call and his desire for intimacy.

14

Felix and Heinrich knew that their father wanted to be with them, to have a normal family life. He gave them what he could: educational opportunity, counsel, encouragement, and most importantly he did give them his love. From him, Felix had inherited a special ear for music and a keen mind. His father's gift had enabled Felix to participate in the choir and, as a very young man, give vocal solo presentations. His mother's gifts, a sincere spirit and gracious manner, had helped him to develop and enjoy many strong friendships. She always insisted that only kindness and charm would overcome prejudice. He could even now hear her saying, "What you are determines who you are."

Both of his parents had contributed to his strong sense of worth. His name, Felix, had been chosen to give him a special identity. Centuries before, Felix and Regula, a brother and sister of Thebes, had come to the region spreading the gospel in the first centuries of the church. Emperor Maximilian had them arrested, tortured, and beheaded on an island somewhere up the river from where Felix Manz now sat. The man for whom he had been named had influenced many persons and he had always felt that he would do the same.

Yes, Felix thought as he picked out a pebble and threw it into the river watching the white tips of the waves swallow it, I have talents and skills that are suited for higher learning, not for some mindless job as a stone-faced guard in Rome.

At seven years of age, Felix had been entered in the Carolina School at the Grossmünster. It was an excellent Latin school named after Charles the Great, the eighth-century Frankish king known as Charlemagne. The school met in the canon house on the northwest side of the Chorherrnplatz surrounding the great cathedral. For six years he had been a diligent student, excelling as one of the best in the school. The areas of study in which he concentrated were Latin grammar and literature and dialectic, to develop the art of disputing.

The other boys did not make fun of him or taunt him about his parentage although he always expected them to. He often

15

thought he saw in their faces a smugness toward him. Perhaps this was what made him try so hard to succeed. Whether the prejudice existed or not, it served as a goad to Felix, spurring him on. The truth was, he found later, that he was well-liked and admired for his thoughtfulness and keen mind, regardless of his background.

He completed his work at the Carolina School with high honors and his graduation day was the happiest in his life, although at that point his future had been uncertain. After the ceremony the schoolmaster had come to him.

"Felix, you have been a fine student and an influence for the good to those around you."

The rare compliment came as a surprise and Felix swallowed the lump in his throat.

"Thank you, master."

"What are your plans now?"

"I'm afraid that I have none, sir." Felix lowered his eyes.

"Then I will ask you to stay and assist me as a proctor."

Had he heard correctly? If so, it would be the one answer to all his questions. It would be the opportunity he craved to stay around the school and be near one whom he greatly admired. If so, the day could not have been better.

"Do you mean you want me to stay on? To teach here?" He spoke too loudly in his excitement and the schoolmaster smiled, also a rarity.

"Yes, that is what I mean," he said. "Then you'll stay?"

"Oh, yes, sir. Yes, sir, and I'm very honored, sir!" Felix turned quickly and ran to find his mother. As he darted off he stopped, embarrassed at his poor manners. He had forgotten to bow before leaving his teacher's presence. He turned to correct his behavior but the man had gone. He had forgiven Felix this time.

Those had been good years: years that had given him self-confidence, years that had built in him qualities of leadership and strength, years that had given him pride. Now, he knew he could go further. He wanted to pursue university studies, especially in

16

Latin and Greek. His heart fluttered as he thought of the challenge of conquering those difficult languages and adrenaline seemed to propel him to his feet.

The town clock suddenly broke into his thought as it struck with nine reverberating tones. He knew that this would be the best time to visit the school. Some of his former students would be there, certainly the schoolmaster. Felix's hands went into his pockets stretching his pants as he walked the path beside the river, still staring into the water as though he were expecting an answer to float to the top.

He had scarcely entered the doorway of the school when the familiar voice called to him, "Master Felix! Welcome back. We've missed you."

Felix looked into the smiling face of Conrad Grebel, a former student, no longer a lad, but now a young man. Grebel was about the same height as Felix, but with dark hair in contrast to his own light brown locks.

"How good to see you, Conrad." Glancing at the others with Grebel he added, "I've missed you fellows. How are you?"

"It is the same here; nothing changes," Conrad laughed.

Felix well remembered his first meeting with Grebel. While Felix was proctor the young student had come to them from the castle at Grüningen. Conrad's father, Jakob Grebel, was a Zurich senator and a member of the highest Zurich Council. Conrad brought the aristocratic airs of his background with him into the school. At first, Felix had envied the young man, and even resented his precocious manners. But as the weeks went by he came to appreciate the quick mind which the young Grebel evidenced, and he respected the fact that Conrad was achieving in his own right and not simply riding on the reputation of his father. Perhaps to retreat from that prestige, he was something of a playboy. Felix could even now see the mischievous twinkle in his eye.

"What are your plans, Conrad?"

"I hope to go to Basel and study at the university. From what I hear, they have a very strong program in philosophy, languages, and riotous behavior!"

"Ah, Conrad, I see that time hasn't tamed you." Felix remembered his feelings when it was his responsibility to monitor the boys. He had found himself on many occasions settling disputes between students and trying to motivate them to more serious study. It was an irritation to him at that time: their perpetual card playing, their games of violence with knives, daggers, and even the short swords with which they delighted in seeking to dominate each other. It was ironic how he could now look back on it so lightly.

"How was your service in the military, Master Felix?" Grebel wanted to know.

"Rigorous; very demanding. Quite physical for one who would rather be a scholar."

"Perhaps we will meet again at the Basel University," Conrad said and shook Felix's hand vigorously as he took his leave.

The several reunions at the Carolina School that day were warm and there were many questions about Felix's future plans. The day was as he had hoped it would be and he left feeling good. The schoolmaster though older was, Felix could tell, as sharp as ever. "You will have your dream and continue your studies, Felix. You must! One so gifted as you will find a way," he said.

Felix made his way down the street to the Grossmünster, for some reason impelled to find his father. When finally they could talk, Felix let it all out. Hans Manz listened with deep interest.

"Felix," he said. "You must have an opportunity for university study. You have the intellect and the discipline to achieve. I will do my best to find some way to get you a stipend for such study."

"But, Herr Manz," Felix hesitated to call him father, "that may take quite some time."

"Yes, it could be a year or two until your name would come up for consideration, but there are other things you can do meanwhile."

18

"Such as?" Felix's tone revealed his discouragement.

"Well, you could go back to tutorial work in Latin. You are good at that."

"Yes, I suppose I could but," he paused, looking at his father, "there is another possibility I would like to ask you about."

"Yes, what is that?"

"The legate from Rome is here contacting soldiers who have returned from their service. He is inviting us to join the Swiss guard in Rome."

"That would be quite an honor," the father leaned toward his son. "And it could be just the service you need at this point."

"But it involves another two years of my life, at least."

Felix's father, recognizing the urgency of youth, the feeling that life was too short to do everything that it offered, mused as though to himself.

"But life can be enjoyed while you are in the service," he said. "It is not as though you must live only for the future."

"I know that," said Felix. "But what are the advantages of being a part of the Swiss guard, especially of being in Rome? You have been in Rome. What would it have to offer me?"

"You will have many opportunities, being exposed to all the best in the holy city. Guarding the pope will take only part of your time. There is much that you can learn while there. Not only that, Felix, but you can build your own reputation and identity and return with credentials from the papal legate in Rome." Hans pulled his shoulders back and raised his head showing pride when he said these words, but then his body drooped and he hung his head. "Perhaps by this you can surmount the limitation of always being known as … as an illegitimate son of the choirmaster at Zurich."

Felix looked at the pain behind his father's eyes. He saw what he had suffered, being locked into the structure of the church in a way that had robbed him of the freedom to enjoy a marriage and a family. Felix had become a man in the military—enough of a man to put his arms around his father and embrace him, tightly.

Without further words, he left his father for a hike to Zollikon along the Zurich Sea. He wanted to talk with an old friend, Felix Kienast, with whom he had formed a close relationship during his studies at the Carolina School. The sun was high overhead and the air invigorating. Felix enjoyed the sights of farms and orchards on the slopes along the north side of the sea. Kienast was excited to see him again, and they grasped each other's shoulders with the warmth of old friends. As Felix told him about the possiblity of going to Rome his friend was exuberant.

"Can't you just see yourself in the red and yellow uniform designed by Michelangelo himself?"

"Michelangelo?" Felix was surprised.

"Yes, didn't you know? He designed them for the Swiss guard. And the women you will attract! They fall all over soldiers, you know." His friend punched him playfully in the ribs. "Think of the glory, the excitement!"

"But Felix," after years of friendship it still felt strange to address another using his own name. "I want to go to school. This is an interruption in my life."

"Oh, you can learn much in Rome, surely more than a dusty old professor could teach you. Rome is the fine arts capital of the world!"

"True," agreed Manz. "I could study in Latin and continue to enrich my language facility." He was starting to see the advantages, and his voice expressed a new enthusiasm.

"Of course you can. And who knows but what you can also pursue studies in Greek or Hebrew at the papal school. I think you should do this, Felix. Go today and tell the legate that you are ready to enroll."

Felix Manz looked at his friend. Kienast had been almost flippant with his advice, but Manz knew that the young man was sincere with his words, even if his tone was lighthearted.

As Felix walked back from Zollikon, he thought about how to break the news to his mother. She was always supportive, always encouraging him to try new things, to take every advantage. But

20

Felix hated leaving her alone again. He was the oldest son and her support.

He stopped by the lake, pausing to study two swans floating gracefully on the water. They arched their necks and raised their wings in protest when he came too near their chosen area. This was apparently their nesting site. He backed away and watched their artistic communication. They faced each other, lifting their long necks and placing their heads side by side, then reversing the position as if they were saying, "You are mine and I am yours." Swans mate for life, Felix knew. How wonderful it would be to have the privilege of belonging to another and having another who belonged to him. Earlier, when he met Felix Kienast, there had been a girl.

He had met his friend at the home of Conrad Hottinger, where Kienast worked. Trini Hottinger, Conrad's daughter, was flitting around the house, at work with the others. He could still hear her laughter and see her smiling eyes. She was beautiful and her dark hair bounced on her shoulders as she moved. Once, he was certain that when he looked at her she was watching him and appeared to blush as she turned away. Perhaps, perhaps after Rome he might try to get acquainted with her.

Chapter 2

Rome and the Swiss Guard

The column of soldiers left Zurich, riding south toward Luzern, then taking the route along the lakes. They were on the way to Rome, boisterous in their gaiety, singing with strong masculine tones as they rode along. The legate had come north with Swiss guardsmen who had completed their term of service and had recruited an equal number of persons to take their place. The row of men and horses moved readily along the roads and paths, almost as if they were on a lazy patrol, with no real place to go. The journey was long and there was no reason for hurry.

Felix could tell the difference between the soldiers who had had experience and those who had not. Their posture and even their vocabulary identified them. As the hours passed, the men became more silent, their weariness reflected in their mood.

"We'll not worry ourselves with training these men until we reach Rome," Felix overheard one of the commanders say. "Then we'll whip them into shape soon enough." Felix smiled ruefully, knowing what that meant.

Felix passed the time by searching the scenery and watching the people. The land rolled into the skyscape on all sides of him: farmland, tilled in even rows now green with vegetables, wheat fields, hay, or vineyards. How the farmers kept the fields so symmetrical, so neat! It was amazing. His admiration for those who tended the earth, sometimes considered peasants, grew with the passing of each plot. The cattle were fat and their brown and white coats shone. It made Felix feel content, as though the economy were safe enough. As they passed the farms, the house and barn combination buildings, a steaming pile of cow manure in front of the barn would tell something of the size of the herd and the wealth of the farmer. Even the smallest pile, Felix noticed, was as proudly and neatly displayed as the largest. The cheerful smiles and chatter of the young women around the houses matched the blooming flowers in the window boxes and the bright, crisp curtains at the windows.

"Did you come from a farm?" asked the rider to his left, noticing his interest. Felix laughed.

"The only dirt that has been on my hands is that which comes from city streets," he said. "You?"

"No, I've spent most of my life behind a school desk."

"Felix Manz is my name." He reached out his hand.

"Hans Spicher."

"We should be getting into the higher elevations soon and into some narrow passes, I understand."

"I'll be glad when we get back to civilization," Hans complained but added, with humor, "That is, my backside will be glad!"

In the next days they left the farmlands behind and the mountains swallowed the column of mounted men. The climbing was more rigorous, for both horse and rider, than Felix had expected. Hour after hour there was only the monotonous sound of the plodding of the horse's hooves on the ground and the creak of the saddle leather. Once in awhile, at a clearing, he could look over the valley below, spread out in greens and browns with yellow patches of sun and shapes of gray on the land where the clouds cast shadows. Felix felt that he missed a lot of the scenery because the passage on the mountain path now took his full concentration. He was pleased to be near the front of the row of

23

soldiers; it made him feel more comfortable to be near the leaders, and the legate was well informed, pointing out historic sights as they made their way.

"That's Mount Pilatus," he said. "Legend has it that Pilate spent the last years of his life, exiled to this area by Caesar, following the crucifixion of Christ in Jerusalem." He told of the unusual faithfulness of Pilate's wife in coming with her husband and standing by him to the end.

As they journeyed south, their vantage in the higher altitudes allowed them a spectacular view: at times they could see the Jungfrau rearing its majestic peak into the sky. When it was visible, they would pause to view the beautiful snowcapped mountain, a symbol of strength that marked the land which they loved. The air, though thinner, was cold and refreshing. Felix enjoyed the exhilaration of the heights and the panorama of snowy peaks. Still, it was a relief to come out of the mountains and be traveling over less rugged ground again. Just the change itself was refreshing, and they were headed to Milan where they would change horses. Also, they would be given at least a day to rest before continuing their journey to Rome.

To think of spending time in this famous city excited Felix. He soon found himself acting as interpreter of the fine arts to the group, telling them of some of the things to be seen in Milan. However, in this group of soldiers he did not find many who responded with interest.

Once settled in at the Milan barracks, Felix and Hans took to the streets trying to see as much as they could in one day. The high point was their visit to the dining hall of Santa Maria delle Grazie, on a wall of which Leonardo da Vinci had painted "The Last Supper." For a long time they stood gazing at the face of Christ and at the twelve apostles, noting the positions in which the artist had placed them. Their postures and facial expressions told the story.

By the time they left Milan, Felix and Hans were planning their stop in Florence. While the legate seemed to be more hurried

24

now, they approached him with a request that they spend at least a day in Florence to enable them to view some of the works by various artists. They especially wanted to see more of the works of Leonardo da Vinci and of the younger artist who had studied under him, Michelangelo. The legate seemed pleased to have men in his command who were more than guts and brawn; he consented to spread the journey out by a few hours.

Their excitement grew as they approached Florence, its red-tile roofs visible from a good distance. Felix and Hans had a whirlwind tour, fairly running from one famed spot to another. The legate had told them to call at the home of Giocondo, the leading merchant of Florence, if they wanted to see one of Leonardo's great portraits. Several years earlier Giocondo had employed da Vinci to do a portrait of his wife. Here, they found that being recruits for the Swiss guard was an advantage, for while they were unknown, they were given gracious entrance by the servant and soon stood before the painting, "La Gioconda," the painting which later came to be known as the "Mona Lisa."

"What do you think she is smiling about?" Hans whispered.

"Perhaps the merchant would like to know the answer to that as well," Felix said behind his hand.

"Well, it is, no doubt, her secret and will remain so," Hans smiled.

The servant must have overheard their conversation for as he showed them to the door he said, "Your question of her smile is one that everyone asks when standing before the painting."

"We will not forget it," Felix assured him. "Thank you so very much for your kindness."

The works of Michelangelo were easy to find. He had become a sculptor and although this was not as popular as painting, the sculptures that he had produced were so impressive that everyone knew of them. If they stood in awe before Leonardo da Vinci's paintings, they were overwhelmed by the realistic, larger-than-life statues created by Michelangelo. His prisoners in stone were communicating meanings that drew them into quiet contemplation. As they stood in front of the eighteen-foot marble "David" done ten years earlier, Felix was amazed at the beauty, the youthful yet majestic form, and the expression of strength and honesty embodied in the sculpture. Even when he stood gazing at Michelangelo's "Pieta," he could not forget the amazing skills of the artist expressed in the one figure of David. It was time to return to the barracks, but Felix said to Hans, "I want to go back one more time to see the 'David.' "

It was good that the horse on which Felix rode was a follower or it would not have know where to go. As they rode into Rome, Felix was searching every building and fountain, trying to see each minute detail. The architecture was so different from Switzerland. Ornate pillars with scrollwork dominated the facades. The marble and granite were symbolic of the strength that Rome was, again. Each street exuded a love of art, and Felix immediately knew that he would like it here.

With so much to do, Felix was now certain that the two years in Rome would go by rapidly. He soon found himself too busy. He entered enthusiastically into the discipline and drill of the Swiss guard, and found himself enjoying the training and the regimen. The red and yellow uniform about which he and Felix Kienast had talked was striking, and he received special attention as a guard of the pope himself. In the past, there had been a representation of soldiers from all over Switzerland, but since Pope Julius II had secured a treaty with the Swiss cantons of Zurich and Luzern, most of the guard now came from these two areas. Felix was relieved to find so many with whom he had much in common.

During his first day off he enrolled in the papal school. To his great pleasure he was able to pursue study in Greek and Hebrew. When he wasn't touring the city he was working on one language or the other. As soon as he felt comfortable with his job as a soldier, he carried notes with him so that he could be memorizing vocabulary words while he guarded secluded doorways, pieces of art, jewels, or old books. There were times when he stood by during an official dinner or a gathering of dignitaries from church and state, and he could not study. At these times Felix found himself becoming the most tired. It was exhausting to put on the best form and be "seen but not seen." He was usually not close enough to hear the conversation and the buzzing of muted voices was irritating.

Without question, Felix's favorite place to guard or to visit was the Cistine Chapel. During his second year, Michelangelo himself came to work with the paints, high on the ceiling and upper walls of the inner sanctuary. (Pope Leo X some years later would commission Michelangelo as well as many other artists, including Raphael and Bramante, to design the new church of St. Peter, which was to become the center of the buildings of the Vatican.)

When on guard at the Cistine Chapel, Felix would always position himself so that he could overhear Michelangelo as he grumbled to himself with frustration or gasped with a new idea. Often, Pope Leo X walked around in the large room, his fists on his hips, looking up and circling around and around. One day, Felix overheard a conversation between the two.

"Michelangelo, your colors are too dull."

"But, Your Grace," Michelangelo responded with seeming patience, "I want you to look at the figures, at the story, not at the beautiful colors. And besides, dull or not, they are my colors."

"Speaking of the figures," complained the pope, "do you not think that God looks too human?"

"Would you like to climb up here and paint him as you see him? And perhaps then the guard over there would like to paint his impression of God and soon we would have paintings of God all over the ceiling and my work would be finished!"

Felix, seeing that Michelangelo had pointed his brush at him, was pleased that the artist had at least recognized his presence. His professionally trained face cracked into a pinched smile. The artist and the pope had heated arguments often, but Felix knew that each of them held a great deal of respect for the other. He suspected that it was somewhat of a relief to Pope Leo X to have someone he could challenge, someone who was not afraid to talk back to him.

When the pope left that day, Michelangelo chuckled and from his perch on the scaffolding told a story, almost for anyone to hear, but Felix was close by and so dared to think that the artist was talking to him.

"I am reminded of the day when I was just finishing the sculpture of David in Florence," he began, still painting the face of one of the figures. Felix wanted to say, "Oh, yes, I have seen it," but he kept his place and looked straight ahead.

"The duke came in and stood there in the marble dust looking at the sculpture, exuding pride in his pompous stule. Suddenly he said, 'I think his nose is too long.'"

Michelangelo dabbed more paint from his palate and continued, a smile in his voice. "Without a word I rearranged the ladder, scooped up my hammer and chisel in one hand, a handful of marble chips and dust in the other, and crawled up to the face of David. Reaching out with the chisel and hammer I acted as if I were chipping on the nose, at the same time dropping some of the chips and dust which I held in my hand. After a few moments, I drew back as though I had now finished my work and asked the duke, 'How is that?' The duke cried, 'That is better, much better, much better!' I crawled down the ladder and laid the hammer and chisel down, took off my apron and walked out of the room without his ever knowing that I had not touched the nose."

Michelangelo let out a laugh that reverberated throughout the chapel and continued with his work.

That evening, Felix told Hans the stories of the day and they both laughed heartily.

"I too have a story you will enjoy," Hans said. "I overheard Leonardo da Vinci talking to someone today. The man told him that he had been in Milan to see his wonderful painting of 'The Last Supper,' as well as to see 'La Gioconda' in Florence."

Felix nodded, remembering both pieces clearly, as Hans continued.

"Da Vinci raised his eyebrows and smiled. 'And what did you think of them?' The man said, 'Both impressed me in a way that I shall never forget. I was especially struck by the painting of The Last Supper.' Da Vinci kept asking what impressed him most. He said that he was amazed by the expression, first in the face of our Lord, also in all of the apostles' faces, and the way in which da Vinci had them arranged. He felt that the painting showed the interaction of the group that Jesus had drawn around himself for his mission. Da Vinci said, 'Thank you for such astute comments. You have an artist's mind. You will understand my story.'

He paused a moment, then continued, 'While doing the painting of The Last Supper, I had painted two realistic silver goblets on the table. One day the merchant Giocondo, from Florence, came to see me about painting the portrait of his wife. Observing the painting on which I was working, he made comment about the beauty and design of those silver goblets. I grabbed my brush and quickly painted them both out. I turned to the amazed merchant and said, 'It is the face I want you to see, his face, not the goblets!' "

That night as Felix lay on his cot trying to sleep, the words he had heard that day rang over and over in his mind.

"It is the face I want you to see, his face. . . . "

As Felix reflected over his time spent in Rome, he realized he had not really seen the face of Christ. He had seen the silver goblets, the gathering of riches and wealth from all across Europe, but the face of Jesus had somehow been eclipsed. Where was the message of Christ? Was it in the church, structured as it was into the church-state? Felix shook his head. He had seen how the church-state operated, ruled by its own corrupt desire for wealth and power. Surely that was not the expression of Christ. Was Christ to be seen in Rome, or heard in the words of the pope? They were eloquent words, surely enough. But they hardly spoke of the peace of God, of feeding the poor, of loving enemies, of serving one's neighbor. Perhaps, Felix thought ruefully, Christ was best seen in the work of the artists.

29

Chapter 3

Study and Trini

"You have done a lot in the last two years," Felix's mother was saying. He looked across the table into her warm eyes, feeling the comfort of being back at home in Zurich.

"Yes, I'm so pleased that I was able to study while in Rome, especially the languages, as I had hoped. Since I've been home, everyone has praised me for having been a member of the Swiss guard," his voice was somewhat sarcastic, "but, you know, that was incidental. What will live on for me will be my language studies and my exposure to art, and all its meaning. Mother, I have a more clear purpose now." Felix's eyes were bright. "I'm ready for university study."

Anna Manz smiled and nodded, but Felix could see that her face was blank. She didn't fully share his passion for study nor his inner drive to achieve. They had been living in different worlds. She moved to attend the kettle, for the stew she was preparing for dinner had started to boil. She stirred it and when she put down the spoon, Felix went to his mother and embraced her. It was good to be home and for a moment the years fell away and he was a young boy again, feeling her comfort. His mother's face was wrinkled with the lines of increased years, but her love was the same.

"Felix!" The exuberant shout came from his younger brother. There was an awkward hesitation while each decided how to greet the other in a way befitting a man, and then, a firm handshake and a clasp of opposite shoulders.

"Heinrich, you're as tall as me!" Felix exclaimed, "and more robust."

"That will make it easier to beat you at wrestling," Heinrich said and laughed, throwing his arm around his brother's shoulder and locking his head in the crook of his elbow.

"Oh, we'll see about that," Felix gently punched his fist into Heinrich's stomach before they broke apart. Their mother watched out of the corner of her eye as she went about tending to the stew. Her smile showed pleasure at having both of her boys home. She seemed relieved that they had outgrown their need for her control and she could simply enjoy them.

"How are your studies at the Carolina School?" Felix asked.

"Oh, Felix," Heinrich groaned in a young man's tone, "there is too much work."

"What do you expect, if you're going to grow?" Felix asked smiling. "And what do you want to do?" he added. "Are you interested in music?" It almost seemed logical that he would be, since their father was so involved.

"No, it's too complicated—diatonic this and chromatic that. I have lots of other interests."

"Well, there is plenty of time, Heinrich."

"Yes, I suppose so," said the boy. Felix could tell by his expression that at his age, he didn't care whether there was plenty of time or not.

On the day after his return when they had just finished the evening meal, Felix's father came to the house for the evening. As always, their pleasantries were somewhat strained.

"And now, Felix, what is next?" asked Hans Manz. "You are still counting on university study?"

"I am more determined than ever." Felix passed the bowl of boiled cabbage to his brother. "I have saved considerable funds to help me through a year of study, perhaps two."

"That is excellent," his mother joined the conversation. Felix was suddenly aware that the circle of people around the table represented what might have been a family if the orders of the church had allowed his father to enter into matrimony.

"And where do you hope to go?" continued Hans. "Are you still dreaming of Vienna, or will it be Basel?"

"That I do not know," Felix answered. "What is your opinion?"

"There is a studious young man at the Carolina School by the name of Jörg Binder. You may remember him, although he is a little younger than you. He began studies at Vienna with Conrad Grebel, but they returned and Grebel went to Basel and Binder stayed here. He has been serving as a proctor in Latin for the last several years, just as you did earlier. It is my understanding that he is leaving in a few weeks to return to Vienna to continue his studies. Perhaps you would want to talk to him about the two of you going together and sharing expenses."

"That sounds like a good possibility," Felix responded. "I must go by tomorrow and get acquainted with him. I'd at least like to discuss it with him."

The next morning it was not difficult to find Jörg, and soon they were speaking in the privacy of the schoolmaster's office.

"Your reputation has lived on here," Jörg said and smiled with the comment. "I have been told again and again what an excellent scholar you are."

"Thank you," Felix nodded modestly but with detectable pride in his voice.

"And you plan to go to university?"

"That is what I am here to talk to you about. I understand that you are going to Vienna to study, and I came by to chat with you about the possibility of our sharing in travel and expenses. I have some monies that I have saved from my service in the Swiss guard, but that will not stretch very far if I am not frugal."

"Of course, this can help us both. I do plan to leave in a few weeks and we can go together. We must make the arrangements." Jörg was delighted and his enthusiasm easily excited Felix about the opportunities that would be theirs in the Vienna academic community. They continued to visit, speaking of studying under Wolfgang Hailigmaier and Joachim von Watt of Saint Gall, a young professor commonly called Vadian.

"He is a new professor in Vienna, is he not?" Felix asked.

"Yes, his reputation is that of a humanist," Jörg said in a matter of fact way, and Felix could not determine from his expression whether he felt that it was good or not to be a humanist.

Somewhere during their conversation the two did make some sketchy plans to leave for Vienna in early September, hoping to arrive in time to begin school with the opening of the term in October. This meant that Felix would have several weeks around Zurich before they were on their way.

During the next week, Felix made several trips to Zollikon, ostensibly to visit his old friend Felix Kienast, but he had continued to remember the girl at the Hottinger's. Kienast had become a successful farmer in the several years that Felix was in Rome and had a more settled air of security about him. He was deeply involved in the Zollikon community and seemed to know everyone by their first name. As Felix thought about it, it seemed most fitting that Kienast would be so popular. He always seemed to have the personality of the politician, mediating between two conflicting parties, making all he met feel as though they were the subject of his full attention.

Felix tried to make his inquiry about the Conrad Hottinger family as nonchalantly as he could, but Kienast did not allow it.

"Would it be Trini in whom you are really interested?"

Felix tried to squelch a grin, but he felt the blood flush his face. "I have noticed her."

"Noticed her? Ah, my friend, you are stricken!" Kienast slapped his embarrassed friend on the arm. "She is as vivacious as ever and has grown into quite the young woman. You really should get to know her."

"I will stop by and visit the family," Felix agreed.

"The family?" Kienast threw back his head and laughed heartily. "This is no time for social amenities; you have only a few weeks. Now go find that girl and reacquaint yourself with her!"

Kienast opened the door with one hand and shoved Felix firmly out with the other. Felix laughed and turned to go back inside, but his friend had closed the door on him. He shrugged his shoulders and set off. It was just like his friend to be so bold. Maybe it was the push he needed.

Felix's first visit led naturally to the next and the next. Trini was a wonderful girl. Not only was she beautiful, with dark hair and large brown eyes, she was also happy, inquisitive, and energetic. She looked at the world through eyes that saw detail, things Felix had not noticed. She saw the good in every event and the best in people. She helped Felix to appreciate the beauty of so many things around him, things he had seen before but not really seen: the flowers and trees, of which she knew every name; the farms and gardens, which shaped the life of the community. On their walks into the city Felix, in turn, interpreted the fine architecture and intricate carvings of many of the old buildings of Zurich. Sometimes Felix found himself staring at Trini, wondering if she were real. There was so much good in her. There was a certain shyness that showed especially when she looked up at him, tilting her head down and to one side a bit. Still, she was bold in speaking her mind and insistent on Felix doing what was best for him, even if it were at her expense. She was never demanding on his time—at least not verbally—but had a way of making him want to be with her.

"Felix, you must not let this opportunity go by! You are so intelligent, so talented. Your life is before you. You can become one of the great teachers if you have the proper training."

"Oh, Trini, I have so many dreams and there is so much that I want to learn and do. I am driven by my own questions." Felix leaned back on his hands and let go a long sigh. They were in an open field, respectfully within sight of the Hottinger house.

"But, Trini," he hesitated, "what about us?"

Trini put her head down and watched her fingers pulling at some weeds. There was silence and Felix was afraid that he would have to say the next words.

The girl lifted her eyes and looked into his face. "I'll be here when you return," she said. "You could never be satisfied to remain in some simple role where you would work only to make a living, and I would never ask you to do so."

There was silence again but this time no words needed to be spoken. Felix leaned over to Trini and lifted her chin with one finger. Ever so gently, he kissed her.

While Felix was in Zurich he attended mass regularly, occasionally at the Fraumünster but usually at the familiar Grossmünster, saying his prayers with routine discipline. But, there remained an emptiness, a lack of meaning to his life. He felt as though he needed answers for the endless questions that seemed to rise from some inner hunger. Yet he held off looking for those answers in the hope that in his university experience he would find satisfaction through his studies and in the achievements that he visualized for himself.

In his alert and quick mind more and more questions began to take form, questions about the essential nature of the church. While at the cathedral, Felix watched his father with new interest. He wrestled with the question as to why the man had stayed with the orders of the church if celibacy were too large a burden to carry. And yet Felix knew that many men in church orders had a mistress or concubine. They only needed to pay monetarily for the privilege, while the women in their lives paid with their reputations and with the hard work that was necessary to keep their families going.

In late August Felix and Jörg Binder left for Vienna. The days moved by slowly as they traveled mile after weary mile. The fact that Jörg had been through much of this territory before was a help to them. They found lodging wherever they could, saving their money by doing chores around a farm to earn a meal and a night's rest. Felix was thankful that his muscles were in good condition from his discipline with the guard. They made their way north and east, traveling through Bavaria until reaching the Danube. Here they were able to secure work on a barge; they spent days on the blue waters of the Danube, sailing to Passau, on to Linz, and finally to Vienna. Felix thought to himself that these were the experiences he would one day describe to his children; these were times that brought zest to his life.

Arriving in Vienna, Felix and Jörg shared feelings of exhilaration as well as nervousness, for they were finally walking the streets of the city, Vienna, making their way to the university. Jörg knew the city from having been at the university for a year of study previously. Felix was openly excited, continually comparing this new setting with his experiences in Rome. Enrollment in the university was routine and they soon found their housing in the Brücken Bursa with the Swiss student group.

Felix plunged immediately into his studies, somewhat overloading himself with work in his enthusiasm. He was able to secure opportunities to tutor others in Latin while he involved himself in advanced studies of Hebrew and Greek. He, with several others, spent a rewarding time reading Plato. Somewhat to his surprise, he found himself more intrigued with the humanities, delighting in the humanism of his excellent teacher, Vadian. This young professor had an incisiveness and excitement about his teaching which inspired his students to diligence in their own reading and study. While he admired his professor, he was self-conscious about being a few years older than the other students and remained somewhat aloof.

Vadian presented his humanism with a strong spiritual core and unity. Yet his first concern was not in ecclesiastical or religious affairs. His primary interest was in poetry and geography. He was a scholar, a humanist with aesthetic appreciation and an engaging interpretation of classic antiquity. Along with this, Vadian carried a Swiss patriotism which inspired his students to think of themselves as exiled Swiss scholars temporarily living abroad. His goal, and he told them so, was the development of young Swiss scholars who would help their fatherland achieve a greater future in the field of learning. Felix began to think of the possibility of developing a university in Zurich.

With his background of military service, including his period of service in the Swiss guard, Felix entered wholeheartedly into philosophical and political discussions with fellow students. Somehow, looking at the world in this new way that was focused in Vadian's class was tying up loose strands in his mind, giving him a more defined purpose. It seemed to provide him with a personal sense of importance that he had not felt before, settling the uncertainties about the value of his life.

The newfound humanism he was embracing led Felix to a much more detached position in relation to ecclesiastical matters and to spiritual exercises. He was less frequent at the cathedral mass. He began thinking more with a kind of fatalism, seeing the world as a place where God was working out his own purposes, where he would also reward his people out of his own mercy. It was important, Felix thought, to conduct himself as a Christian purely for the benefits that would come because of a merciful God.

With his artistic interest, Felix found himself pursuing the fine arts as something of an avocation along with his studies. This was especially true of music, as he reveled in the organ recitals on the magnificent instrument recently installed in the cathedral. The organ, created in Bavaria, was a new development in music and seemed to be the most popular artistic attraction in the city. While he enjoyed the expressions of art in the paintings and sculpture prominent in Vienna, at no point did he find himself as impressed about the works available in this city as he had been over all he had seen during his time in Italy. His introduction to Leonardo da Vinci, Michelangelo, and Raphael, he knew, had exposed him to the very best.

The two years in Vienna moved by rapidly. In the spring of 1518 Felix and Jörg found themselves delighting in the status that their studies afforded them. They could not return to Zurich and enter the field of teaching. Jörg's goal had been to prepare himself to be schoolmaster at the Carolina School, and he was now ready for this position should it open. Correspondence over the last several months had given certification that he could return to the position of assistant headmaster. He hoped to become the master of the school within a year or two. Felix had in mind teaching language at another level, not with the young students, but with those who were preparing to go on to university study. Perhaps, he dreamed, in the future there might be the development of a university in Zurich itself! And he could be a professor of linguistics.

The trip back to Zurich repeated much the same pattern that they had followed two years earlier, but in the reverse order. There was a pleasant variety in the familiar sights, previously viewed with a certain amount of tenseness and uncertainty about the future, but now with both insecurities and much hard work behind them, they were relaxed. They sang and joked with the other men as they worked their way up the Danube.

It was August when they arrived in Zurich. They walked hurriedly up the street to the famous Grossmünster, in which so much of their lives had been shaped. Their quick steps revealed their excitement. Felix was anxious to turn into Neuenstadt Street to see his mother and brother. However, he first stopped with Jörg at the Carolina School. Here they were met with the joyous exclamations of young students who remembered Jörg with obvious fondness. To his surprise Felix was welcomed by a group of older fellows, former students who found the school a good meeting place. Among them was Conrad Grebel, the young chap whom Felix had taught in language school. Grebel had just returned from Basel, where he had studied under the famous professor, Glarean. Now, he and several others were making plans to leave for Vienna to study.

As they greeted each other, Felix turned to Grebel with interest. "And what brought you from Basel?"

"Glarean closed his bursa," Conrad replied. "He is going to Paris. As far as I'm concerned, I have no more reason for being in Basel."

"But is not the famous Erasmus in Basel?"

"Yes, of course, but my studies were with Glarean. I was not especially interested in switching to another group when their philosophies are so different."

"Philosophies? Different?"

"Yes." Grebel's posture showed his distaste, "Erasmus is so committed to the church and to the Scriptures that he scarcely understands the humanism of Glarean."

"And if you go to Vienna," Felix wanted to know, "you will continue in humanistic studies?"

"That is my intent. I want to study under Vadian. Did you sit in his lectures?"

"Yes. He is an excellent professor, my favorite." '

"Is he actually as great as we hear?" Conrad asked excitedly.

"He is an excellent teacher, a gifted poet, and a loyal patriot. If you are not committed to the Swiss fatherland before you sit in his classes, you will be by the time you are through." The laughter following his comment caused Felix to notice how many young men were listening in on their conversation.

"Yes," Jörg interjected, "Vadian has created a little Saint Gall in Vienna itself."

As the interchange continued, Felix excused himself and slipped off across the Chorherrnplatz, heading down Neuenstadt Street to his mother's home. Even for a man of thirty there was a strange, warm glow in his heart as he thought again of his mother and her gracious, sacrificial spirit; her support of him and her unquestioning love. Many had been the time when, mocked for his lack of a normal home and parentage, he had gone to her after school, placed his face in her apron, and cried, feeling her soothing hand and her tender voice reviving his spirit. He would never forget her words.

"Felix, it is who you are and what you become that is important and God will enable you to be a man as worthy as any other."

The reunion was warm. He sat that evening with his mother and younger brother telling story after story of his time in Vienna and his studies. Heinrich's eyes sparkled with special excitement as Felix told of the experiences of travel to Vienna, especially on the barges. It was obvious that Heinrich's interest in the world and its people was much stronger than his interest in books and the arts.

Felix was anxious to get to Zollikon, for he wanted to see Trini. But it was too late in the evening and the trip would need to wait until morning. Shortly, Hans Manz arrived at the door. Felix rose from his place and greeted his father. A firm pat on the back said, "It's good to see you again."

"I have missed you, son," Hans said, preceding him to a chair. "I have been so anxious to hear of your experiences. I did want to get here sooner but I could not get away."

"I understand," Felix said, but he dropped his eyes to the floor. Even after all this time, he realized that he really didn't understand. Still, he reviewed what he had shared moments before and added his hopes for the future.

"I believe that you are in a good position to establish a teaching role," his father told him. "I have seen many young men going through the Carolina School who should be prepared for further study at a university by the teaching that you could offer. However, I do not think that this is the most opportune time."

"What do you mean?" Felix was concerned.

"From what I know, from the inside," he said and smiled, "of ecclesiastical leadership here, in the next several years they will call a senior priest to minister at the Cathedral Church. This person, whoever he will be, will have a lot of influence on the direction the church program will take in the future. Until that appointment is made, there is little chance that a university will be born."

"And what am I to do in the interim?" Felix rose, suddenly angered by the thought that his preparation could have been for nothing.

"That is hard to answer, Felix, as there isn't much to offer just now."

Felix sighed and shook his head. He combed through his hair

with his fingers and then turned abruptly to his father.

"What would you think of my going to Basel, doing some further work at the university, working part time to support myself?"

Herr Manz was taken by surprise. "Why are you talking of Basel?"

"Well, today I was talking with Conrad Grebel, and he has just returned from studies there. I asked him about Erasmus, to find that Conrad was not really exposed to his teaching. I do have quite a lot of interest in discovering what he has to offer."

"Erasmus is much more of a churchman than the humanist, Glarean, under whom Grebel studied," the choirmaster responded.

"And at this point," Felix said, "I have had so much exposure to humanism and the arts, that it would do me good to discover how one such as Erasmus interprets ecclesiastical and religious thought in the humanist setting of the university in Basel."

Felix looked over to his mother, whose brow was wrinkled with concern. He could tell that she wanted to speak and so he allowed a lull in the conversation to give her the chance.

"Felix," she began, "you have been gone so much the last few years. Do you really want to go again? Can't you teach here?"

"I know I've been away, Mother, but Basel is not so far. It is much closer than Rome and Vienna. I could come home much more frequently and keep in touch with you, and Heinrich," he added, glancing at his father as though to apologize for not adding his name.

The choirmaster was looking down at his hands as he interlaced his fingers in his lap. He looked up at Felix and said, "My son," and paused with a deep expression of feeling. "There is not much that I have been able to offer you except my support and my love. If you choose to go to Basel, I will assist you in doing so. In the meantime, I will do my part to promote your ideas of a school for advanced study here in Zurich."

The choirmaster soberly bade each good night. Bending low

41

over Anna, he kissed her cheek in a rare expression of affection before their sons. Turning with what was undoubtedly a sigh of pain, he walked out the door into the night.

In one day, Felix's plans had again been altered. Early the next morning he walked the familiar paths to Zollikon to see Trini. As he passed through the familiar market gate the strides he made were long and quick with excitement. Before he knew it, he was walking up the worn path and knocking on the Hottinger door. His heart hammered as he waited. Trini herself appeared at the door and suddenly they were in each other's arms. Felix buried his face in her hair, enjoying the feel of her body in his arms. He had not realized how much he had missed her until now. No words needed to be spoken. In their long separation, they had skipped the steps most relationships take, and each had silently committed to the other. It was easy to talk of loving and of how they wanted to be part of each other's lives.

Trini seemed to be expecting Felix's news that he would not yet be staying in Zurich. She was satisfied to wait for him, with the knowledge that she was continuously in his mind and heart. Enjoying her life on the farm, and being with her family, she was in no real hurry to leave her home.

"We have our whole lives," she said.

"Yes, we do," Felix responded, but in his mind he added, You are young, and don't know how long I've waited.

The next weeks passed rapidly with the pleasure of their time together. In the late fall he journeyed to Basel, enrolling at the university for several classes under Erasmus. Here he found himself involved in a new expression of humanism, one which was built on a religious and spiritual base. To his surprise, Erasmus began to open for him a new understanding of the Scripture, especially of the teachings of Jesus.

To help meet his financial needs Felix made contact with one after another of the various well-known printers in Basel; Froben, Amerbach, and the famous printer, Cratander, searching for work. Other students already held the jobs for most of them, but

Erasmus himself, recognizing Felix's facility in the languages, asked Cratander to give him employment proofreading manuscripts for publication. This assignment had the special benefit of enabling him both to read and be of service to Erasmus, helping the professor to put his writings into final form for printing.

One afternoon Felix was straightening the stacks of paper that crowded his worktable, ending his labor for the day, when he overheard his name being mentioned across the large room that was the printer's shop. He looked up to see a messenger coming toward him.

"Felix Manz?"

"Yes."

"From Zurich?" Felix nodded, and was handed a piece of paper.

It had never even crossed his mind. He had no idea what the message might be and still, as he slumped down into his chair, he could not believe it. His father had died.

As he walked the hills back to Zurich he thought of how he had not truly known his father and that now, he never would. He thought of his mother, and how she had devoted herself to the man; of his brother, and wondered if they had been close. Mostly, he thought of living at a distance from his father for all the years of his life and how better it was than living without him at all.

He should not have been surprised at his mother. The same brave spirit with which she had conducted her life was evident in the way Anna Manz accepted her sorrow. She had loved the choirmaster deeply, and had been a source of strength to him, but their relationship had been so limited that she accepted the loss almost as though she were released from something that had been of bondage to her—bondage endured with love, but it had made a hard life.

Felix's homecoming, while tinged with grief also had a feeling of well-being. The strong sense of family which his mother had over the years worked so hard to develop, now strengthened the three of them. Felix had decided to stay in Zurich and Heinrich was relieved that some of the burden of the family would be taken from him.

Jörg Binder, upon hearing of Felix's return, immediately engaged him for assistance in teaching the older students at the Carolina School. Jörg was now master of the school and was well liked as an effective teacher and a good administrator. Felix felt comfortable in his relation with him and enjoyed the opportunity of a regular schedule of teaching.

Coupled with this good relationship was the excitement that the Cathedral Church was now negotiating with a new parish priest. The council was calling to the Cathedral Church a priest from Einsiedeln, Ulrich Zwingli, a very successful pastor. The new priest arrived in January 1519, and assumed his responsibilities with dedicated enthusiasm. Felix was impressed with Zwingli and surprised to find that they were practically the same age. Zwingli had achieved his master's degree at the University of Basel in 1506. Currently he maintained a correspondence with Erasmus and read everything the great humanist printed. Having studied at Vienna toward his doctorate, their common experiences now served to initiate a friendship between Felix and the new pastor.

Felix first became acquainted with Zwingli through his involvement at the Carolina School. The more they conversed the more they found common ground, especially in their discussion of Erasmian thought. Since Felix had recently come from his Basel studies with Erasmus, and Zwingli had been following Erasmus through the written word, they had a common interest. His awe for Zwingli and his imposing personality as well as his education and talent made it difficult for Felix to approach him with a proposal for a school for advanced studies. Instead, Felix asked Zwingli's counsel about pursuing further university study. To his amazement, Zwingli proposed that he should study in Paris and further prepare himself for possible university level teaching in the Zurich community! Felix was elated, particularly when Zwingli suggested that he concentrate his studies in languages and the classics.

"Master Zwingli, that is one of my dreams!"

Together they talked and planned for the future development of a university in Zurich. For Felix this was an invigorating vision. It revitalized his spirit as he thought of the future.

The scholarship program arranged by the Zurich Council and the King of France had a significant list of applicants year after year. While Felix had been in Basel, his friend Conrad Grebel had returned from Vienna and had then gone to Paris on such a stipend. Now, Zwingli brought Felix Manz's name to the council with many positive comments, recommending a two-year stipend to enable Felix to study in Paris. Felix had often thought of this, but scarcely had he dared to entertain the consideration. He knew that the more aristocratic young persons were the first recipients of these scholarships. But Zwingli defended Felix as a prime candidate for this stipend, and word came from the City Council in the spring of 1520 that he had been named to the scholarship. Although there were political tensions between France and Switzerland, arrangements were made which would enable him to begin in the fall term. Felix was overjoyed not only to receive an opportunity to study, but to have such an affirmation of his own worth and dignity.

During the next months, Felix completed his work at the Carolina School. He attended the School of Prophecy, as the classes Zwingli taught were called, listening intently to both Zwingli's formal presentations as well as his informal conversations. The recent happenings in Saxony, where the priest, Martin Luther, had defied the church and resisted the papal decrees, had become a main topic of conversation in ecclesiastical circles. Zwingli was especially interested in Luther, an interest which seemed almost like an obsession. As Zwingli discussed Luther's ideas with men such as Heinrich Englehart, pastor at the Fraumünster, and Caspar Grossmann, known as Megander, chaplain of the Zurich Hospital, it became evident to Felix and the others who listened to these animated discussions that Zwingli had a personal identification with Luther.

The disease that had taken the choirmaster, Felix's father, did not die out in Zurich. Over the months that followed there continued to be serious cases of illness and an increased number of deaths. The plague was so threatening that Felix was cautious about making frequent trips to see Trini, lest he carry something unwittingly to her. The City Council, concerned over the continuing number of persons contracting the plague, called for special attention to health matters.

It was a great shock when, in midwinter, Ulrich Zwingli, their new and beloved papal priest, came down with the illness. Felix was distraught. Their friendship had grown immensely. The man had deeply stimulated him by the discussions of Luther, and they were together attempting to recover the New Testament gospel and work for the renewal as well as the unity of the church. With Zwingli's illness, their opportunities of interchange were interrupted. Felix found himself regularly attending mass, saying his "Hail Mary's" with deep concern for his new friend and highly esteemed pastor. In the spring of 1520, Zwingli recovered from his illness sufficiently to be about some of his duties at the Grossmünster. Now, they could resume their conversations.

Felix found a different person in Zwingli. There was a change in his spirit as well as in his perspective. Zwingli did not refer to it as a conversion in the same way that he had spoken of an earlier change in his life. In 1516, he had experienced an intellectual conversion when he had moved into the thought of Erasmus. But it was evident that during his illness he had undergone a spiritual change. Now, Zwingli spoke of his faith and experience in a very personal way, from commitment born in the crucible of suffering when he had been at the point of death. There was a new intensity in his life when he spoke of the church, of the need for renewal, and for a recovery of the meanings of the New Testament gospel. His conversations with Felix now emphasized the importance of Felix's own involvement in the work of the church.

"There is a new day dawning, with new demands on the faithful," Zwingli said. "The church is a little flock in a hostile world, a group of committed people who will need to suffer persecution to be true to the gospel of Christ. And you shall be one of its leaders."

News came up the Rhine to Zurich that Martin Luther was in exile at Wartburg, protected by the Elector of Saxony.

"How fortunate for Luther," Zwingli said. "The Elector has saved him for the present."

Frequently Zwingli talked of Luther with Felix and with Jörg Binder, expressing his fear that Luther might be martyred as John Hus had been. With deep conviction in his expression he said, "I intend to follow down this same path, even though it could mean suffering." Reaching over to his desk he picked up a letter.

"I have just written to my friend Myconius in Luzern. I would like you to hear this." He began to read to them. "Born in blood, the church can be restored no other way but by blood . . . ." As he read, the words gave Felix chills. They were lofty and poetic words but frightening in that they left no clue as to how they might manifest themselves. The possibilities were sobering.

The arrangements that Zwingli had worked out with the Zurich Large Council providing for his study in Paris remained a clear direction for Felix. Still, he had some fear about going. All reports said that the plague continued to rage in Paris. He and Trini talked of this with common anxiety. Finally, word from Paris suggested that the plague was abating, although thousands of Parisians had lost their lives. Communications also revealed that some of the current Swiss students, including Felix's acquaintance, Conrad Grebel, had fled Paris to live out of the city in Melun, capital of the region Seine et Marne. The smaller city was twenty miles up the river Seine from Paris. Glarean, with whom Felix would study, had moved his pupils a bit farther to Marnay on the Seine. There he was continuing his instruction in Greek language and literature.

Felix did wonder whether his own stipend for study in Paris may have come about because of the plague and the hesitancy of others to accept a scholarship for study there. But with Zwingli's encouragement that he accept the stipend, he set out for Paris.

The trip was long and tiring. For most of the journey he traveled alone and lacked the pleasant company he had known on the trip to Vienna with Jörg Binder. But he enjoyed going north through the black forests of south Germany, dense with gray-green life. It was like an enormous painting that stretched on and on, he thought, a masterpiece. His path next took him west to the Rhine and north to the region of Freiburg. To cross the Rhine he secured passage on a ferryboat. He observed at some distance the jovial and robust peasants who were sharing the ride with him, kept his privacy, but all the while remained close enough to overhear their conversation. From time to time the largest man, his nose red with the evidence of overindulgent living, would tell a joke and then look to Felix as though to see if he had enjoyed it. Felix would smile and chuckle under his breath, mostly to be polite.

The tall cathedral spire of Strasbourg welcomed him long before he entered the city. He felt comfortable in being among the many people after his days of traveling alone. His few days of rest were interspersed with social interchange and attendance at the cathedral. Visiting the markets he learned of a merchant who ran a supply route to Paris. He hired on to a supply wagon, working for food and the privilege of riding part of the journey. Felix welcomed the interlude of laboring with the crew for the next several weeks. Upon arriving in Paris he stayed only briefly in the city and soon made his way to Marnay. His limited facility in French allowed him to converse with many along the way. Although Glarean and his circle of young scholars were only temporarily located here, it was not difficult to find them. Glarean himself had just returned from a trip to Basel and had brought with him several other Swiss students for his fraternity. When Felix discovered this, he was much relieved. He had found that he did not understand the French people, but now he was among persons with whom he had much in common.

Quickly becoming a part of the group, Felix delved into his studies. It was as though he were not at one of the most exciting cities in the world, as though he wore blinders and could only see his books. He did go sight-seeing from time to time, but mainly to the collections of art and to the great Notre Dame Cathedral. The spireless Gothic architecture gripped him. It was a study in human genius: the massive flying buttresses, a tribute to man's understanding of the symmetry and order of God's creation. The building was an inspiration to Felix and he visited it more frequently than any other building in Paris. Another of his enjoyments was attending mass at the Church of the Sacred Heart, high on a hill overlooking the city.

His study in what was actually a Latin institute was a new discipline for Felix. Even the community life was conducted in the Latin language. Since Glarean gave special instruction for those more advanced students who were working in Greek and Hebrew, he formed a close friendship with this smaller group. But during the nearly two years that he was in Paris, Felix was a scholar, not a socializer. He read Homer in Greek, Livy in Latin, and numerous scholars of the Old Testament Scriptures in Hebrew. He found that he had a growing interest in Hebrew, as a language, but an even deeper interest in the study of the Old Testament prophets.

There had been no opportunity for Felix to meet with Conrad Grebel and his friends in Paris, although he had thought that he might. By the time Felix had arrived in Paris, Grebel was already on his way back to Zurich with his cousin John Jacob Grebel. Felix soon learned the unpleasant story. In a drunken bout on January 1, 1519, Grebel had impulsively broken completely with Glarean, and had pursued no further study under the professor. Glarean told Felix of his disappointment, of the lack of discipline and interest in study among Grebel's little circle. He was especially displeased with their revelry and riotous living.

"Intelligent and as good a poet as he is," Glarean said, "Conrad wasted much of his time during his two years in Paris."

The talk around the school was that Conrad left Paris planning to follow his friend Johann Ammann to Bologna, Italy, and study at Milan or another of the universities in Italy, Padua, or Pisa. A recent letter from Jörg Binder shared the news of the death of Conrad's brother, Andreas. The younger brother had served King Ferdinand as a courtier in Innsbruck, but had come home suffering from the plague. He had died early in September. But from all that Felix heard, Conrad's reason for leaving Paris may have been more out of fear for his own safety.

Several months after breaking with Glarean early in January 1519, Conrad had been involved in a brawl in which two Frenchmen had been killed. They had apparently been bandits robbing the Bershof. In the fight which ensued, two of them had been killed and it had not been easy to clear this with the French authorities. Conrad and his partners had been in a dangerous position that could have led to their execution. An appeal to the king kept them from being condemned, but even this did not provide security from the bandits. Conrad, having lived in fear of their plots of revenge, had decided to leave the region.

Felix's education followed the normal patterns of university study with one exception. The university students now had many intense discussions about Martin Luther, the revolutionary German monk he and Zwingli had so often discussed. While Felix had reservations about Luther's open defiance of Rome, he recalled with disturbing clarity Zwingli's comments of support for Luther's reformation. Thinking it best to participate in these discussions in order to better understand what the issues actually were, he soon found himself admiring Luther for his convictions, reevaluating the monk's charges against Rome.

Felix was diligent in keeping up correspondence with his friends at the Grossmünster. He was watching for any indication that Zwingli might be taking steps toward developing a university in Zurich. From Jörg's letters, he soon learned that Zwingli had instead increased his activity in religious reform. Zwingli's sermons now contained outspoken expressions against the injustices he saw in the church of Rome. As a church leader he had even publicly abandoned his papal pension. But now, in a more radical move, he led Zurich to withdraw her alliance with Catholic France. And committed to humanistic pacifism, Zwingli was now crusading to prevent the sons of Zurich from serving as soldiers. Jörg wrote Felix that Oswald Myconius, a good friend of Zwingli, who fully identified with him, had written a classic dialogue, "On Not Going to War," to support Zwingli's position.

Felix began to feel like a foreigner, not only in Paris but as he thought of Zurich. He saw his own time in Paris as limited. Zwingli, it appeared, had practically moved into Luther's camp, a matter of great concern to Felix. He was not fully convinced of Luther's stance and would need to hear Zwingli for himself. Perhaps he should not take secondhand news so seriously, even if it was coming from a person for whom he had high respect.

Jörg Binder, in his most recent letter, expressed his own enthusiasm for Zwingli as a good student of the Scripture, and a strong preacher. Zwingli was currently preaching systematically through the Gospel of Matthew, emphasizing Christ's expectations for the life of the church. He planned to follow this with sermons from the Acts of the Apostles, from Timothy, and from Galatians. Binder's confidence in the man as an expositer of the Scripture was well warranted and there was little cause for anxiety. Still, Binder admitted in a concluding comment, there were representatives of the Roman Church who were quite critical of Zwingli's evangelicalism.

In the summer of 1522, Glarean, his professor, terminated his teaching in Paris, and returned to Basel to work with Oecolampad in reform. Felix bid farewell to numerous friends in Paris and accompanied him. The group made its way across France to the Rhine and into Basel. Felix again bid farewell to close friends and to his professor, then journeyed on to Zurich. He had a deep sense that he was not only going home but that he was going to his work.

Chapter 4

In Partnership with Zwingli

It was a different Zurich to which Felix returned. He could almost feel it in the atmosphere as he walked along the streets.
Again and again he encountered comments by different people
on what was regarded as the new evangelical emphasis in Zwingli's preaching. The effectiveness of Zwingli's leadership was
reflected in the attitude of the people. Felix was hardly prepared
for the number of persons that were attending the Grossmünster
to listen to the sermons.

His young friend, Conrad Grebel, was back in Zurich after a
brief time in Milan as well as Basel. Much to Felix's surprise,
Conrad was now married. Felix met Barbara, Conrad's wife, for
the first time after the preaching service at the Cathedral Church.
He chuckled when Conrad introduced her, calling her his
"Holokosme," his whole world. Felix had not imagined his
young, impetuous friend as a settled husband, but now Conrad
was saying: "Felix, you should get married. This is the heart of my
life."

Felix laughed, looking discreetly at the woman who had captured Grebel so completely.

"Perhaps, but I first must find the person who would have one
such as me," he joked.

"Oh, she's around," Conrad said. "Just open your eyes."

Felix thought of Trini and his eyes felt misty.

"I am doing that," he said softly, "but first I must have something to offer her." He paused a moment then asked, "Where are you living, Conrad?" He wanted to change the subject.

"We are living with my parents for the present, but I am not sure how long this will last, especially with so many family members there. As you can see, we are expecting our first child within three months."

"Yes, congratulations to both of you."

"And now that you are back from Paris, will you be working with Zwingli?"

"That's what I have anticipated. I had a chat with Leo Jud, Engelhart's associate at the Fraumünster, and learned of the fine group of scholars who gather for study and discussion here at the Grossmünster. In fact, Jud and I have similar backgrounds and being illegitimate sons of priests, well, we have found a common bond between us."

"Yes," Conrad said. "I can understand that. For some months now I have been involved with the scholars and I am excited about what is happening. You must come."

The next morning at seven, Felix went to his first session of the scholars' meeting with Zwingli. It was held in the choir of the cathedral. Welcomed by Leo Jud, Felix was introduced to each of the others. Among them, Felix felt drawn to Simon Stumpf, a very interesting and expressive person who was a pastor at Höngg. But further acquaintance would have to wait, as they soon found themselves in intense conversation with Zwingli, intrigued as he led them in a careful study. His exegesis required the application of new insights of the gospel to the life and work of the church. These sessions he called the School of Prophecy, for they involved the participants in very careful interpretation of the Bible.

In the group process, the respect that was given to Simon Stumpf suggested that he was a very successful and popular preacher. And to his surprise Felix sensed a similar esteem being shown to Conrad Grebel. In fact, there was a mutual admiration among all the members of the group which seemed to free each of them in their sharing.

During the next weeks, Felix was regular in his attendance of Zwingli's services although he was increasingly frustrated by the fact that any discussion regarding his desired university program in Zurich had been eclipsed by the present focus on reform. As a preacher, Zwingli's presentations were impressive. One listener described the impact by saying, "I felt as if somebody were lifting me off the ground by my hair!"

Felix's response was more intellectual, and steadily the sermons, the School of Prophecy sessions, and the reading of the Scriptures in Greek and in Hebrew awakened in him a new sense of the enormity of the faith to which he was being exposed. When he first realized it, Felix did not know, but in his mind the need for a personal faith now stood in contrast to the conceptualizing of doctrines, to the routine orders of the life of the church, to the administering of the sacraments and the observance of monstrance and celebrations.

Zwingli's deliberate actions in rejection of church tradition led Felix to respect him as one who insisted on thinking for himself. He and Binder chatted about it. Jörg said, "Felix, change is all about us. One shocking incident occurred during the Lenten season before you returned. Some of the workers at Froschauer's print shop ate sausages for lunch on a day that Zwingli had been in the shop, and he had quietly approved."

"Sausages? During Lent?" Felix exclaimed.

"Yes, during Lent. I'm sure this led to Zwingli writing his pamphlet on 'The Choice and Freedom of Foods'—especially since the bishop of Constance, Hugo von Hohenlandenberg, sent two men to admonish Zwingli. They were men of stature, Bishop Melchior Wattli and theologian Nicholas Bredlin. Zwingli has referred to them as 'that unnecessary, magnificent delegation.' And that's not all. On July second, Zwingli, with ten other priests, wrote a supplication to the Most Reverend Lord Hugo,

Bishop of Constance! They asked for freedom to preach the evangelical gospel and for freedom for priests to marry!"

Hearing this, Felix began to contemplate his own role in the future of this movement. His mind quickly moved to his abilities in scholarship and then to his own experiences of spirituality. Zwingli was acting on issues that Felix had contemplated but had not allowed his mind to pursue. He would need to put action to thought if he were to be a participant in Zwingli's movement.

Jörg's voice brought him from his reverie. "It is known," he was saying in an undertone, "that Zwingli wants to marry. He is known to be an admirer of the widow, Anna Reinhart."

Felix felt uncomfortable with the way their conversation was bordering on gossip. "Is this common knowledge?" he asked.

"No, I would not say it is public knowledge, but the council knows that he had a sexual liaison with the barber's daughter in Einsiedeln. However," Jörg threw up his hands, "the bishop permits this for a fee." Felix's thoughts went to his own father, and Jörg, knowing of the situation, decided to change the subject.

"You must have heard of Grebel's summons before the council last July?"

"No," Felix responded with interest, "Grebel, before the council? This is news to me. What happened?"

"Well, on July seventh the Zurich Council summoned Conrad along with others you will soon come to know, Claus Hottinger, Heinrich Aberli, and Bartlime Pur. The council censured them sharply for confronting the monks. They had made public their comments against them, and Conrad especially became so bold before the council, with pointed statements, that one of the councilmen said, "The devil himself is in the council chamber."

"Referring to Conrad, I presume?" Felix chuckled.

"Yes. But Conrad answered, 'The devil is not only sitting in the council chambers, he is sitting on the bench where the councilmen sit, for one of your councilors has said that one might as well preach the gospel to a dung heap! If the councilors stand in

55

the way of the progress of the gospel, they themselves will be destroyed.' "

"That was confrontive enough!" Felix exclaimed. "Conrad seems to be quite taken up in Zwingli's attempts at renewal."

"That he is," Jörg replied, "at least in reform."

As summer turned to fall, Felix's trips to Zollikon took on a regular pattern. His joy in being with Trini now made the walk to the Hottinger farm more normal than going to his home. But early fall found Felix almost obsessed by his own work in the Scriptures. He was increasingly aware of a relevance in the humanism which he had studied, for it was a bridge from sacramentalism to the presentations from the Gospels which Zwingli was sharing in his sermons. A restlessness grew within Felix and questions formed one after the other, demanding satisfaction. His keen mind led him to an in-depth search of himself, driven on by the hunger in his soul.

"What is my relationship with Jesus Christ? Is my religion, as Zwingli preaches, little more than form and ritual?" And the questions moved him to ask again and again, "Have I, as Zwingli says, taken seriously the call of Christ to take up the cross and follow him? Am I a disciple and not just a scholar?" Trini heard his questions, but she waited patiently for him to find his own answers.

As Zwingli's group of scholars continued their discussions, Felix became a prominent voice in the conversations. He was convinced now that there was a birth by the Spirit that he had not really experienced. The more they studied the letters of Paul, expecially Ephesians, the more evident it became to Felix that his need was to commit himself totally and personally to Jesus Christ. At the Carolina School one morning, he shared this conviction with his friend Jörg. Binder's frank admission that he too had felt such a conviction added to Felix's sense of urgency.

"Jörg," he said. "I may not understand it all now, or what it might mean in the future, but I must give myself completely to Christ and his way, with all of the honesty with which I can commit myself."

Jörg stared at the floor and pushed a piece of lint forward with one foot. Felix wondered what he was thinking, then Jörg spoke up.

"I will join you," he said, "I must face this truth."

There, in a classroom where both of them had spent so much time learning of spirituality but not really experiencing it, Felix and Jörg knelt together and began to pray.

As Felix prayed, it was as though a light dawned within his spirit. The heaviness that he had borne so long was taken from him, and in his head was ringing the joyous strains of the "Gloria." He rose from his knees with a new radiance. He and Jörg embraced in their excitement.

"For once I am sure that I'm a child of God, a member of his family!" Felix exclaimed.

Jörg burst out, "It's wonderful to be able to say, 'Jesus is my Lord,' to be sure of our commitment to Christ!"

"Yes, for, 'If anyone is in Christ,' " Felix quoted, " 'he is a new creature.' "

Felix went about his teaching that day with an inner calmness that showed in his increased patience with his students. He went to the next meeting of the School of Prophecy with new enthusiasm. He could hardly wait to share the experience that had changed him. But how could he describe what had happened, how could he describe a complete rebirth?

As he was approaching the door of the Grossmünster, Conrad Grebel came hurrying toward him from the adjoining street. As he came up to Felix there was something different about his expression. He had always been a boisterous man but there was an energy and a glow in his face that was new. Perhaps the baby has been born, Felix thought. But when Grebel was near enough, his first words revealed what had happened.

"Felix, I am a new man! My life has been transformed." He paused, then continued modestly, "I have literally been born by the Spirit."

"I know what you mean, Conrad!" Felix took Grebel's hand

firmly in both of his and his voice trembled with excitement, "I have experienced this same miracle!"

Grebel looked at him with amazement.

"Do you mean that you also have been changed by the Spirit of God?"

"That is just what I mean, Conrad. I have become a follower of Jesus Christ, a child of God by faith."

The two men threw their arms around each other and Conrad exclaimed, "Then we are brothers!"

At that moment Felix felt closer to Conrad than he ever had felt to anyone. They walked into the church with unchecked smiles on their faces. There was a loss of inhibition in their excitement, mixed with a completely new sense of peace and joy in a common faith. Those who had already assembled in the room looked at them, expressions of curiosity on several faces over the excitement Felix and Conrad evidenced. Felix addressed Zwingli loudly enough for everyone to hear.

"Ulrich, something has happened to us. Your preaching has led us to new steps of faith, to a new commitment to Jesus Christ."

Zwingli jumped to his feet, stepping quickly across the room. He reached out one hand to Felix and grasped Conrad's arm with the other.

"This is what I have been praying for! I have come to believe very deeply in the importance of each person coming to Christ in faith, actually becoming a priest before God through Jesus Christ." Turning to Conrad he said, "And you, my friend? Is this true for you?"

"Yes, in my own home, sharing new biblical discoveries with Barbara, it suddenly dawned on me that I needed to take further steps of faith for myself, to move beyond the ideas which I was sharing with her into the reality of my own experience of the righteousness of Christ."

Zwingli smiled and spoke in pastoral directness, "As you do this, Conrad, all of the studies and experiences which have been your privilege will fall into place in a new way."

The small group that day, their discussion in Romans, focused on the meaning of justification by faith. Slowly others in the group began testifying to the new awareness of faith that was dawning within them. Zwingli was visibly moved.

"This is not just a change happening to the structure of the church," he said. "It is a change in the very understanding of the nature and meaning of the church. We are becoming a fellowship of faith. We will want to teach this to others, for there are many who need to be introduced to this reality."

Later that day Felix made his familiar trip to Zollikon to be with Trini. The trip seemed longer in his haste to be with her to share the new meaning of his faith in Christ.

"Trini, all of my life I have felt like an unnamed person, one who had nowhere to belong. But now I do belong. I am a true member of God's family."

"Felix, you have always belonged. You are the son of the famous choirmaster of the Cathedral Church. His position and your education have enabled you to walk with the best in aristocratic, scholarly circles. You have always been more than welcomed and respected in our home."

She paused, looking into his face, then added, "But I have known that you had an emptiness in your life, and I am glad that you have found fulfillment."

Felix could see the sincerity burning in her eyes, and he felt the inner lift this gave to his own spirit.

With Zwingli's support, Felix now began a Bible study in his own home. With his skill in Hebrew, he began teaching from the Hebrew Bible, translating it and interpreting it into their own German language. At first only a few friends attended the Bible study, Conrad Grebel and his wife, Jörg Binder, as well as Felix's mother, Anna, and his brother, Heinrich. Although they could not understand the Hebrew words, they entered with enthusiasm into the interpretations Felix gave on the passages.

Within a few weeks the group expanded to include friends

from Zollikon and the new parish priest, Wilhelm Reublin. Wilhelm had come to Zurich from Lauffenburg on the Rhine, having been born at Rottenburg in south Germany, and having studied at Freiburg. Prior to his present assignment, he had been the people's priest at St. Alban's Church in Basel. Conrad had met him during the brief time he had been in Basel, having been part of a group that had shared dialogue with the famous Erasmus.

Their acquaintance with Basel led Felix and Conrad as well as some others in the group to ask Wilhelm many questions about his work there, especially his parish experience at St. Alban's. There was no lack of modesty on the priest's part as he told them that he had enjoyed remarkable success.

"The crowds attending my preaching services often numbered up to four thousand persons," he said; then he added with evident irritation, "My popularity with the people was not shared by the City Council. Having espoused Luther's evangelical doctrine, I began to preach strongly that the Scriptures are the only sacred object, and that the monstrance contained only dead bones. And on the twenty-seventh of this past June, I was expelled from Basel by the City Council."

They all appreciated Wilhelm, and within a few weeks his gifts and abilities had made a place for him in Zurich. He frequently preached in the Fraumünster, the cathedral dedicated to the virgin Mary, and they went to hear him. Then he was assigned by Zwingli and the council to be an assistant preacher in Wytikon and in Zollikon. Especially in Zollikon his preaching was drawing large crowds. Felix joined Trini and her family on several occasions to hear his presentation there. While Zwingli was the primary attraction at the Cathedral Church in Zurich, Reublin was popular in the surrounding towns. He was less sophisticated than Zwingli, more homespun and forward in his expressions, and the rural populace flocked to hear him.

Early on Reublin developed a close relationship with Johanns Brötli, the associate pastor in the Zollikon Church, and they worked together quite harmoniously. Together they befriended

Andreas Castelberger, a book salesman who had come into their community from the eastern part of Switzerland, had opened a bookstore in Zurich, and had begun holding Bible classes. Andreas had also become a friend of Conrad Grebel, who dealt with him in the purchase and sale of books and who had shared in some of his earlier Bible study gatherings.

Reublin brought Castelberger along to visit the class which Felix was conducting. As the discussion progressed, Felix found himself admiring Andreas for his commitment to faith and his strong emphasis on the authority of Scripture. Castelberger, walking with a cane and called "The Cripple," immediately impressed all who met him with his agility and constant activity. He seemed to have no lack of energy, telling them stories of how he had been a colporteur working for Zwingli between Einsiedeln and Glarus. He had traveled not only from Chur across eastern Switzerland, but quite extensively in the areas surrounding Zurich and west to Basel. His Bible classes had actually begun as an interest in the evangelical preaching which had spread south from Saxony, extending Luther's emphasis. His extensive book market included printers in Frankfurt and Nuremberg and had given him further understanding of the Reformation voices. Still, his teaching was uniquely his own, for he excelled in exegeting passages of Scripture in his own straightforward style.

With so many different people coming together to study the Scripture, increasingly the religious awakening in Zurich appeared to be taking its own form. Felix recognized that the group was in no way a simple extension of Luther's work in the north. This was evident in August, when Zwingli's *Apologeticus/ Archeteles* was published. Felix's group, under Conrad's leading, spent time reading and discussing the implications of this new publication. Zwingli had honored Conrad by including a poem Grebel had written in the conclusion to his book. In this poem Grebel had attacked the hierarchy of the Roman church. Having an appreciation for Conrad's poetic gifts and knowing that he had associated in Basel with the famous poet, Kasper Ursimus

Velius, Felix complimented Conrad on being included in the publication. Conrad responded simply, "My regret is that at that time I did not know the meaning of personal faith in Jesus Christ. I wish I could have included in the poem a witness to justification by faith in answer to the emptiness of religious form." Felix, not struck by his humility, did admire his conviction.

Felix himself was increasingly excited about being a partner with Zwingli in church reform. Like never before, he now felt vital and motivated. Sensing the importance of his involvement, he now believed that he might even be influencing the future of Christianity itself. Zwingli's encouragement imparted increased enthusiasm for Felix's study of the Scripture in the original languages. Urging him to continue study with the group of young scholars, Zwingli asked Felix to provide him private tutorials in the study of Hebrew. Language was not a field in which Zwingli had excelled and so Felix became a special tutor to his theological mentor.

At one of their group meetings early in October, Zwingli surprised them with a note from Macrinus, a friend from Solothurn. His friend had written of his joy in the evidence that Conrad Grebel had become a distinguished patron of reformation, an advocate of the gospel. Zwingli read the note to them with evident satisfaction and, looking at Conrad Grebel, then at Felix, Jörg, and Leo Jud, he remarked, "One of my greatest satisfactions is this circle of scholars who are committed to the new life in Christ. And I am grateful that you are supporting me in the bold undertakings on which we have embarked."

During the late months of 1522, Zwingli began shaping, ever more openly, a new direction in theology. He believed that his biblical interpretation and preaching were headed for a confrontation with Rome as surely as had Martin Luther's teaching in Saxony. Zwingli began to prepare his circle for the showdown which he saw as inevitable. He suggested that he might need to resign from his pastorate as a Romish priest. But he hoped that the support in Zurich from the populace as well as the council would reinstate him as the people's priest at the Great Church. "This," he said, "will allow me to build the kind of program which will be consistent with the gospel which I have been preaching."

In his zeal, Zwingli sent a copy of his *Archeteles* to Erasmus at Basel. His disappointment was evident when he received only a brief letter of caution over the appearance of arrogance in his defiance of Rome. Zwingli told his group that following Christmas activities he would make a trip to Basel and seek opportunity for interchange with Erasmus. He wanted to challenge the scholar who, like the earlier Luther, hoped that in the renewal of the church the unity of the church could still be maintained.

Zwingli's position was clear to his friends: By its opposition to Luther, the Roman church had declared itself as disobedient. He was not on the same path as Erasmus, and the circle of Zwingli's scholars in which Felix participated were in agreement with him. They must now be prepared to pay the same price that Luther was paying. The question before them was whether they could inaugurate a new church true to the Scriptures. The issue, Felix believed, was the authority of the Scripture itself as they stood under the direction of Jesus Christ.

"Christ said to the apostles," Zwingli preached, " 'in the world you will have tribulation'; and at another time, 'you will be hated by all men for my name's sake,' and 'the hour will come when those who kill you will think that they are doing a service to God.' So there will always be people who will persecute us Christians because Christ is in us even though they likewise may boast of coming in the name of Christ. Such, however, as obey the law of men rather than the law of God, manifestly lack the marks of Christ. If they place his commandments lower than their own . . . is this not the fire which will make the work of each man manifest and bring to light whether he is fighting for the honor of the world or for the honor of Christ?"

Felix listened intently as Zwingli discussed his understanding of a church true to the authority of Scripture. It was stimulating but not comforting to hear Zwingli say:

"Never will the world accept Christ, and even the promise of rewards by Christ is accompanied by the promise of persecution. He sent out his own like sheep among wolves."

By the end of 1522, Felix and his associates who surrounded Zwingli understood clearly that he now intended to break with the church of Rome. Zwingli cautioned them, however, that not everyone who was against Rome was of the same mind. At one of the School of Prophecy meetings, he distinguished three classes of evangelicals among them.

"The members of one class are merely anti-Catholic, negative protesters whose whole faith consists in not being Catholics any longer. There is a second class who are the libertines who see in the gospel a charter for freedom to indulge their own desires. But there is a third group, which characterizes those of us who work in the Word of God, the evangelical pastors and scholars here in Zurich. Not all in the church here in Zurich can understand this spiritual renewal of which we speak, but I am so thankful for those of you who join me in the work of the Word of God."

Felix held similar concerns, wanting to distinguish those who deserved identification with their group from those who did not. He asked Zwingli, "What direction do you have for the Bible schools that are being conducted across the canton? With my education and concern for scholarship, I may be somewhat prejudiced, but are all of those who are leading the schools competent to do so?"

There was an intenseness in Zwingli's gaze at Felix that was hard to interpret. The leader's eyes moved with the same fervency to Grebel, to Castelberger, Jud, Binder, Bartlime Pur, the baker who had joined them, and Bolt Eberi, a pastor at Zollikon, before he said, "Multiple leadership is a risk we will have to take. I am in full support of the Bible schools. Recently my friend, Vadian, wrote me from St. Gall of such groups gathering around Johann Kessler. He says that a significant renewal is happening in that community through the study of Scripture. I believe that the common man should drink at the fountain of life." He paused, then continued more firmly, "We will need to be prepared to take those steps necessary to enhance the faith and obedience of all people who take the Word of Christ seriously. From the uprisings of the peasants in Bavaria, in Schaffhausen, and even here in Switzerland, it is evident that they need to be informed in the Word of God. This is the time for the development of a new people's church."

Chapter 5

The Search for the True Church

It was early January 1523, and the city of Zurich was all abuzz. There were now definite plans for a disputation on Catholicism, and it was being prepared to convene at the end of the month. For nearly three years Zwingli had been preaching reform. Teaching the evangelical faith, he had encouraged the Bible schools and the participation of the laity in the search for truth as it is found in the Scripture. The trip to Basel and his conversation with Erasmus had only served to reinforce his conviction. His emphasis on *sola scriptura,* the authority of Scripture alone, was being heard by more and more persons in the church, although most still thought of themselves as affiliated with the Roman church. But this disputation was now rumored to be between Zwingli's church and the church of Rome. The question was in the air: Is a break with Rome in the offing?

Even with the spirit of reform that permeated the city and in spite of Zwingli's forceful preaching, the patterns of church life had remained the same. Zwingli repeatedly attacked the worship of images and exposed the economic and social injustices of the times. He attacked the rites of infant baptism, the spital, the exorcism of devils, the use of oil, all as offering a false security for persons who failed to enter into the meaning of salvation by faith.

However, Zwingli delayed in acting to change the patterns in the church, and this hesitancy created unrest among those within Zwingli's circle and also among the evangelical people who attended his preaching. Felix and Conrad were very active in their small group and kept urging Zwingli to carry forward on the break with Rome and to establish a true church, a free church. As their group discussed this with Zwingli he said, "We will need to make a decision as to whether we proceed without the consent and support of the Zurich Council or whether we will carry the council with us and have their support and authority in establishing a new church."

"But if the Large Council authorizes the character of the new church, then it is still tied to the civil state and will limit us in being a church under the authority of Christ," said Grebel.

"That is true," Zwingli replied, "unless we can carry the council with us into the meaning of Christian faith. Then their faith would add to the resources which their office offers in the strength of the new church."

"This means then," Felix joined in, "that we need to help the Zurich authorities to become a Christian authority, a council composed of believing members of the church."

"Yes, that is exactly what I mean." Zwingli's response was emphatic.

Felix leaned forward in his chair, his hands on his knees.

"But, Ulrich," he said, "what is to guarantee that the decisions will be decisions of faith rather than of expediency on the part of the council?"

"This is a risk we will need to take if we are to break from Rome."

Felix's sigh showed his wariness. Still, he was convinced that they should try.

The next weeks were busy with the preparations for the "Council of 200" to host the disputation on Catholicism. As a first act in their reformation the Zurich Council nullified the authority of the Bishop of Constance over Zurich. Now the Zurich region stood under the direction of the council, of the civil authorities. Zwingli saw this as the appropriate time to resign from his priesthood in the Roman church. His friend, Heinrich Engelhart, pastoring at the Fraumünster, had already resigned as canon of the Grossmünster chapter so that Zwingli could be appointed to that position. With that as his security, in a dramatic step, Zwingli announced publicly and deliberately in early January that he herewith relinquished his role as the people's priest in the Cathedral Church. Stepping away from the pulpit to stand among the people, he listened to their response. It was exactly as he had expected and hoped. Immediately the people appealed to the City Council to rehire Zwingli as parish priest and to structure the city of Zurich as an evangelical church.

The Large Council still regarded itself as a Catholic civil authority, but with this event they were not certain as to what was developing in their relationship with the Roman church. Being convinced that they needed Zwingli as a leader in the church life of Zurich, they negotiated with him to continue as the parish priest. Included in the negotiation was Zwingli's plan for a disputation on Catholicism. The confrontation was now set for January 29, 1523, and the days were filled with excited conversation among the friends with whom Felix associated.

Early in the forenoon of the 29th, the Large Council convened the meeting in the City Hall of Zurich. Six hundred persons could be accommodated in the hall itself, and the crowd filled every seat and actually spilled over to stand around the outside. Supporting Zwingli in the presentations were several of his close associates: Leo Jud, who had been installed as the parish priest at the Church of St. Peter; Heinrich Engelhart, who was parish priest at the Fraumünster; Jörg Binder, the schoolmaster at the Carolina School; as well as Conrad Grebel, Felix Manz, Simon Stumpf, Wilhelm Reublin, Ludwig Hätzer, and others of Zwingli's circle. The council sat, in full formal attire, to hear the presentations from the city church and from the representatives of Rome.

Burgomaster Röist, with both the Small Council and the Great

Council of 200 identifying with Zwingli, now confronted the delegation from the Roman church. It was led by the very able Vicar John Faber, their highly qualified and competent disputant. Zwingli had drawn up sixty-seven articles as his declaration of faith. These articles opposed almost everything that was distinctively Catholic: the mass, fasts, pilgrimages, indulgences, purgatory, saint worship, auricular confession, clerical celibacy, monasticism, the propriety of infant baptism, and popery.

After reviewing the articles, the Council of Zurich opened the session with Röist as Burgomaster making a lengthy declaration of support for Zwingli. He stated that the council was asking that charges against Zwingli by the Roman church be dropped. In the hours that followed, the discussion between the vicar and Zwingli was intense, often heated. Zwingli was bold, almost heroic, in his defense of a new church.

"But there is another church which the popes do not wish to recognize; this one is none other than all righteous Christians, collected in the name of the Holy Spirit and by the will of God. That church depends and rests only upon the Word and will of God. That church cannot err; it is the right church, the spotless bride of Christ governed and refreshed by the Spirit of God."

At the conclusion of the disputation, the City Council voted to support Zwingli in the reformation of the church in Zurich. Felix and Conrad with the group of men that had so hoped for this moment could hardly contain themselves. They embraced and shook hands with expressions of elation. A new church was being created with a clear evangelical faith.

"This was history in the making," Felix said to Conrad. "This is the will of God."

Changes immediately began to happen in Zurich and in the surrounding areas. Many of the monks from the Dominican, Franciscan, and Augustinian monasteries opposed Zwingli and stayed by the Roman church. But a number of cloisters were soon deserted and the council turned the buildings into hospitals. Priests and nuns were getting married, and new holy orders were being formed to allow the unmarried to relate to the orders of the church with new identifications.

Zwingli now announced his own marriage. Felix had anticipated this. Although Zwingli had been discreet, his respect and love for the lovely Anna Reinhart was obvious to those close to him. Felix wondered how Ulrich had found time to court and to build a relationship solid enough for marriage. Felix himself had not been free enough to do so. He had seen Trini only three times in the last month and he was so consumed with thoughts of change in the church and of new theologies that there was little room for those of marriage. Now, certainly, he thought, there would be so much to do it would be difficult to find adequate time for getting to Zollikon.

Changes at the Grossmünster were actually quite minimal. Zwingli, while able to encourage others in their change, made very few himself. The observance of mass was held as before, along with the continued baptism of infants and the festival celebrations outlined by Rome. Orders were issued from Zwingli that all preachers in the canton were to preach "only what they could prove from the word of God." The worship service itself now became primarily an exercise of hearing the Word of God read and expounded. In spite of his love for music and his own excellence with lute and viol, Zwingli excluded congregational singing from the city churches. He spoke against those whose music was a hypocritical performance and not a ministry.

"As the Scripture cautions, like David, they make instruments of music to themselves rather than to God. Above all, worship should be inaudible, an experience of the heart," Zwingli preached. "In neither Old or New Testament is there commandment where God specified music in corporate worship."

Felix and Conrad could hardly believe that the reform was moving with such hesitancy. They continued to urge Zwingli to carry out a reformation that would deal with the more substantive issues: to stop the mass, to have only a membership of believers, and to use the practice of the ban or discipline in the full renewal of the church. Zwingli was diplomatically seeking to carry the Great Council with him, and he cautioned them against zealous and enthusiastic actions which would do more harm than good.

"Remember," he said, "there is a difference between the external symbols and the true inner meanings of faith. Let us emphasize the meanings and the symbols will change."

"The mass is only a symbol then, Ulrich?" Felix asked.

"Well, let us take baptism for the illustration. There are two baptisms, the outer baptism with water and the inner baptism with the Spirit. It is not the outer baptism which saves a person, but the inner baptism with the Spirit."

Felix and Conrad were in full agreement with him on this. But they urged him to move more decisively in the changing of practices which would conform the church to Scripture. Zwingli appealed to them, "Please be patient and ask the people to respect the care with which I am working for reform." He expressed his concern that more radical actions would cause the City Council to back away from supporting the direction in which he was moving.

Felix boldly interrupted. "But, Ulrich," he was surprised by his own tone, quiet but intense. "We serve Christ, not the council, and unless you move with the conscience of the people, they may lose heart in your leadership."

Conrad added, "Already many people who have been awakened to faith are afraid that, without a full reformation, we may fall short of obedience to the gospel."

"That is a risk I must take," Zwingli said, shrugging his massive shoulders and closing the discussion.

Felix and Conrad strolled along the cobblestone street. Felix, walking with Conrad, went out of his :vay so that they could speak together before Felix turned back to head for his own home. They walked slowly, Conrad limping because of his sore feet, "a consequence of my profligate youth," he told Felix, "partly frozen while drinking beer and bundling in the forest one night." He made a few comments of regret for the way in which

71

he had conducted himself in Vienna and in Paris. Felix did not pursue the matter with further question, but empathized with his friend.

They were both quiet as they approached Conrad's home, thinking over the conversation they had just shared with Zwingli. Then Conrad stopped and turned to Felix. "Zwingli has his risk, but perhaps we have our own that we must take," he said. "We will continue our studies and see how God leads us."

The home Bible study movement continued to spread in Zurich. In the summer of 1523 Felix and Conrad, cooperating with their friend, Andreas Castelberger, continued their several classes. It was soon evident that many lay people knew more of the Scriptures than some priests and preachers. In these studies, Conrad and Felix provided leadership, actually developing language facility on the part of a number of their friends. Grebel regularly led studies in the Greek New Testament, beginning with the Gospel of Matthew. The studies in Hebrew were taught by Felix, with readings in the Old Testament prophets. He constantly emphasized their call for renewal and its relevance for the church. He would ask his students to follow the model the prophets had expressed for Israel.

A very intense group continued to meet for Bible study at Felix's home. It was a circle, quite diverse in makeup even as it became more united in faith. During the summer, a weaver from St. Gall, Lorenz Hochrütiner, returned to the city and joined them. He had traveled to Zurich frequently, attending Zwingli's sessions. On those trips he had developed a friendship with Conrad. Lorenz was a zealous man whose Christian faith was bold and his zeal contagious. He now became a close partner with Jacob Hottinger, from Zollikon. They both were very articulate and quite bold, speaking out against continuing the use of images and the practice of the mass as a repeated sacrifice.

Zwingli was so busy with the council that he had little time with his scholars. As the brethren continued their discussions, they became more confident. Most of them felt that they were now beyond Zwingli in confronting issues to which he had not yet addressed himself. In the late summer Felix and Conrad, accompanied by Simon Stumpf and Wilhelm Reublin, arranged a session with Zwingli. It was a meeting of friends, and in the freedom of their conversation they each encouraged him to stand with the community of faith alone, to build a free church, let the council say what it would.

In the intensity of the dialogue and with nervous chuckles, they reminded Zwingli of his statement in January. "You stated then," Felix reminded him, "in worldly things and actions I know well that on account of resistance judges are necessary, and I would be very glad to accept my lords of Zurich as judges. But in matters concerning divine wisdom and truth I will accept no one as witness and judge except the living Scriptures and the Spirit of God which speaks out of the Scriptures."

Zwingli mulled over the reminder for some time. Felix held his breath, hoping that the discussion would not become heated and divisive. Finally, Ulrich spoke. "Yes, basically that is what I believe, but I have come to understand that the Scriptures are not for private interpretation, and that the judges as well are responsible to work with the authority of Scripture. For example," he continued, "I had felt deeply that tithes should be abolished, but when the council decided that tithes are necessary for the sustenance of our program, on June twenty-second I supported that action. In a similar way we will need to work with the council as to the nature of the changes which we should carry out in Zurich."

Zwingli had a way of putting an end to a conversation by his authoritative tone and words. Felix and Conrad, though they had more to discuss with him, left his presence with uneasiness. There was relaxation in Zwingli's tactics for change, but Felix and his colleagues felt a sense of urgency for reform that clashed with Zwingli's seeming submission.

The group in the Bible class was anxious for a report and so Felix and Conrad gave them one, though disappointing, at the next meeting. The group evidenced their deep concern and desire for more immediate action. In September Felix's friends, Claus Hottinger, a brother of Jacob, and Lorenz Hochrütiner, took matters in their own hands. Early in the month they, along with a few others, tore down some of the icons and statues of saints at St. Peter's church where Leo Jud was pastor.

As a token act of law and order, Claus was imprisoned by the council with a sentence of one week. To support him, Hochrütiner and another friend, Wolfgang Ininger, destroyed the oil lamps at the altar of the Fraumünster. They were soon arrested and similarly imprisoned for a few days. Upon their release, Lorenz, Claus, and Hans Ockenfuss, another supporter who had joined the rebels, went to Stadelhofen and tore down the crucifix, proclaiming boldly that this hindered people from faith in the risen Christ. They announced their plan to sell the material and give the money to the poor. Their decisive act elicited cheers from the gathered crowd. But the wrath of the City Council was aroused by this deed and by the preaching of Simon Stumpf against images in the church at Höngg.

The Council now called Zwingli before them, making it clear that they held him accountable, saying that the men had acted on the basis of his teachings. Zwingli was furious. But diplomatically he appealed for a second disputation. Agreeing to his request, the council set the date for October 26-28. Zwingli assured them that this would enable him to correct the radical position of the enthusiasts and move ahead in good order in the reformation of the church.

During the next several weeks Felix, Conrad, and Simon met often at the Green Shield Inn for conversation. One of their concerns was how they should relate to Zwingli and to his compliance with the council.

"His is a strong man," Simon said, "and his hesitancy is not out of fear. He is a politician at work with the council."

"Yes, it is clear that he feels that he needs to identify his work with the City Council to have their full support for his ministry at the Grossmünster," Conrad added.

"True," Simon continued, "he did not respond favorably when I shared my proposals for a church of believers."

Felix rose to his feet and brought a fist down on the table in front of them. "But the reformation of the church is far larger and more extensive than what happens here in Zurich! We must draw clear proposals for reform according to evangelical truth and the Word of God and submit these to Zwingli. The cause we share is larger than his position at the Grossmünster."

They were agreed. During the next days each of them wrote proposals to submit to Zwingli for the reformation of the church according to their understandings of evangelical truth and the Word of God. Only when they had discussed the papers together and were unified in their presentation did they ask for an audience with Ulrich and with Leo Jud, his associate. Their request granted, Conrad and Simon each in turn first presented their statements to the reformer.

Finally, Felix had the opportunity to share his proposal, which he called a "Petition of Protest and Defense." He appealed specifically to Zwingli to abandon his attempts to organize and constitute a church according to agreements of the City Council, and instead to set up a church of believers that was more in keeping with the ideal they had discussed months before.

"Such a church would be one of genuine faith," he said, "one in which there would be integrity, where sin would be dealt with by the action of the church in responsible discipline. Righteousness and sanctification are to be promoted in the life of this church. The ministers of the gospel should be supported by voluntary gifts from the church rather than from tithes and benefices. Let the goal be a united church in Zurich where the different assemblies of the Grossmünster, the Fraumünster, and the other churches are in fellowship as the church of Christ, rather than having a separatist church apart from the big church," he urged. "We must build a church of ture faith, not one which is filled with persons who have only a nominal Christianity."

Zwingli and Jud were attentive, hearing each of them in a surprisingly friendly manner and responding kindly to each. However, just as kindly, Zwingli rejected their proposals in turn, saying that if they would just work with the civil authorities, they could bring about change in the church.

"In the New Testament," he reminded them in a somewhat patronizing tone, "Jesus taught that the tares and the wheat grew together until the judgment."

When Felix heard his words he insisted, "But, Ulrich, the field in which the tares grew is the world, not the church!"

Zwingli only shook his head. He was not interested, he said, in moving in a direction which could exclude many persons who lacked evangelical faith.

Zwingli's disagreement was not easy for Felix to accept. They had long been friends and had discussed their ideas with freedom. But now, Felix was aware that either Zwingli and his associates would change, or he, Conrad, Simon, their friend Wilhelm Reublin, and other close associates would have to conform. His own convictions had grown and solidified over the last weeks. It was unthinkable that he should give up now.

A few days after the meeting, Felix was walking from the marketplace when Zwingli stepped out of Hujuff's shop in front of him. They greeted each other with a certain tenseness but stood in front of the shop as if there were things one wanted to say to the other. As others were crowding the sidewalk, Zwingli said, "Let's step into Hujuff's garden for a moment."

As they walked off the street and into the garden, Zwingli began speaking. "Felix, I admire your zeal," he said, "and your facility in biblical interpretation. You make an important contribution in the gathering of the School of Prophecy."

"Thank you, Ulrich. I do enjoy teaching and I'm excited about the exercise of biblical study. It is especially meaningful since we have new freedom to work at developing a church in accordance with the Scripture." His words were forceful and his eyes piercing.

"And we must stand together in unity," Zwingli replied, "even if we don't present our interpretations in the same way."

"But," Felix countered, "I remember some important words from the Chinese leader, Confucius, that I learned at the University of Paris. Let me recall them. . . . 'If language is not used correctly then what is said is not what is meant, then what ought to be done remains undone. If this remains undone then morals and art will be corrupted. If morals and art are corrupted, justice will go astray. If justice goes astray, the people will stand about in hopeless confusion.' "

Zwingli was silent for a few moments, then replied, raising one finger in a characteristic gesture, "But we must be realists about the character of the church and not get carried away in perfectionism."

"You are right, Master Ulrich, that we cannot expect perfection with our sinfulness, but we can call for repentance and a break from the deliberate practice of sin." As he spoke Felix thought about his words and about the awe he had felt for this man that kept him from speaking his mind. Now, his disagreements with the leader had raised his own self-esteem enough to mandate frankness. Zwingli did not like it.

"And are you living so perfectly, Felix?" he asked.

"Master Ulrich, my life in grace is a forgiven one, but I seek not to presume on God's grace."

Zwingli smiled and said, "We must talk again," and turned toward the cathedral. Felix watched him go, feeling the victor in their conversation, and yet feeling a great loss.

Together, Felix and Conrad along with Wilhelm and Simon agreed that they should extend their interchange beyond the Zurich community to persons involved in evangelical emphasis. The word from Waldshut was that Dr. Balthasar Hubmaier, a friend of Reublin's from university days, was preaching eloquently for reformation in the Waldshut Cathedral. From St. Gall news came of evangelical awakening there. The report came through Vadian, who had married Conrad's sister and was a political leader in that community. Discussions with Ludwig

Hätzer, long an associate of Zwingli, made them aware that the well-known Dr. Sebastian Hofmeister and others in the area of Schaffhausen and Hallau had become articulate in their commitments to evangelical faith.

Beyond the leaders, the peasants, especially in Bavaria, were actively engaged in calling for change. There was even a report from Pastor Benedict Burgauer of St. Gall, that some families were refusing to have their infants baptized lest they give them false hope. They said it was better to call them to personal faith when they came to an acceptable age.

As they reviewed these reports, Conrad declared that he would write his former acquaintance, Pastor Burgauer, and call him to openness, to an honest hearing of evangelical faith. As brothers, they agreed together that they must discuss this new development on infant baptism with Zwingli. Actually hearing this news from St. Gall might help him to rethink the nature of his reform. They planned to remind Zwingli that he had preached in 1521 that "the little children who are not baptized will not be damned." Also, that in May 1523, he had agreed that children should not be baptized until they were instructed in the faith. Felix was confident that, with their support, Zwingli could find the freedom to develop a free church and not be intimidated by the City Council.

The second disputation was convened Monday morning, October 26. As the brethren walked along the Limmat to the City Hall, people were streaming into the street, hurrying to the hall to secure a seat. Felix looked at the dark blue waters of the Limmat flowing through the city from the Zurich Sea; he recalled Zwingli's words that one could no more stop the impact of the Word of God than that one could stop the waters of the Rhine! The brethren entered the hall and were taken to seats opposite Zwingli and his associates. Burgomaster Röist opened the meeting, having appointed Vadian and other esteemed delegates to preside. Zwingli's friend, Dr. Sebastian Hofmeister from Schaffhausen, served as the discussion chairman. He had earned his doctorate in Paris and was well known as an evangelical voice in north Switzerland. He actively promoted the new understandings of faith, assisting the "Lutheran" preachers who had come to his area.

Over eight hundred clergy and laypersons came to the Rathaus, or Council Hall, filling the hall and standing in aisles and entrances. As Felix scanned the faces, he was pleased to see that among those present was Dr. Hubmaier of Waldshut, well-known for his work of reformation in southern Bavaria and for his itinerant preaching in St. Gall. Much of his emphasis was similar to the current thinking of Felix and Conrad, and they were pleased that he was present.

The discussion began with a review of the 67 theses which Zwingli had presented in the January disputation. It soon moved on to the particular issues that had emerged relating directly to the nature of salvation. Here, there were two primary areas of focus. The first concerned the abolition of the mass, with the awareness that faith in the risen Christ and fellowship with him had an altogether different meaning than the way the crucified Christ was presented as a repeated sacrifice in the mass. The second issue was the question of baptism and its relation to salvation, especially as it related to infants who could not enter into the covenant of faith.

The discussion moved now between Zwingli and the more radical group rather than between Zwingli and the Roman churchmen. While Dr. Hubmaier engaged effectively in the dialogue, Conrad was the most prominent spokesperson for the radical brethren. In his deliberate style, he represented Felix and their associates, interpreting the meaning of a more total reform than that which Zwingli proposed.

By the second day, it was clear that there were two parties. On the one side were Zwingli and those who supported his position, identifying the City Council as the authority by which the new church should be constituted. On the other side Manz sat with Grebel, Stumpf, Reublin, Castelberger, Hätzer, Claus Hottinger,

Lorenz Hochrütiner, and other supporters.

On the third day, the discussion became heated. Zwingli rescinded his previous position and moved deliberately to silence the opposition.

"The council," he said, "will decide the nature of the change in the church. They will set a time for dealing with images and the mass, a change which will come in the near future."

Suddenly, Simon Stumpf leaped to his feet and shouted, "Master Ulrich, it is not in the power of your hand nor of this council to decide this issue. The Spirit of God has already decided it by his Word. If my lords adopt and decide on some other course, that would be against the decision of God; I will ask Christ for his Spirit and I will teach and act against it."

Zwingli's reaction was emphatic. "I too stand for *sola scriptura* but interpretation is not a private matter. I will also preach and act against it if they decide otherwise. I am not putting the decision in their hand. They are not over the Word of God, and this goes not only for them but for the whole world!"

The disputation ended with an irreconcilable distance between the two groups. Felix felt sick in the stomach over the long period of tension. He noticed that his knees were shaking as they left the City Hall. Simon Stumpf was singled out and retained by some members of the council. Felix waited outside, anxious to know what was happening to Simon in his interchange with Zwingli and the council.

When Simon was finally escorted into the street by several of the guards, Felix took his arm and they walked off together.

"Felix, I am finished in Zurich," Simon managed to say.

"You are what?"

"I am finished in Zurich because I won't stop speaking against images. I have been told to complete my affairs here. I am to leave Höngg and my pastorate in November."

Felix felt helpless. He was caught up in a movement that had snowballed and suddenly was getting out of hand. He still could not believe that he and Zwingli were on opposite sides.

80

"I must talk with Master Zwingli apart from the council," he said, "and see whether he really believes what he was saying before them. He surely doesn't support this."

The very next morning Felix met Zwingli at the Latin School. When he questioned Zwingli, the response was a question.

"Felix, do you not believe that in situations of difference one cannot be, by himself, even secretly, a true Christian?"

"No, my friend, for Christianity and brotherly love must be expressed publicly and cannot be a private matter. We are called to walk daily with Jesus."

"Do you mean to apply this to all members of the church?"

"Yes, for as Paul wrote, 'Fornication, covetousness, adultery, and such like are not to be tolerated among Christians.' We ought to discipline such offenders of Christ and ban them from his table."

"Felix, you try that and see how far you get in the church. Go ahead," Zwingli spat, "put out of the church those who have such vices; set up this genuine church that you talk about."

"But, Master Ulrich," Felix was holding his temper well, "I am not a bishop like you. That is your authority."

"And I do not see it as you do, Felix, so we will accept the church as it is given to us."

Felix joined a very somber group that evening as they met for the Bible study. The time given to study was actually quite brief. A major question faced them. Could they work with Zwingli and his associates? Most still felt that they needed to work further with Zwingli and the council to achieve mutual understandings of the Scripture. They were agreed that their growing contacts with other evangelical leaders could be a significant influence. As a group they committed themselves to continue to work to this end. They closed their meeting in prayer, seeking God's guidance for their next steps.

Chapter 6

The Breach Beyond Repair

"Trini, if it weren't for being so excited about my new faith, I would be very sad." They were walking by the lake, Trini's hands in her apron pockets, Felix picking at a piece of dry grass.

"I have lost a friend. I have lost a mentor."

"Felix, you must think of Zwingli as the man who brought you to this new understanding of Christianity, not as the one who abandoned you when you got there."

"Yes, you're right. It's just that I'm so disappointed. Trini," he jumped ahead of her a step and threw out his arms, "so many are discovering the meaning of faith and are studying and dreaming together. I'm telling you, Bible study has opened a whole new world to people!" His enthusiasm had caught Trini off guard. She had stopped and was looking at the lake water. For a moment, he had forgotten that while he was in Zurich, immersed in working for reform and enlightenment, she was in Zollikon, working on her father's farm. He resumed his place beside her and they walked on.

"Did Hochrütiner leave Zurich as he was asked?"

"Yes," Felix sighed. "Conrad wrote his brother-in-law, Vadian, and asked him to receive Lorenz in St. Gall and give him every support. And Zwingli himself wrote Vadian, as he likes Lorenz very much, urging that Lorenz be received graciously, even though he is too outspoken and rebellious for Zurich at this tempestuous time."

"And Simon has gone, also?" Trini was trying to keep herself informed about those who were important to Felix.

"Yes, he had to be gone before Christmas."

"Banished?" Felix heard fear in Trini's voice. There was nothing he could say to console her. The possibility of being arrested was all too real. Trini had stopped walking, so they sat on the cold ground.

"There were a few days after he was released from prison when we were able to meet. We actually drafted a plan for an evangelical believers' church in Zurich."

"Is that all you ever think about?" Trini was looking straight into his face, the corners of her mouth turned down.

"Yes," he said, "when I'm not thinking of you."

She tilted her head down and smiled slightly. There was silence except for a group of wild ducks that had flown up from the opposite side of the lake. Felix admired her beauty, her clear complexion. Finally, Trini spoke as if she had decided that if she were to be part of Felix's life, she would need to accept what he was doing.

"Who is left in your study group?"

"Conrad, Wilhelm, Johann Brötli, and a few others," Felix said, relieved to be speaking again.

"Wilhelm was married in August, wasn't he?" Trini had dropped her voice. Felix hesitated, wondering if she was disappointed that the wedding was not hers. His chest tightened at the thought that he may be hurting her by avoiding the subject of their future.

"They're expecting their first child." He knew he shouldn't keep talking about the controversial issues which so obsessed him, but the words came out. "Wilhelm and Conrad are constantly discussing the question of infant baptism since they both have or will have children. Many in the parishes of Wytikon and even here in Zollikon are accepting Wilhelm's counsel and are delaying the baptism of their children."

"Pastor Brötli supports this?" Trini's face showed disbelief.

"At first, no, but Wilhelm has been persistent in his teaching and now Brötli is an open advocate of the position."

"What was all the rioting we heard about at the beginning of the month?"

"Well, I was not involved, but as I understand it, a number of evangelical laymen took action in opposition to the continuation of the mass. Some of the men took liturgy books and tore out the pages on the mass and placed them before the door of the provost's house. Then they went to the place of capital punishment and cut down the gallows in protest."

"I heard about what they did, but what was the result of their actions?" Trini wanted to know.

"Well, it brought a response. On December tenth, Burgomaster Röist and his councilors heard a memorandum by Zwingli, Jud, and Engelhart. They, as the three 'people's priests,' intend to abolish the mass and introduce a new evangelical communion by Christmas Day," Felix explained.

"The council had patience and listened, and Zwingli had patience and spoke." His sarcasm showed. "And the council held to moderation and a continuation of the mass and postponement of any revisions."

"Well, I certainly don't see why these things are so important," Trini said. "But I do hate to see all this divisiveness."

"Yes, you are right. Zwingli has called a third disputation for next month partly in response to the disunity."

"Well, tell me about your teaching. Is it going well?" she wanted to know.

"Oh, quite well, except the income is limited and, as always, my financial situation gives me little security." He showed some embarrassment. "Come, let's walk."

Things moved slowly with the turn of the year, but on January 20, 1524, Zwingli stood before the council. Felix and Conrad attended with high expectations, only to find that the dialogue continued to be focused on the issues that had been raised in the previous disputation. Even with the increasing public interest in believer's baptism, the issue was not pursued in any length. Zwingli specifically addressed the group of theologians who were gathered.

"Think of what will happen if we push a perfectionist Christianity on a people who are only beginning to understand what Christ really taught," he said. "People must be made ripe for the gospel."

Zwingli did make a compromise, however, with those he saw as radicals. He supported decisive action on the removal of relics and images from the church buildings in Zurich. Addressing the assembly he said, "The buildings were meant first to be meetinghouses for the proclamation of God's word, not 'fully' temples."

The council accepted Zwingli's position, and by early spring the works of art, the holy relics, the altars, the candles, and crucifixes were removed from all of the church buildings. Workmen whitewashed the inside walls to cover the pictures and images. Felix was pained over the destruction of some of the more impressive art, although he agreed with Zwingli's interpretation of the function of church buildings. Still, he and Conrad felt that Zwingli was making only token changes. Conrad challenged Zwingli in a personal confrontation. In a burst of honesty and well-planned words, Conrad laid out the disagreements he had with him.

"When," he asked Ulrich, "will you release the Christian church from its captivity to the tax system? How can you be an employee of the city of Zurich and a free prophet of Christ? Who will break the news to the people that Christ calls his followers to lay aside violence, even the common sword of self-defense? How long will you wait for the council to let you abolish the repetitive sacrifice of the mass? What keeps you from giving up the baptism of infants who can't possibly repent and believe the gospel?

When will the rule of Christ become the rule of the church?"

Zwingli, with an expression of frustration, said, "And when, Conrad, will you and your friends trust me? I'm trying to do my best at reform."

The disagreements continued. Felix gave himself more to his own study of the Scripture. He was thoroughly convinced that the New Testament called for a responsible voluntary decision in one's commitment to Christ. This was a step of faith which an infant could not take. Therefore, infant baptism had no real meaning for the infant but only for the parents. It seemed to him that parents should dedicate their children to the Lord and give themselves to bringing up the child in the fear of Christ, but baptism should accompany the child's own commitment when old enough to be held accountable.

By the spring of 1524 the matter of infant baptism was no longer a private consideration. It had become a topic of common discussion in the Zurich community. The City Council expressed its concern that its authority was being threatened by the act of parents withholding children from baptism. They began holding discussion on how best to require the baptism of infants. As to the mass, Claus Hottinger, Felix's good friend and a relative of Trini, had been arrested and expelled from Zurich for his bold statements against its continued observance.

On March 9, the community of Zurich was shocked by news from Luzern. Claus Hottinger had been executed by the Roman Church for his position. The Zurich Council, reporting his death, informed the Zurich residents that they had tried to intercede for Claus but to no avail. There were many who had been associated with him and who grieved his death. He had been an activist in Zwingli's reform. In March 1522, he was one of those who had eaten sausages on Ash Wednesday at Froschauer's house. He and Felix had shared closely in Bible studies. And he and Conrad had been together in taking over the monk's pulpits and in preaching against the monks in July 1522. His had been a strong voice for reformation and he would be missed.

Felix first went to Rennweg, where Claus had lived, to comfort Margaret, Claus's sister. Then he made a hurried trip to Zollikon to see Trini. He knew that she would be bereaved and frightened over her uncle's death. He comforted her as best he could, although he too was confused, angered, and horrified. Reminded of the Beatitudes, he quoted to her, " 'Blessed are you when men persecute you for my sake,' the Scripture says." But, he could tell, words meant little to her and were inadequate assurance against Felix's own future. He managed to push his own fear into the background and decided that if the "Pharisees" were angered, the brethren must be doing the work of Christ.

He resolved now to concentrate even more on sharing the faith of Christ. In addition to calling on many of his old friends, he was able to lead Hans Hujuff, a goldsmith from Halle, Saxony, to a new experience of faith. Hujuff had been turned to faith by the Lutheran movement and now came to accept the meaning of the believers' church emphasis on a voluntary adult faith. Felix found it satisfying to be an evangelist. His dialogue with his colleagues and his witness to others helped him to systematize and articulate his convictions of faith.

Conrad was doing much the same. The two of them were recognized as the primary leaders among the brethren and both were greatly influenced by Jakob Hottinger. Grebel had written earlier to Luther, especially on nonviolence as the Christian lifestyle. While Luther did not answer in writing, he did send words of encouragement through a friend to the Bible-studying brothers and sisters in Zurich. Conrad had also written and published a tract on adult believer's baptism.

In June, Ludwig Hätzer, whom they considered to be vacillating on their cause, was preparing to travel to Augsburg. He hoped to arrange the publication of his expositions of the Epistles from Ephesians to Hebrews. Even though he had also become impatient with Zwingli and his writings showed some differences with the reformer, Ulrich had agreed to write a letter of recommendation to a friend, Johann Frosch. Zwingli also included a letter of introduction to his friend, the reformer, Urbannes Raggius. Before leaving, Hätzer made a special visit to their Bible study to tell Felix and Conrad of his trip and to bid them farewell.

"Perhaps," he told them, trying to encourage them to patience, "with the relics destroyed and the pictures removed in the church and with the emphasis on the hearing of the Scripture as it is preached, Zwingli will soon be ready to remove the mass and institute the Lord's Supper."

Felix had little time with Conrad during the first weeks of June. Conrad's youngest sister, Dorothy, only 15 years of age, married Conrad's friend, John Jacob Ammann—against the wishes of Conrad. Ammann was insistent, and being closely associated with Zwingli, he had Ulrich's support as well. Dorothy's parents reluctantly agreed, with Conrad caught uncomfortably between his parents and his friend. To Felix he commented, "This is not at all like my interchange in getting my sister Martha married to Vadian."

Felix held back his words for he watched Conrad's family relations with interest but with limited understanding. As the weeks passed into summer, Felix could see the opposition to the free-church aspects of reform continually increase. Reublin's open teaching against infant baptism at the churches in Wytikon and Zollikon was getting much attention. In August, the council acted. They had both Reublin and a baker, Heinrich Aberli, arrested in Zollikon and held in prison in Zurich. Felix and Conrad were astonished that the council had gone so far, and Conrad went to his father, a member of the council, to plead for tolerance. But it did no good. Felix felt helpless. Burying himself in study during the weeks of June, he edited his earlier writing, "Petition of Protest and Defense," hoping to have it published.

Wilhelm's imprisonment gave Felix a strong sense of urgency to put into print his statements about their position. Beginning with repentance and faith, he explained the basic character of New Testament faith and the reasons for rejecting the various practices of the Roman Church. At the same time, Conrad was in dialogue with Dr. Hubmaier of Waldshut and with his brother-in-law, Vadian, of St. Gall. He sincerely hoped to gain Vadian's support for what their growing circle of committed disciples were attempting to achieve in Zurich.

In late August, Grebel shared with the group at the Bible study a report of a reformation voice from the North, one Thomas Müntzer, who was now in South Germany. Müntzer, having been converted by the evangelical teaching of Luther, had left the reformer because he held a more radical stance. With the counsel of the group, Conrad drafted a long, ten-page letter to Thomas. He urged him to faithfulness to the New Testament and the Word of Christ. He expressed the interest of the group in Zurich to dialogue with him. Stressing the importance of the example of Christ in love and obedience to the will of God, he affirmed their support of Müntzer's emphasis against presenting a "sweet Jesus" who approves persons without obedient discipleship.

On the evening of September 5, Felix, Wilhelm (who was now out of prison), Jacob Hottinger, Andreas Castelberger, and Hans Ockenfuss joined with Conrad in signing the letter. Conrad asked the brethren whether it might be wise for him to travel into Saxony and talk with Müntzer and other persons who were formerly with Luther; they advised him against making the trip. They reminded him of his problem with his feet and the difficulty he would have walking. The letter was enough for the present, especially as they didn't know the man.

The idea of meeting with persons from Luther's circle materialized from another source. At the end of September, Dr. Gerhard Westerburg came to Zurich from Saxony. He had a letter from Doctor Carlstadt, his brother-in-law, who had previously been Luther's associate; and he had script for books which Carlstadt had written. This was his first concern, to get them printed. He first met with Zwingli, describing the nature of the works and asking for his help. But Zwingli, upon learning that Carlstadt had broken with Luther, had no interest in getting involved in the publication of such materials. "Especially," he said, "if they might lend support to the position of the radicals in his own movement."

When Dr. Westerburg learned of Conrad and Felix and their associates, he came to them with the materials, asking for advice about the project. They welcomed him warmly, Conrad saying, "We regard Dr. Carlstadt as one of the finest proclaimers of the pure Word of God."

Felix was interested in Westerburg's comments on the continuing reformation of the church.

"Carlstadt," Westerburg said, "wanted to achieve a more genuine expression of the believers' church rather than simply a separation from Rome."

Felix asked for several of the manuscripts for review, and after careful reading he was impressed with their content. He discussed with Conrad and Wilhelm the possibility of helping Carlstadt get them printed. Both Conrad and Felix, during the time they had spent in Basel, had worked for Cratander, the well-known printer. It was agreed that Felix should go to Basel with Dr. Westerburg and help him arrange to print the manuscripts.

Felix was enthusiastic. He could, while there, check about getting his own writing printed. This project excited him, but his eagerness to lobby for Carlstadt was short-lived. On October 24, Carlstadt himself came to Zurich and he and Felix's group were able to share in more detail their vision for a believers' church. In their discussions, Felix sought to interpret the position of the Zurich brethren to Carlstadt. It soon became evident that the man was not with them on the nature of the free church. In Felix's opinion, he was not clear as to how the church could be a believers' church and be separate from civil authorities. However, they decided that even with limited support for Carlstadt's emphasis, Felix should help arrange the publication of the work.

A few days later they set out for Basel. The air was fresh and cool, the fall crops an interesting evidence of planned farming. It was familiar territory for Felix, and he enjoyed guiding Westburg and Carlstadt across the country. As they talked of the university city, both of them wanted to meet Oecolampad the scholar who had returned to Basel and was now the leading reformer in the city.

Arriving in Basel, they went first to the printing house, where they were warmly welcomed by Cratander. Felix was impressed that the old printer still remembered him. Perhaps he could have some influence with this man. Before long, and to their delight, they discovered that Cratander was himself caught up in the debate between Erasmus's work in the church and the reform of Oecolampad. He would publish any material which would enhance the movement for renewal in the ecclesiastical community.

Felix had much more confidence now, and after arrangements were made for Carlstadt, he discussed with the printer the possibility of publishing his own writing. To this Cratander was agreeable and encouraged Felix to complete his work. Elated and now anxious to get back to Zurich and continue writing, Felix felt an inner urgency to finish the manuscript. Reflecting on Wilhelm, who with his frightening prison experience had not altered his teaching against infant baptism, Felix was sure that the issue would not long go unchallenged by the council. He wanted his interpretation in print.

Once back in Zurich, he used the Bible study group as a sounding board for his material. They met frequently to study and to seek direction for their future. Occasionally Trini would now attend, coming from Zollikon with her Aunt Margaret and Uncle Jacob. Felix looked forward to those evenings when the woman that he loved became involved in the cause he espoused. Her interest had ·grown with their friendship. He had been surprised when she suggested making the trips from Zollikon. He had purposely not mentioned it before.

"Felix, would you mind if I visit some of the Bible studies?"

"Mind? I would be thrilled!" He couldn't help reaching for her hand.

"I couldn't make the trip for every meeting but I could visit Aunt Margaret and come along with her."

"It would mean so much to me," he had said. And it did. He watched her every reaction in hope that she too would fully own the convictions that he held.

In mid-October, a priest from Chur named George Cajacob was added to the group. He was brought by their friend Hans Ockenfuss of Zollikon. Heinrich Aberli, the baker who had been imprisoned with Wilhelm, had also become a close friend to George. His wife and George's wife had been immediately drawn to each other. Cajacob was a large man, very outspoken, often eloquent in his extemporaneous statements. His aggressive spirit added considerable encouragement to the brethren as they sought ways to best represent their position to Zwingli and the several people's priests. Their hope now was to get the Zurich Council to take a more moderate position on reform, especially in the dispute about baptism. They understood the council's fear. If only believers were baptized into the church, then the church-state would be denied and would eventually be replaced.

The first step was to try again to reach Zwingli, to meet with him and the other Zurich pastors to discuss their conviction on believer's baptism. They hoped that the church leaders could be led to at least negotiate some moderation on the part of the council. To the surprise of Felix and Conrad, Zwingli agreed to meet with them not once but each Tuesday for the next several weeks, providing time for careful study of the Scripture. It seemed almost like the earlier days of the School of Prophecy meetings. They were encouraged and went with high spirits, but at the first meeting, Zwingli and his associates dominated the discussion. Zwingli said,

"Be patient. The Word will take its course. We can't change everything at once."

"Master Ulrich," Conrad responded. "Nowhere in the Scripture do we read that the apostles baptized children with water."

"Not specifically, but the Word is not lacking, for baptism is our outward circumcision," was his reply.

After a lengthy discussion on this interpretation, Felix commented, "But when the apostles baptized, they first examined applicants as to their faith."

"Yes, sometimes, but it did not always happen in that manner." Zwingli was argumentative. "Jesus gave sight to a blind man without first examining his faith, for later he met him and asked him if he believed in the son of God, to which the man responded, 'Who is he, Lord, that I might believe?' "

Conrad broke in, "But we are told by Jesus, 'He who believes and is baptized shall be saved; but he who believes not shall be damned.' "

"These words cannot be applied to the question of children, for they cannot be among the group who hear the gospel, so clearly, this doesn't apply to the question." Zwingli responded.

"It would be a far more powerful and effective act," Conrad insisted, "if everyone openly confessed his faith before he is dipped into the water."

"It is easier to learn to know faith if one has been baptized as an infant," replied Zwingli. "Salvation is not in the baptism but in the grace of God; therefore, to have baptism as an infant is a basis to call the growing child to learn the law of God and come to faith."

As they left the meeting, Felix turned to Conrad, "I could barely talk. They choke my speech in my throat."

As he looked up, he saw Jörg Binder at a distance. He was certain that Jörg had seen him, but he had quickly turned a corner and disappeared. They were on different paths of faith. Felix missed his old friend, yearning for him to follow through on his earlier commitment to Christ in full discipleship, but Jörg was fully with Zwingli. He was above all committed to his position at the Carolina School, and he wasn't about to rock the boat.

The second weekly discussion with Zwingli was held in early November, and was to be the last. In the discussion, Zwingli was especially confrontive with Jacob Hottinger, the elder from

Zollikon who accompanied them, for he was known to be a very spiritual man and a very influential person among the radicals, as Ulrich called them. It was evident that Zwingli and his associates would not give them the opportunity to share their understanding of the Scripture but wanted them only to listen to the council's position. Sensing that the issue was becoming increasingly divisive and anticipating that the next step would be a meeting with the Large Council, Felix turned his attention to completing his written disputation. He stated unequivocally that he and his friends stood by the first mandate of the January 23 disputation of the council: all actions must conform to the Bible. He followed this with his own careful exegesis of Scripture.

It was mid-December before he was able to make his presentation. He hoped that the council, which had recently changed its position in regard to church images, would also be willing to change its understanding of baptism. Felix had outlined five points to show that infant baptism did not correspond to the New Testament picture of the meaning of baptism: it did not follow repentance; it did not issue from faith; it was not the confirmation of a new life; it was not the sign of personal covenant; and it was not a voluntary commitment. He emphasized the call to an adult decision.

As he reviewed his writing before the council meeting, he decided that it was good. He began his introductory letter, "Dear Lords and Brethren, in virtue of the common name which we all together bear, I appeal for a similar common and open study of Holy Scripture . . . ."

"Infant baptism," he had written, "is against the example of Christ, who was himself baptized at thirty years, although circumcised at eight days! Now Christ has given us an example that as he has done so also ought we to do."

In the conclusion of his statement he appealed to Zwingli to put in writing the reasons which he held in support of infant baptism.

There was tension in the atmosphere of the many-windowed

Council Hall of Zurich, where Felix and his colleagues met the Great Council. In the discussion which followed his presentation, Zwingli first agreed with Felix as he emphasized the call to repentance, repeating the references to John the Baptist and other passages quoted from the New Testament. Zwingli also affirmed Felix's emphasis on baptism as the rite which "launches men on this new life," the rite of introduction to a new life. But Zwingli rejected emphatically the necessity for adult baptism alone. He did not articulate his reasons for infant baptism, but said that he would put them in print.

Burgomaster Röist adjourned the session and each group filed out. The council left solemnly in their long robes, and then the brethren of the believers' church persuasion left. They were perplexed but confident as they walked from the City Hall along the Limmat toward Conrad's home on the Neumarket. After a few farewell words, Felix turned and made his way past the Grossmünster, along Neuenstadt to his home.

Felix waited anxiously for some response, but the days passed with no word. In late December Zwingli published a booklet entitled, "Those Who Give Cause for Disturbance." The booklet, rather than providing a full discussion of the question of infant baptism, discussed the views of divergent groups. Zwingli noted seven types of troublemakers. He at least paid his former associates the respect of identifying Felix and Conrad as sincere religious persons with whom controversy was really unnecessary. While they were radically evangelical, his differences with them, he wrote, were mostly a matter of timing, as they were presumptuous and impatient. Felix knew as he read the words that this was the council's answer to the brethren, given through Zwingli as spokesman.

In his discussion of infant baptism and the Lord's Supper, Zwingli emphasized that the Catholic ritual accompanying both of these ceremonies would, of course, disappear in Zurich—not by action of the council, but through the inner developments of faith. He affirmed these to be only external rites and not the basic elements of faith. He appealed for Manz, Grebel, and their associates to get rid of their spiritual pride, to leave the difficult office of interpreting the orders of the church to the pastors, and to work for unity in the evangelical movement.

Felix was indignant. His own writing had received little attention and Zwingli, he saw, was avoiding the issues once again. Suddenly, he found himself laughing out of frustration. He made his way to the Neumarket and Conrad's home to share his reaction. To their surprise, the next discussion between the brethren and Zwingli's circle was called a week later. Zwingli asked that only one of the persons be the spokesman. Felix and Wilhelm urged Conrad to speak for the brethren. This severely limited Felix, as well as Wilhelm, and their new colleague, George of Chur, but they respected Conrad's role.

George had been pastor at Trins in the diocese of Chur, but had left the Roman Church in 1523. Under persecution for this move, he had actually come to Zurich to talk with Zwingli. This he tried, but found little response from him. He had found his way to the Bible study led by Felix and had identified with the brethren. He was nicknamed, "Blaurock." At the October 28 disputation, George had enthusiastically leaped to his feet to share his comments and someone in the court had asked for identification as to who was speaking. The reply was simply, "George, with the blue coat." From that time on, he carried the nickname of George of the Blaurock.

Since then, through the weeks following that October disputation, a close friendship had grown between George and Felix. Blaurock was tall and large-boned, very dark, with deep set, piercing eyes. At first Felix held him at a distance, a bit inhibited by his aggressive manner, but mainly, seeking to discern his nature and motivation. But by the time of the interactions in mid-December, when Felix had presented his defense to Zwingli and the pastors, he was thoroughly convinced by George's consistent support that he was a man of sincerity and faith.

As spokesman for the brethren, Conrad called upon Felix to

present again statements from his "Protest and Defense" (*SSA*, pp. 311-312). He began.

Wise, considerate, gracious, dear lords and brethren:
It is well known to your Honors that many strange opinions have appeared. First, some hold that newborn infants are to be baptized as they come from the womb and that this can be proved from the Holy Scriptures, others that infant baptism is wrong and false, and has arisen from and been invented by that antichrist, the pope and his adherents, which is true as we know and believe from Holy Writ. Among whom I too have been held and accused by some as a rioter and wretch, which is however an unjust and ungracious charge that can never be raised and proved on the basis of the truth, for neither have I engaged in rioting nor in any way taught or encouraged anything that has led or might lead to rioting (which all those with whom I have ever been associated can testify of me). For this reason the charge is unjust. Since, however, I have been accused of being such a person, it becomes necessary for me to give to you, my gracious and dear lords, an account and reason for my faith as follows. . . . "

Felix felt that the members of the council were listening to him carefully, but then, he had felt the same the last time. The entire session seemed repetitive. The brethren were discouraged when, after a cursory review, they were told that there would need to be another meeting to discuss the same issues. Exhausted by the feeling that they were making no headway, they prepared themselves to meet Zwingli again on January 10, 1525.

Barbara and Conrad heralded the birth of a third child, Rachael, and now the question of infant baptism was for them and for those in their fellowship, an immediate one. The Bible class became a prayer meeting in anticipation of the discussion with the council. They decided to press Zwingli at the next meeting to give them scriptural reasons for the continuation of infant baptism in the evangelical church. They would go with scriptural reasons for the cessation of this practice and the introduction of a true believers' church.

January 10 dawned cold but bright. Their meeting was to

convene at the Grossmünster, just a short walk for Felix from his home on Neuenstadt Street. In the early morning they met in the familiar choir hall of the great church of Zurich. Felix had frequented this hall from his early boyhood, but now the confrontation with Zwingli made the majestic halls seem ominous. The people's priest was accompanied by the other parish priests and several representatives of the Small Council. The brethren made their appeal to Zwingli, on the basis of Holy Scripture, calling for a church that was truly founded on the Word of God. If he did so, they maintained, they would be fully supportive. The brethren assured him that they committed themselves to honest presentations of their interpretation of Scripture. The Scripture alone, they claimed, can bring understandings and reunite the divergent emphasis.

But the meeting left them as far apart as ever. It was evident that Zwingli and his associates were not committed to solidifying their church reform under the City Council. Conrad, Felix, George, Wilhelm, and their associates were committed to a free church and to a ministry of evangelism which would call people across the country to faith in Christ. They sought not only to bring reform into the church but to be a free church as an expression of the kingdom of Christ in society.

Following this disputation, Felix felt that he should try one other approach. He sent a petition to the City Council asking for opportunity to present his written testimony to the Great Council. He requested that it be read apart from Zwingli's or his own presence. He explained, "Zwingli overpowers us with his fast talking so that we are not truly heard."

In response, the City Council assumed responsibility for a bold answer to Felix. They set a meeting for January 17, and a mandate was issued to Felix and the brethren for response.

"All who hold the error that infants should not be baptized" shall appear before the council in the City Hall the morning of Tuesday, January 17, 1525, to give reasons "from divine Scripture" for their position.

The brethren did not back away from this invitation. They called a special session to pray and converse together, outlining their strategy. This was their high opportunity. It was agreed that three of them would be the primary speakers, those who had been leaders in their movement and associates of Zwingli through the years of their developing faith: Conrad Grebel, Felix Manz, and Wilhelm Reublin. They were, of course, supported by George Blaurock, Andreas Castelberger, Heinrich Aberli, Hans Ockenfuss, Hans Hujuff, Jacob Hottinger, and others.

As they spoke and prayed together, they each had the sense that the coming meeting would determine their future. Felix felt a profound responsibility to be true to the spirit of the New Testament and to the will of Christ. He spent many hours alone, rehearsing answers to possible questions, reviewing Scripture and praying. Finally, as the week drew to its close, he felt saturated. He was ready.

Chapter 7

The Beginning of the Free Church

"The freedom of the individual is not to be compelled by the councils of the state!" Felix declared emphatically. He and Conrad were discussing the issues facing them in the struggle for a believers' church.

They sat at a rough wooden table in a corner of the Green Shield Inn, a favorite eating place for them. Usually they were served by the maid Regeli, but today, the matron herself, Anna Widerker, waited on them. They were slightly bothered by her repeated trips to their table until they realized that she was interested in their conversation. With this encouragement, they spoke more loudly, knowing that others would hear them.

"We are not simply wrestling with the question of infant baptism," Conrad replied. We are wrestling with the question as to whether the church can be free in its obedience to the directions of Christ as we understand them."

"And obedience in faith is the logical expression of our commitment to Christ," Felix added.

Conrad nodded his head. "To hold people accountable, the community of believers must develop a disciplined congregation," he added.

"But not with the sword, as the City Council seeks to do," insisted Felix. "No Christian smites with the sword, or resists evil actions against himself. And further, since Christians do not kill, no Christian should be a government official."

"I agree," Conrad responded. "The sword must be left for those who live outside of the perfection of Christ."

Felix had been sharing daily conversation with Conrad. The tension had increased since Conrad and Barbara had refused to baptize their newborn child. They were facing intense pressure not only from Zwingli, but also from Conrad's father, Jacob Grebel, a member of the elite Small Council (Senate). He wanted them to agree to the child's baptism and to identify fully with the church. Zwingli himself spoke to Conrad of how important his contribution was in the life of the church.

"Conrad," Zwingli told him. "You are looked to as a leader, and your leadership can help bring your circle of brethren into harmony with the church. Consider your influence, Conrad, as you decide to baptize your daughter."

The issue was now public. Zwingli was preaching passionately against the impatient radicals who did not wait on the responsible leaders of the church to guide them. Felix and Conrad, discussing the issue, were not only convinced of their position, but were keenly aware of the support of the group identifying with them in the same convictions. The brethren were of no mind to surrender their stance to the City Council. As they met to prepare for the disputation scheduled for January 17, they encouraged one another.

"A church governed by the City Council is no more free than the Catholic Church governed by the pope in Rome," said Felix.

The group was encouraged by various reports of the spread of the evangelical faith in other regions. They were not alone in the quest for freedom to be true to their convictions as disciples of Jesus Christ. Dr. Hubmaier of Waldshut was also a challenge to Zwingli, teaching against infant baptism. They sent word to him of the public notice, inviting him to be present on the seventeenth.

The leaders of the brethren went early to the City Hall on the day of the public disputation. As they took the familiar walk along the Limmat River, many of their associates walked with them. They were greeted by friends along the way, for the streets were filled with people seeking to gain entrance for the discussion.

When they entered the Hall, Conrad, Felix, George, and Wilhelm were escorted, as before, to seats on one side and facing them were Zwingli, Leo Jud, Heinrich Engelhart, and a young theologian by the name of Heinrich Bullinger.

Bullinger had recently come to the city as an assistant to Zwingli. They soon discovered that his comments led Zwingli to interject a rather recent theological position into the discussion.

"The initiation of children into Christianity by baptism," he said, "is comparable to the initiation of infants into Judaism by circumcision. It is the mark of covenant, of being one of the people of God."

Conrad spoke to this.

"We are not initiating persons into Old Israel, nor into a national body, such as the Jewish nation, but into the fellowship of Jesus Christ. The Scriptures tell us: 'He that believes and is baptized shall be saved.' And a child does not believe nor enter into covenant until he or she is of the age to understand the teachings of Christ. Baptism," he continued, "should be administered to believers to whom the gospel has been preached, who have understood it, and who of their own accord desire baptism, and who are willing to mortify the old self and lead a new life. Of all this infants know nothing whatever; therefore, baptism is not intended for them."

The discussion was soon in full swing. Felix and Conrad, with their associates, cited numerous Scriptures on baptism from the Gospels and the Acts of the Apostles. They showed that the apostles did not baptize infants but baptized those who had come to an age of understanding.

In response Zwingli said, "You cannot show one place in the Bible where a person was baptized twice!"

Felix responded kindly, although it took great restraint to do so.

"Master Zwingli, I'm sure you have overlooked the account in Acts 19. Paul baptized a dozen men who had been baptized earlier with a baptism of repentance. We hold that baptism is to be administered according to the Scripture; therefore, as in this passage, believer's baptism, not infant baptism, is to be practiced. It is necessary for persons to make their own commitment to Jesus Christ and thereupon to accept baptism for themselves.

"And our Lord confirms this by his baptism with the Spirit. Christ did not teach and the apostles did not practice child baptism, but only this which baptism signifies, that those should be baptized who mend their ways, take on the new life, die to the old vices, are buried with Christ, and through baptism arise with him in newness of life."

Commenting on Peter's experience with Cornelius in Acts 10 and Paul's experience in Acts 22, Felix added, "From these words we see very clearly what baptism is and when baptism should be administered, namely, when one is converted through the Word of God. Afterwards, he desires to walk in newness of life as Paul clearly shows in Romans 6, 'dead to the old life . . . .' To attribute these experiences to infants is itself unscriptural and even contrary to all Scripture. 'Baptism is nothing else than a sign of the dying of the old and the putting on of the new.' "

Although each of the leaders of the brethren spoke profoundly and each challenge, Felix felt, was answered in a manner adequate to satisfy any logician, it was evident by the end of the dispute that the council would support the position of Zwingli and his associates. Felix was taken aback by the force with which Zwingli had fought. At one point he had taken issue with Felix, addressing him personally. He heatedly denounced him, claiming that he was an irresponsible idealist. Felix had addressed the council, angered and hurt by the man who had once been his friend.

"My lords," he said somberly, "speaking extemporaneously does not come easily for me, especially to reply when attacked, for I must have time to develop a fair presentation of my understanding of Scripture. If there is anyone at all, whoever he be, who holds from divine Scripture," and here he became more emphatic, "that newborn children should be baptized, and can show all this to you, my lords, scripturally and in writing, I will give an answer. I can't do much in disputation and don't desire to, but I wish only to deal carefully with Holy Scripture."

The burgomaster soon adjourned the meeting, stating that the council would go into session and would publicize its decision the following day.

As they made their way from the City Hall, Felix and his friends were weary. Their posture showed it; their faces showed it. Were it not for the support of so many, the four leaders would have felt mortally wounded. Among the colleagues who walked with them were Johann Brötli the associate pastor at Zollikon, Lorenz Hochrütiner the weaver, Jacob Hottinger of Zollikon, Gabriel Giger of St. Gall, and Andrew on the crutches. As they walked and thought, they discussed the weight of the arguments in the disputation, and agreed that the council would not relent. They could expect severe action.

Hans Hottinger, night watchman of the Augustinian jail in Zurich and one of Jakob Hottinger's brothers, came across the street and joined them. He told them of a conversation he'd had that morning with Rudolf Asper, who was complementing Zwingli's sermons.

"I told him that I do not know why he should be happy. Today Zwingli preaches one thing and tomorrow he retracts it. Years ago he preached that little children should not be baptized, but now he says that they should be baptized. And when he says God has commanded that children be baptized, he lies like a rogue and a heretic. Asper reacted and told me that Zwingli would be told of my statements, and I am sure he will! I am so sorry for my anger. This won't help us at all."

"No," Felix replies. "We'll hear about your words again."

Early the next morning the council's decision was posted. It came sooner than they expected. Several of the brethren had been watching for it at the City Hall and copied it for Conrad and Felix (*SSA,* p. 336).

> Whereas an error has arisen in the matter on baptism, namely, that young children should not be baptized before and until they have come to their days of accountability and know what faith is, and some have consequently left their children unbaptized, our lords and burgomaster, the Small Council and the Large Council called The Two Hundred of the City of Zurich, have permitted a disputation to be held on the matter on the basis of Holy Scripture, and have decided that notwithstanding this error, all children shall be baptized as soon as they are born. And all those who have hitherto left their children unbaptized shall have them baptized within the next eight days. And anyone who refuses to do this shall, with wife and child and possessions, leave our lord's city, jurisdiction, and domain, and never return, or await what happens to him. Everyone will know how to conduct himself accordingly. Effected Wednesday before Sebastian's Day, 1525.

Felix and Conrad shook their heads in disbelief. They had prepared themselves for the worst; still, the finality of the decision was a consternation. They had already decided what the next step would have to be. They would need to adjust their strategy from seeking a more radical reform of the city church to developing a separate free-church movement.

They were committed to Christ and to the spread of the evangelical faith. Zwingli had brought them to an evangelical understanding of the gospel, and they would continue to share this gospel across the land. Perhaps the believers' church would not need to be a structured organization such as Zwingli was developing. It could be made up of small fellowships of committed disciples, fellowships of the newborn who put off the old life and walked in the new life of Jesus Christ. They would meet in homes, in forests, in caves, wherever they could, but they would be a people of Christ.

On January 21 they had a further surprise. The Great Council posted another notice. It was a resolution of the council following

St. Sebastian's Day, drawn up in the presence of Lord Röist and the Small and Large Councils. Its concluding mandate read (*SSA*, p. 338):

> Conrad Grebel and Felix Manz are to be silent, and to refrain from holding further meetings of their Bible schools. Leaders in the Bible study groups who are not citizens of Zurich are herewith banished from the city: Wilhelm Reublin, Ludwig Hätzer, Johann Brötli, and Andreas Castelberger, and they shall leave within eight days.
> We call upon the citizens of Zurich and its environs to attend the services of the established church, and to seek the unity of the peace.

Notices were posted on every church in Zurich and in the surrounding areas of Wytikon, Zollikon, and beyond. As a deliberate show of authority the council's action against Reublin and Brötli had not only banished them from Zurich but from their pastorates at Wytikon and Zollikon.

For Felix, the mandate to close their Bible schools forced them to make a choice that was definitively a losing one.

"The issue is no longer our speaking out for reform in the Roman Church, nor for our calling for a new evangelical church-state, Heinrich." Felix was addressing Heinrich Aberli of their group, who had been in prison briefly on four different occasions because of his pronouncements. "You were arrested simply because you were less patient in your demands for the removal of the images and Catholic patterns from the new evangelical church of Zurich. But we are now no longer with that church, no longer under the protection of the City Council. We are now facing what it means to be a separate people of God, disciples of Christ who have no support other than our faith."

Aberli was insistent. "You cannot compromise your position. You must continue to teach."

Conrad looked at each of the men as he said, "We should meet tonight as scheduled. No doubt God will show us the direction we should take as we meet together to pray."

It was a solemn group that gathered that evening on Neuenstadt Street. They met at their usual place, a few doors from the Grossmünster, in the home which Felix shared with his mother, Anna, and his brother, Heinrich. Conrad led them in the study of the Scripture and later in the evening the group prayed. They asked for God's help to enable them to carry out their convictions to be his true church and to give them wisdom about facing the opposition. They prayed fervently, emotionally.

There was a sense of holy awe, of the Spirit's presence, as the 15 men arose from their knees and again took their seats. Felix was torn and drained. He felt as if every limb were stretched with the pain of his need for guidance. Suddenly, George Blaurock stood from his chair and walked over to Conrad Grebel saying, "Conrad, for God's sake, will you baptize me with a true Christian baptism upon my faith in Jesus Christ and my knowledge of his will?"

He knelt on the floor before Conrad. Grebel sat in silence for a few moments, then got to his feet, walked over to the water bucket, took a dipper full of water, and walked slowly back to George Blaurock. He stood there a moment, deep in thought, weighing the implications of what he was about to do. Placing his hand on George's head, he led a short prayer and then poured water down upon his head, affirming that in doing so he was baptizing him "in the name of the Father, and of the Son, and of the Holy Spirit."

Giving George his hand he helped him to his feet, and used words from Paul in Romans, chapter 6:

"Like as Christ was raised up from the dead by the glory of the Father, even so you also shall walk in newness of life."

George's face was radiant. As Conrad stood before him he suddenly said, "George, will you now baptize me?"

Immediately he knelt before him and George took the dipper and proceeded with his baptism. As Felix watched, the tension drained from his body. It was replaced by a sense of certainty, a sense of peace. He felt himself moving to the two men and kneeling before them. He heard himself asking to be baptized. As Conrad and George joined together in this important act, Felix felt as if it was the culmination of everything for which he had been working. He felt as if it was more than right, it was total commitment to Christ. The Holy Spirit seemed to fill the room, fill his heart.

One after another, each of the fifteen men were baptized "in the name of the Father, and of the Son, and of the Holy Spirit" by the pouring of water as a symbol of the inner baptism with the Spirit. Following the baptisms, Felix brought bread and wine from a cupboard, and reverently they shared the Lord's Supper, each contemplating silently what was happening to them.

Long into the evening, they talked together of the beauty of the experience. They had truly expressed what they had shared together over the last months. Ironically, they quoted Zwingli's words.

"There are two baptisms, the outer baptism with water and the inner baptism with the Spirit. The outer baptism is only a symbol; it is the inner baptism with the Spirit which changes one's life."

"There is no turning back at this point," Conrad said. "We have embarked on the course to build a free church, free in the grace of Christ. This we must do by God's grace."

"And to do this," Felix said, "we need each other. We need to support one another in the ministry to which God has called us."

"The ministry!" Conrad exclaimed. "This is exactly what we must face next. God is calling us to be ministers of the gospel, to teach and practice the faith to which he has called us."

For the next moments they discussed the unusual thing of ordaining one another to the ministry of the gospel. They read from Paul's letters to Timothy, and answering to one another they made commitments to be faithful teachers of the Word. They vowed to be loyal servants of Jesus Christ, to build a church that was none other than his body, a fellowship of believers born of the Spirit and committed to walking in newness of life. They now commissioned one another, although rather informally, to this high and holy calling, in the name of the Lord Jesus Christ.

As Felix and Conrad shook hands at the door in parting, Felix's eyes turned to the Grossmünster which stood at the end of their street. It was the symbol of Zwingli's power, of an authority which was no longer for them. He said, "It is not the word of Zwingli on which we build, but the Word of God."

Conrad nodded in agreement and turned for a moment to gaze at the big church. They shook hands again, and Conrad walked away into the night. Felix was moved by the sense of destiny that had brought their lives into this common service.

Felix did not sleep much that night. His excitement and the rushing of thoughts kept him awake. The group of fifteen had acted deliberately, countering practices the church had followed for more than a thousand years. They were called of God, he was sure, to reawaken a New Testament church free from the powers of a church-state, of the political forces of the magistracy. Their act of ordaining one another to the ministry of the gospel gave him the exhilarating feeling that they had answered the City Council! They were not about to surrender! They were committed to moving aggressively forward, building the church of Christ.

It was this Saturday evening, January 21, 1525, that Felix now saw as the birthday of the free church. He fell asleep thinking that on the morrow, on Sunday morning, the brethren would attend the churches in Zurich, Wytikon, and Zollikon. They would share their faith unashamedly with all persons with whom they would have opportunity of conversation. They were now convinced that the church of the future would need to be made up of many free congregations operating by the authority of Scripture in the freedom of Christ.

Chapter 8

The Free Church in Zollikon

Sunday morning dawned bright and crisp with the Manz household already astir. George Blaurock, having accepted the hospitality of Anna Manz, had spent Saturday night in their home. As they sat around the breakfast table, eating too much bread and cheese in their excitement, Felix and George talked about the meaningful event of the evening before. The night had not robbed them of their enthusiasm. They were both convinced that they had acted properly, according to their new insights of Scripture. They had been baptized as believers, they had taken the Lord's supper as laymen, and then they had been ordained as ministers of the gospel—the priesthood of believers.

As they talked, Felix noticed that his mother and especially his brother were paying close attention to them. Heinrich had been asking more questions in the past weeks, and Felix was proud that he was taking such an interest in things of the spirit and of the church. His mother's commitment remained as firm as ever, and although she was not verbal about it, she seemed to be gaining new insights by being around the Bible study group from time to time.

"You men have embarked on a radical course of action," she said in her motherly tone. "I am sure that you have not heard the end of opposition from Zwingli or the council. You need to walk

110

prayerfully before the Lord, carefully seeking his guidance."

Felix was sensitive to his mother's concern for him.

"Yes, mother," he responded "We do mean to be prayerful. But the time has come to act. I have never felt more certain of anything in my life. God is calling us to build the church anew."

George added, "You see, for twelve hundred years, since Constantine, the world has had a fallen church. It is by God's grace and the intervention of the Holy Spirit that the true New Testament church is being born again."

Felix and George planned to attend the Grossmünster for the second of the morning services. They wanted to hear Ulrich Zwingli's sermon, and be able to discern any further implications for their movement which might arise out of Zwingli's position. As they left the house Felix told his mother not to expect them back for lunch as they would be going to Grebel's house, then on to Zollikon. She stroked his cheek and managed a half smile.

Quickly they made their way the short distance down Neuenstadt Street to the Cathedral Church. They quickly joined the crowd entering the sanctuary. Zwingli's message was excellent, as usual. His gifts in exposition of the Scripture held the audience in rapt attention. He made a strong appeal for unity and for support of the evangelical, reformed church. He made brief reference to a need for the church to distinguish its position in freedom from those who were less circumspect in their opposition to the patterns of the past.

"Such," he said, "need to be held accountable by the City Council."

When they left the service, Felix and George went to Conrad's home in Neumarket. Conrad and Barbara welcomed them heartily. Felix found himself ravenous, commenting to George that there was nothing like a Sunday afternoon hunger. He was relieved when Barbara set out a tray of cold meat sandwiches.

They had barely begun to eat when there was a quick knock at the door. It was Hans Ockenfuss, the tailor of Stadelhofen, and he was excited. Conrad invited him in and his story spilled out in

111

rapid words. He had left his home early that morning in Sta-delhofen to take a suit to Wilhelm Reublin. Hans had wanted to talk to Wilhelm, and took the occasion to deliver his suit to him before he would have to leave Wytikon. Passing through Hirs-landen, Hans had witnessed a moving scene by the village well. Johann Brötli, the associate pastor in Zollikon who had been banished by the Zurich Council, was standing by the well talking with Fridli Schumacher, the shoemaker of Zollikon. Schumacher was Brötli's landlord, Ockenfuss explained, and they had, of course, shared previous discussions on the position which Brötli had taken. Brötli had, as everyone knew, been teaching in the parish in support of the believers' church movement.

Ockenfuss had heard Fridli say, "All right then, Johann, you have shown me the truth. I thank you for it and ask you for the sign." Without hesitation, Brötli had taken water from the bucket at the well and baptized Fridli "in the name of the Father, and of the Son, and of the Holy Spirit."

"This was a public happening," Ockenfuss said. "It is already known all over Zollikon. What happened last night in the privacy of your home, Felix, is now public knowledge!"

Conrad stood and leaned on the table with the ends of his fin-gers. "It must be made public," he said. "Our course of action is clear. We have embarked on this venture in faith as led by the Spirit of God. And we will take it as he leads."

Felix also stood. "George and I are on the way to Zollikon. We will visit the Jacob Hottinger home. Perhaps we can call together others of the brethren for an evening meeting and encourage one another in our walk in the Spirit."

"Don't you want to stop by the Conrad Hottinger farm on your way, Felix?" Barbara interjected, a sly smile on her face.

"Well, as a matter of fact, I had planned to if that's alright with you, George."

"Certainly, my friend," George kidded, slapping Felix on the back. "There are still other causes which need our attention as well!"

112

They all laughed and said their good-byes. Hans Ockenfuss headed for the house of Gabriel Giger to find Andrew of the crutches, and inform them of the evening gathering.

As they walked the path to Trini's home, Felix's mind was not really on what George was saying. It was on something about the future of the movement in which they were now so heavily involved, but Felix barely knew what. His mind was filled with the picture of Trini, smiling almost impishly, laughing lightly. His stomach was filled with butterflies and his legs with energy.

"Do we really need to walk so fast?" George asked with a chuckle. Felix noticed that his friend was short of breath and they slowed their steps.

"Oh, excuse me," he said.

When they arrived at the farm, Felix introduced George to the woman he loved and to the Hottinger family. George immediately began a conversation with Conrad Hottinger and Felix took the clue. He and Trini wrapped themselves in heavy coats and walked to the garden together. There was a thin layer of snow on the ground, enough to hide the dry earth but not enough to make it difficult to walk.

"Tell me all that has happened in the last few days," begged Trini. Felix was only too happy, and he began by relating in detail the events of the disputation, his own statements to Zwingli and the council, and the distance which had emerged even more clearly during the debate.

"Trini," he said, "I had hoped that the council, which had changed its position in regard to church images would also change its conception of baptism. I appealed to them, especially to Zwingli, to give answers to our position from the Word of God. This did not happen. And then they publicized their acts of condemnation. With their judgments upon our group we had no other recourse than to meet and obey the Lord."

Trini's expression did not give away her opinion and Felix continued.

"Last evening was the most moving experience of my life. In

our mutual confession of Jesus Christ as Lord and head of the church in which we share, we had a service of baptism." Felix had rehearsed in his mind how he would tell her about what had occurred. He wanted Trini, more than anyone, to understand. He told her how George had asked Conrad to baptize him and that in turn Blaurock had baptized Conrad and then of his own request for the sacrament. He related how they had sat together around the Lord's table, in awe over the decisions that they had made.

"It was clear to us that we are beginning what may be a believers' church movement," he explained. "We ordained each other to serve as ministers of the gospel of Christ in building this church. Trini, I have never found such deep satisfaction as I came to know last night. As you know, for years I have sought an identity. I have sought to be connected; to know who I am and what my life is about. Well, I have found this in Jesus Christ and his calling. I am a child of God, a disciple of Jesus Christ, and I am free now to be a minister of his gospel of the kingdom. I cannot imagine any greater fulfillment in my life than in the joyous proclamation of this gospel." His voice rang and his face was aglow. Almost embarrassed, he looked at Trini, not knowing how she would respond. But he found her eyes sparkling and a broad smile on her face.

"Felix, I believe you," she said. "This is of God. Something is happening which will affect the whole country, even the world."

Felix took her in his arms and pulled her to him. He felt her arms reach around him and they stood, holding each other, wordless, for a long time.

Hearing voices from the house, they returned to find that Hans Ockenfuss had arrived. Felix explained that they were going next to the Jacob Hottinger's, where a number of persons were gathering for a meeting. Conrad Hottinger took his coat from a peg and said, "We will go as well."

As friends and strangers gathered, the group began to share in worship. Felix led them in singing familiar psalms of praise.

114

Conrad led in prayer and meditation from the Scripture. Suddenly, Conrad turned to Felix and said, "We have shared baptism and the Lord's Supper in our smaller circle. Let us share the Lord's Supper here in the new freedom which is ours. We have rejected the form of the mass. Now let us celebrate the death and resurrection of our Lord together."

Felix and George responded affirmatively and Jacob and his wife brought bread and wine to them. George, and then others shared their understanding of the Lord's Supper. They emphasized that as Christ had given himself to the death for them, they in turn should be willing to give themselves to the death for the cause of Christ and his followers.

Conrad lifted the bread and broke it, offering thanks to God. Then he placed it back on the tray, and it was passed around the circle. There was a silence in the room that was almost audible. It was a group of more than fifteen and each, individually, was in meditation and prayer.

Trini watched as the tray reached Margaret Hottinger and the older woman took the bread and broke a piece for herself. When it came to her, Trini did the same. She handed the tray to Felix, and the warmth in her smile told him that she was one of them.

When Conrad lifted the cup of wine, he passed it to Felix and nodded that he should share this symbol. In simple words, Felix said, "Let whoever knows the meaning of God's forgiveness, who knows that his sins have been washed away in the rose-red blood of our Lord, drink together of this cup."

Offering a word of thanks to God for the new covenant in the blood of Christ, he passed the cup. Each person drank, reverently, of the symbol of the Lord's death.

There was a sense of wonder among them, for they had taken a radically different step from the pattern in which the sacrament was administered from the altar at the Grossmünster. There, for centuries, only the priests shared the wine, while the congregation was given the wafer. Here, in the simplicity of this farmer's parlor in Zollikon, the believers broke ordinary bread together

115

and shared it along with the wine. As the participants, they were aware that they were voluntarily sharing in the Lord's Supper.

Felix and Conrad invited persons to share the meanings of this experience to them. One after another, they affirmed that from now on, they wanted to live in keeping with a Christian way of life. Jacob Hottinger expressed his intention for their fellowship, "that we will always have God in our hearts and think primarily of him."

Felix nodded to Jacob and then added, "These symbols are a sign of brotherly love and peace. This kind of service is an occasion for us to express to each other the love of Christ in which we are redeemed."

Late in the evening just before Trini left with her father, Felix took her aside and behind the door he kissed her good-night.

"I do love you," he said.

It was a cold night but Conrad, George, and Felix seemed unaffected as they traveled back to Zurich. They would return to Zollikon on Wednesday to the home of Rudy Thomann, an elderly and prosperous farmer. There would be a farewell supper for Reublin and Brötli. The two had been given one week to leave and would do so following the Wednesday gathering. Thomann was inviting numerous friends to join for this time of fellowship.

The first days of the week passed slowly for Felix. He was so anxious to see Trini. He spent time each day with Conrad. As he passed the Grossmünster on his way to Neumarket, he wondered how Zwingli felt about what had happened. Finally Wednesday came and Felix along with Conrad and George arrived early at the Thomann homestead in Zollikon. As they walked up to the gate they paused for a drink of the cold spring water running into a huge trough. They were warmly welcomed at the door by Thomann's son-in-law, Marx Bosshart. He introduced them to Thomann's brother Heinrich and to Hans Bruggbach of Zumikon, a neighboring village. Soon many others arrived, among them, Trini, her parents, and a younger sister.

After the meal the group sat around the long table and shared together in a study of the Scripture. Felix led in a meditation from the New Testament, with special attention to Acts 2, emphasizing the importance of repentance from sin and a faith commitment to Jesus Christ. He reiterated the gospel promise that by believing in Christ and being baptized they would receive the gift of the Holy Spirit.

As the teaching continued, the group became aware that Hans Bruggbach was weeping. Felix stopped speaking and, concerned that he not embarrass the man, touched his shoulder and asked if he could pray for him.

Hans stood and in deep anguish cried, "I am a great sinner!"

George asked him, "Do you truly desire the grace of God?"

"I do!" he responded.

The men knelt together and Felix began to pray. Then Hans prayed, asking for God's forgiveness.

Felix rose and asked, "Who will forbid that I should baptize this man?"

George answered emphatically, "No one."

Felix reached to the water bucket and filling the dipper with water, poured it on Hans's bowed head, baptizing him with the words, "in the name of the Father, and of the Son, and of the Holy Spirit."

Some moments of silence followed. Suddenly the elder Jacob Hottinger got to his feet, walked to Felix, and said, "I also believe and would like to be baptized."

Kneeling before him, Jacob received baptism as Felix administered the ordinance. The meeting was soon concluded with prayer, and the room was hushed as the guests slipped out into the night and went their different ways. Felix and those who had come with him remained in the Thomann home for the night, for it was too late for them to travel back into the city.

Early in the morning Marx Bosshart awakened his father-in-law, and the two of them went into the room where Felix and George were sleeping and awakened them.

Marx said, "I could not bring myself to be baptized last evening, but I have wrestled with this all night long. In the early hours, I made peace with God, and in this commitment to Jesus Christ, I now want to be baptized."

George said, "You know, Marx, you have heretofore been very lax, a very reckless young man. This commitment means that you must make a total change in your life. You must put away the old Adam and put on a new man."

Marx answered, "By the grace of God, that is what I mean to do."

With a smile and an outreached hand, George said, "Come here, and I will baptize you." Marx kneeled before him and Blaurock administered the baptism. The new man rose from his knees, joyful.

George then turned to the father-in-law, Rudy Thomann, and reminded him that there were not many years until he would face death. "It is imperative," George said, "that you amend your life and open yourself to the grace of God. Rudy, if you will do this in faith, I will baptize you as well."

Solemnly, Rudy affirmed his commitment to Jesus Christ and kneeled for Blaurock to baptize him.

George was now caught up in enthusiasm over what was happening in this home. He urged Rudy to have his whole family and servants baptized. The farmer agreed to this. "But," George said, "each of them must make their own decision." And so during the morning, Felix and George administered baptism to a large circle of persons from the household.

When they had finished, Blaurock noticed a loaf of bread on the table and lifting it, spoke to the group. "All who believe that God has redeemed them with his death and his rose-colored blood, let them come and eat with me of the bread and drink with me of the wine." Reverently, the group stood around the table and passed the bread and wine from one to another, sharing the symbols of the Lord's death for their redemption.

During the next few days, Felix practically lived in Zollikon. George and his wife stayed in Zollikon, accepting the hospitality of Fridli Schumacher, and on the first day of their visit Fridli's wife asked George to baptize her. Now there were meetings scheduled in different homes from evening to evening. Felix visited Trini each day, but he also had several opportunities to call on his friend Felix Kienast. On one visit, Kienast had gathered a number of his neighbors to his home to hear the message which Felix had to share. One of these was a young, enterprising farmer named Jörg Schad, and in the Bible study which Felix led, Schad had a remarkable conversion. He openly committed himself to Christ and declared himself to be a disciple. Felix baptized him with tears on his cheeks, rejoicing with Jörg in his new faith.

Felix Kienast rose and moved toward the center of the room. "I also believe, and confess Jesus as my Lord. Will you baptize me?" Manz's tears flowed freely now and he threw his arms around his friend, weeping. When he had composed himself, he baptized Kienast "in the name of the Father, and of the Son, and of the Holy Spirit."

By the week's end, Felix and George were so excited about the development of a believer's church in Zollikon that they could scarcely contain themselves. If the church could not be free in Zurich, at least it could express its freedom elsewhere.

Brötli had baptized numerous persons from his parish during the week. Since he was soon leaving, he operated in the freedom of knowing that criticism from the City Council would come after he would have left the community. Among those baptized by Brötli were Trini's father, Conrad, and her brother Rudolf, at a meeting in the house of Hans Murer.

Conrad Grebel had left earlier in the week for Schaffhausen. He wanted to dialogue with Dr. Sebastian Hofmeister, now pastor of the city church. He also hoped to meet with Dr. Hubmaier from Waldshut, for he had heard that Hubmaier was using armed force against the Austrians in defense of his program. After seeing them, he planned to travel east to St. Gall and talk with Vadian, his brother-in-law.

Felix now felt the weight of what was happening in Zollikon resting on himself and George. While he respected and loved George, there were times in which he felt that his zeal over-shadowed his judgment. He sensed also that others in the group looked to him rather than to George for guidance.

On Sunday morning, January 29, they attended the church service in Zollikon, where Brötli had served as minister until his expulsion by the Zurich Council. They were interested in hearing what would be said by Brötli's successor. The preacher, Niklaus Billeter, was just preparing to enter the pulpit when suddenly, George jumped to his feet and in his strong voice, called out, "What are you intending to do?"

Billeter answered calmly, "I will preach the Word of God."

"But," George insisted, "not you, for I have been sent to preach."

Billeter, still collected, looked at George and said, "Not today. I have been sent by the superior canon of the Grossmünster in Zurich." And he turned, mounted the pulpit, and began to preach. To Felix's embarrassment George continued to say that he had the Word from God and wanted to share it. Felix didn't know whether to pull George back to his seat or not, but while he was thinking, Billeter interrupted his message and stepped from the pulpit to close the dialogue with George before continuing his sermon. The congregation, assuming that he was leaving the pulpit, called out to him to go on with his sermon.

George yelled, "It is written, 'My house shall be called a house of prayer but you make it a den of robbers!' " He pounded his fist on the bench in front of him to emphasize his statement. This was too much for Bailiff West, who was present in the church. He called out to George that he either desist or he would take him to jail. Now Felix reached out and tugged lightly on George's jacket. George turned to look at him and, seeing his friend's expression, sat back down and listened as Billeter went on with the message. Felix could sense the hostility and tension in the congregation which George's actions had stimulated.

After the service they walked out of the Zollikon church and down the street in silence. Finally, George said, "I got carried away this morning."

"Yes, I would say you did," Felix responded.

"I hope it does not create more problems for us. It's just that I feel so strongly that the Word which we believe must be heard by these needy people."

"I understand, George. But we will need to be 'wise as serpents and harmless as doves,' as our Lord taught us."

Felix and George went to the Jacob Hottinger home for dinner and enjoyed the afternoon visiting. That evening the circle of brethren and a few of the women who had accepted baptism gathered for fellowship. Trini was not in the group of the baptized, but Felix knew that she was giving it very careful consideration. Twenty-five of the group were local persons from the farms on the slopes along the north coast of the Zurich sea. In Felix's mind there was every indication that a strong church was emerging in the Zollikon community.

But their success in converting people to their movement had not gone unnoticed by the pastors in Zurich. Even more disasterous, the word of Blaurock's uncouth confrontation of Pastor Billeter had reached the ears of the City Council.

Early Monday morning Felix and George were awakened by the sound of soldiers in the streets. Locating the two reformers immediately, the soldiers arrested them. They started marching them along the street toward Zurich, but it was soon evident that the soldiers had a list of names; from one farmhouse after another they took various persons who had been baptized. Nearly the whole congregation was suddenly and without warning on its way to prison.

Chapter 9

From Parish to Prison

The walls of the cell were sweating, as if it were difficult to contain its prisoners. It was cold and the dampness seeped into Felix's bones. The dungeon was in the Wellenberg Tower, which stood in the Limmat River, connected to the shore by a lone bridge. This was the Zurich state prison and had only nine cells. Felix and George were each placed in a small cell with nothing but a bench on which they could sit or stretch out to sleep—if they could sleep.

The prison was too small to house the twenty-five other persons who had been arrested in Zollikon. They were taken to the Augustinian monastery in Zurich, near the Fraumünster. In early December 1524, under Zwingli's reform, the monks had been required to vacate the place. Now all of these prisoners in the Zollikon group were lodged together in a hall of the monastery and a delegation selected by the Great Council cross-examined each prisoner. Their intent was to reconvert them one by one to the Zwinglian viewpoint. The delegation consisted of the city's leading pastors, Zwingli, Jud, and Casper Megander, along with three council members who had assisted in the arrest.

Felix and George, confined in the tower, could only speculate as to what was happening to the other brothers and sisters. They snatched a little news from the prison guards, who brought only bread and water. Finally Zwingli himself with several associates came to the Wellenberg Tower to talk with Felix and George. It was a strange feeling that moved in Felix's heart as he stood in the cell and looked through the bars of the door into the face of Ulrich Zwingli, once such a close friend and admired teacher. They talked of the days in which they had studied together. Felix affirmed the awakening of his faith under Zwingli's preaching. They shared reminiscence of the excitement they had found in studying the Scriptures together in the Hebrew language.

Zwingli said, "Felix, I don't understand what is happening to you. We have been so close, and I have had such great dreams for you and Conrad in the movement I am leading. You know that you have been in line to head the Hebrew division of our theological school, and Grebel could have led the Greek division. This arrest would not have happened if you hadn't embarked on this ridiculous course which you are bent on pursuing." He was appealing to Felix with the powerful tool of flattery.

Felix responded in kind. "Ulrich, this course is none other than that to which you introduced me. I learned the way of Christ from you, and I am only seeking to follow the illumination of his Spirit as I study the Word."

"Bah!" Zwingli exploded. "You learned some things from me, but you have gone on with your own interpretation of the Scripture and you've disregarded the learning and the counsel of those around you. Your friend, Simon Stumpf, has learned better and he has written me of a change in his thinking."

Felix wondered if it could be true or if it were a ploy to weaken him. "I cannot speak for Simon," he said. "All I can say is that I must be true to the Word of God. You taught me that Scripture alone is authority, and by the Scripture I must stand. Show me from the Scripture that the course of faith and freedom in Christ is other than that which I have espoused and I will change."

"But Felix," Zwingli interjected, "there are many of us who have found faith in Christ through the Scriptures, and we have not felt led to renounce the magistracy, to separate the church from the state as you would advocate, for we are sure that all people must hear this Word."

123

"Of that I am sure as well, Ulrich, and to that end I have committed myself: to preach the gospel of Jesus Christ so that all may hear. Conrad has gone to . . . ,"—he hesitated—"share this faith."

"I know he is in Schaffhausen," Zwingli said. "We have sent word, warning Dr. Hofmeister. We have also warned the priests at Waldshut about Conrad and of Reublin and Brötli. Just today, Felix, Conrad's friend Anemund de Coct, the French nobleman, was with us. He had been here in Zurich to adopt a little son, Niklaus, and went with Conrad to Schaffhausen. But he returned to talk to us about the things Grebel has been saying to them about me! Between Myconius and myself, we have helped Anemund to rethink his relationship with Grebel." Zwingli paused, and then added, "If Conrad's father wasn't an esteemed member of the council, we'd have Conrad in a cell, too!"

"The truth will stand, Ulrich, for it is not your word nor mine but God's Word which is the authority. Remember our conversation in Hujuff's garden? It is the Lord's church, Ulrich, not ours, nor the council's."

Zwingli left the prison, and Felix sat alone in his cell, pondering the implications of his situation. During the next days, one of the commission called on him and on George every day to pursue discussion. As the week wore on, the interchange became more heated. Tempers exploded as the men attacked Felix and George for their stubborn stance. Felix could hear them talking with George in a cell down the block and was pleased that they were united in their response.

On February 8, Hans Hottinger, the night watchman at the Augustinian monastery, was able to bring them word that the twenty-five prisoners in the monastery were free. They had agreed to cease their propagation of the new doctrine. They had paid the costs of their imprisonment including their support and had been released to go back to Zollikon. The report by Hans informed Felix and George that on one point the group had felt that they had beaten Zwingli! When he said that there was no case of rebaptism in the Scripture they, as Felix had earlier, brought to Zwingli's attention Paul's rebaptism of men at Ephesus in Acts 19. But they had made political peace and had paid security with one thousand florins. Their release came with the instruction that they should no longer deal offensively "against God and their neighbors."

Felix and George continued to be confronted by representatives of the council. Felix reiterated again and again the position he had taken in his disputation. He sought to clarify for Zwingli and his associates the meanings of his faith. He found it only in Scripture, he explained, which had its full meaning in Christ. He did criticize the pastors of Zurich for misleading the people and for failing to follow through on their own understanding of Scripture. He reminded Zwingli that he had promised them two years ago that he would abolish the mass and institute the Lord's Table as the new way.

"Why," Felix asked, "have you been afraid to move on this? And why have you not developed the ban for disciplining rather than using force? The church needs to be disciplined, so that persons will truly follow the Word of God, and repent from their open sin and vice."

Zwingli, was silent. Then he said, "Felix, I think we understand each other. You stand free in your faith. I have faith as well, but I am also responsible for the church as an institution. If you will just pay 100 gulden and prison costs we can let you go."

"And say by doing so that the council is right in imprisoning me for a matter of faith?" Felix countered indignantly. "In no way, Ulrich; that I cannot do!"

During the second week of imprisonment George wrote a letter to the council, expressing his position. He reminded them that Christ sent his disciples to teach all people, that he had given them power to grant remission of sins, and that he commanded them, as an outward sign of forgiveness, to baptize believers. He informed the council that whenever he had shared the gospel in this way, people had turned to him in tears and had asked him to baptize them.

125

Then George described his instruction to new believers: "I call upon Christ for his mercy upon them, and instruct them to live in love, in unity, and in community as the apostles have taught us in Acts the second chapter. I remind them to always be mindful of the death of Christ and not to forget his shed blood; and I share the practice of Christ in the Last Supper, break bread, and drink wine together with them as brothers and sisters in the body of Christ. This, I submit, is not contrary to the Holy Scripture or to the church of God."

Following this letter from George, the interrogation by Zwingli and his associates was intense but focused more on the authority of the church. George, in his thunderous style, responded by telling Zwingli that he was doing violence to the Scripture and falsifying it more than the "old pope himself." In an attempt to get beyond Zwingli, he then made another appeal to the council, stating that he would like to defend his statement before them.

But on February 18, the council made a decision to dismiss George on the promise of peaceful conduct. They reminded him that he was not a citizen of Zurich and that consequently he was being banished from the city and its environs. Finally, on February 24, he was set free. As he was leaving the prison, he reached his hand through the little window in the bars of Felix's cell. Felix bid his friend farewell, and George assured him that he would be faithful in the teaching of the Word.

"Where will you go, George?"

"To Zollikon first," he answered. "I must find my wife before I do anything else."

"Please pass my love to Trini," Felix said emotionally, but the conversation was interrupted and George was prodded down the hallway and out of the door of the prison.

Now Felix was alone in the Wellenberg Tower. Each day was long and he felt that he had studied every stone in the wall hundreds of times. Yet as he sat on the bare bench in his cell, he knew that he was not alone, for he sensed the presence of God. In spite of all that had happened to him, Felix had an inner sense of freedom and joy in being in the will of Christ. His suffering was for his Lord.

It was late February, an even colder month than January. Felix paced the narrow cell at night to keep warm and tried to sleep during the day. Fortunately he was permitted some visitors and Jacob Hottinger was able to gain permission to visit him. Jacob brought extra clothing and several blankets to him. The meager diet of the prison was supplemented by his gifts of food. On one occasion he had a basket of fresh rolls which, he told Felix, were from the hand of Trini, and, he was sure, with her love. Felix cuddled the rolls in his hand and wanted to weep for missing her.

There was good news of what was happening in Zollikon and beyond. Jacob assured him that the faith was still alive, although needing rekindling for some. He reported that Brötli had written to the Zollikon community from Hallau, where he was working in the region of Schaffhausen. He had gone there with his wife and child after being banished from Zurich. He wrote that he, Wilhelm Reublin, and Conrad Grebel were together in Schaffhausen. They were having great success in the region. Many were responding to the gospel, especially leaders in community life, and were accepting baptism. But they were deeply grieved over the arrests in Zollikon.

"He especially commended you and George, Felix, for your faithfulness, and he pledged prayer support for your release. I can recall his words, 'Oh how strong I hear my brother Felix Manz is, and George, but especially Felix Manz. God be praised.' " Felix's eyes misted. Jacob continued, "He urged the church in Zollikon to renew our commitment to Christ and the new fellowship. And my brother, Hans, our night watchman, was arrested for those statements he made to Rudolf Asper about Zwingli's double-talk," he told Felix.

"And where is he now? What has been done to him?"

"They did not keep him. The council dismissed him from his position as watchman and made him promise to be more respectful in his comments."

"Apparently, Zwingli's spies keep close watch on us."

"Yes, but Zwingli cannot prevent the moving of God's Spirit."

With this, Jacob began sharing with Felix some of George's recent activity in the Zollikon community. From prison he had gone immediately to the home of Heinrich Aberli, the baker of Rennweg who remained a faithful participant in the free church. Hans Ockenfuss and Jacob himself, both of whom had been prisoners in the Augustinian monastery, were present for an evening supper at Aberli's. With them was Anton Roggenacher of Stadelhofen, a newcomer to the circle. He had been impressed with George's spirit and message and invited him to come to his home the next day.

George did so on Saturday, February 25, and stayed until Sunday. And Sunday morning, Roggenacher asked to be baptized! George gave him the "sign," and following the baptism they joined others who were making their way to the parlor of Hans Murer, the farmer in Gstad. Here Blaurock presented the gospel message, and at the close of his talk eight of the women rose and went forward, asking to be baptized. Blaurock baptized them.

Felix was listening intently. "And who were the women?" he asked softly.

Jacob began naming different ones of the group and suddenly broke into a smile, saying, "And, of course, Trini was one of them."

"Oh, that is wonderful," Felix exclaimed, involuntarily raising his arms and clasping his hands over his head.

"Would you believe it," Jacob continued, "the wife of Hans Wuest, the bailiff and president of our village, was baptized as well!"

"Remarkable!" He brought his arms down in a gesture of emphasis. "I am so thrilled that the women are identifying with us in the step of baptism. In the church of Christ, we are all one. But the bailiff's wife?" he grinned at Jacob. "That will present the Zollikon leaders with a new problem."

They sat for a moment, thinking of the implications, until Felix asked, "Where is George now?"

"He left on Sunday, and we do not know for certain where he is. Having been banished from the Zurich region, he could not stay longer. He and his wife went to Wytikon only as a first stop and they may then go on to St. Gall." He was silent for a moment, then his face broke into a smile. "You should know of Marx Bosshart's work, especially in the area of Winterthur. He is having great success, often heard by small groups in the Zum Salmon inn. He has dared to challenge Zwingli, saying, 'M'lords of Zurich wink at Zwingli's faults and Zwingli at M'lords'.' "

The first weeks of March dragged. Felix sought any bit of news from the Zollikon community. He was repeatedly visited by someone from Zwingli's group but on occasion Zwingli himself spoke to him. There were times when they would visit almost as old friends, until the issues which divided them came to the fore in their conversation.

On Ash Wednesday, March 8, Zwingli came to the prison. Felix thought it highly appropriate and reminded him of Ash Wednesday three years earlier and the beginning of reform in Zurich. Once again he confronted him with the commitment that he had made for several years that he would abolish the mass and institute a new order of the Lord's Supper. Zwingli said, "Felix, I'm developing such an order for the service and I plan to institute it during this Lenten season. I fully intend now to make the change. The time is here now, and I will conduct an evangelical celebration of the Lord's Supper by this Easter."

Felix replied, "But you have waited long, Ulrich, and some of us could not see good reason for taking so long to make the changes."

"But it is necessary for us to maintain the unity of the church," Zwingli responded, "and this is the more appropriate time."

"Unity with whom? We of the laity are as much a part of the church as your City Council. Is it not their power which is important to you, more than unity of the people of faith?" Felix was in no mood to mince words.

129

Zwingli responded, "I am bishop and priest in this town of Zurich, and to me is the care of souls entrusted—not the monks."

During the next few days, Felix had no visitors and his loneliness was painful. However, on Monday Jacob Hottinger came again to his cell. His eyes sparkled and he almost quivered with excitement. How out of place such a spirit seemed in a dungeon, thought Felix. Jacob explained that there were more baptisms than he could ever imagine.

"On Wednesday the eighth we shared a beautiful celebration of the Lord's Supper by the lake, in the orchard on the farm of Hans Murer."

Here Jacob paused, and his expression made clear to Felix that he was now ready to relate some special news. "On Sunday, March 12, an unusual thing happened in the Zollikon church. Jörg Schad, whom you baptized in late January, Felix, has become a very forceful witness. Following the morning sermon at the Zollikon church, when Billeter had finished his sermon, Schad stepped to the front and gave his testimony of faith, telling the people of the change in his life. Everybody in Zollikon has known him as a reckless young man, and now he is a model of the new life in Christ. At the close of his testimony, he invted anyone who would like to take this step of faith with him in baptism to come forward! To the amazement of all of us in the congregation, about forty persons stood, and Jörg Schad baptized them—in the Zollikon church!"

Felix responded with open amazement. "That is unbelievable!" After a moment's pause he added, "What a contrast to the last Sunday I was at the church with George Blaurock. Has Pastor Billeter changed his mind?"

"No, he hasn't changed and he left the service while Schad was speaking. No one knows what his reaction will be. But there is another bit of news which I should tell you," Jacob continued. "There are additional persons who have arrived in Zollikon and have joined us. Hans Bichter of the Black Forest is especially active and has baptized thirty persons. With him is a very impressive couple, Michael and Margarita Sattler. Sattler had been prior of the monastery of St. Peter in the Black Forest and has studied at Freiberg. While there is monastic reform that has been ordered by Bishop Hugo, it is seen more as a means of satisfying the peasants rather than a 'genuine quest for righteousness' among the monks. He was tired of the emptiness and perversion in the lives of the monks, as well as being disturbed by their disregard for the poor, and himself being quite sympathetic to the cause of the peasants. He left his monastic position and married Margarita, a clever little woman, who was serving the church as a Beguine."

"He is a learned man," Jacob went on, "He and his wife came here together to visit Zurich and to learn of Zwingli's reformation. After meeting Zwingli, they also learned of the believers' movement in Zollikon and they have come and now identify with us."

"And what is Sattler's stance? Is he truly one with us?" Felix did not mean to be skeptical. "Or is he with the militant peasants?"

"That I cannot answer fully as yet, but he is a believer in Christ and is now in a voluntary church of the reborn. He is learned in the languages and is already involved in the Bible studies which are being held in the Zollikon homes."

"I will look forward to getting acquainted with Sattler. If he is a disciple of Christ, he is my brother."

That the movement in Zollikon was being watched by the City Council and Zurich pastors was evident. Soon after the event at the Zollikon church, the council began making arrests. On Wednesday, Hans Hottinger, the former watchman, and Jacob, who had been communicating with Felix, were arrested for their involvement with the free church. On Thursday, a special raid was made into the Zollikon community, bringing more than a dozen others to prison. This group included the new Bible teacher, Michael Sattler, who had become known to the council for his influence, both from his earlier position as a prior in the monastery and as an effective teacher.

And then there followed the second arrest of his friend, George Blaurock. Apparently, the work of Blaurock and his wife in the Wytikon area had been so successful that they had not moved on. News of his continued activity had reached the council, and they had reached out to the Wytikon community and arrested him as well. Once again, he was back in the tower, placed in a cell down the hall from Felix. As he passed Felix's cell, he said jovially, "Well, my brother, as to be expected, I am back!"

Felix called after him, "We are here for Christ's sake. Indeed, it is to be expected!"

This large arrest had one good consequence. The day following George's arrest, the prisoners were instructed that the council planned a disputation for March 20. Jacob Hottinger, Hans Hottinger, Sattler, and the others were given warnings of the consequences of their actions and a goading promise that, by attending the disputation, they could surely be convinced to abandon their ridiculous views and gain their release.

Zwingli informed Felix and George that they would now be permitted to give a defense from Scripture of their position on the question of baptism. In a show of good grace he informed them that their friend Conrad was back in the Zurich region with his wife, after his stay in Schaffhausen. Out of consideration for Conrad's father Jacob Grebel, and as an evidence of the good will of the church, Zwingli was inviting Conrad to join his brethren for this disputation. He had made a commitment to Conrad of "safe conduct," and had sent it to the Rudy Thomann house.

Felix had a new sense of hope. At least something was happening that brought a change into the routine of his imprisonment. But he was suspicious that this seeming tolerance was Zwingli's ploy to gain concessions from them.

On the morning of March 20, Felix was led out of his prison cell and into the open. He stood for a moment, allowing his eyes to become adjusted to the foreign light. He was weak, but the fresh air was envigorating. He inhaled deeply as he gazed at the blue-green water of the Limmat. Looking toward the sea, he lifted his eyes to the *Oberland* and the beauty of the distant mountains. His heart filled with the longing to be free. George was brought outside also and they were taken across the bridge, down the familiar streets of Zurich, and straight to the City Hall. Conrad was waiting for them.

"My brothers!" he exclaimed, and threw his arms around them both.

The elaborate robes which the members of the Large Council wore were in stark contrast to the common garb of the brethren. As Burgomaster Röist called the meeting into session, the spokesman for the council forthrightly expressed their motives for the meeting. Zwingli constantly addressed his comments to Conrad, who had not been in prison. This also placed Felix and George in a lesser light. It was evident that he was seeking to divide them. He was especially blunt with George calling him a "great, foolish dreamer." At one point, he ridiculed Blaurock because even though he had been a monk for years and trained at Leipzig, he had difficulty reading the German translation of the New Testament which had been handed to him in the discussion with the council. Zwingli also accused him of the presumption of counting no one a child of God unless he were a mad man like himself!

Zwingli finally addressed questions to Felix regarding the separation of the free church from the evangelical reformed movement in Zurich. He charged Felix with being divisive, a separatist, an idealist who envisioned a return to the primitive New Testament church.

"Felix," he said, "you fail to understand what it means to create a church in the sixteenth century in obedience to the teachings of the Scriptures. This is not the first century. We must live today."

Felix cleared his throat. It was not easy to concentrate after months with little food, spent in solitude. "Master Ulrich, it is not a church with a civil religion that we are to build, but a church expressing the kingdom of Christ. I seek truly to stand by the

Scripture and the interpretation which is given to us by the guidance of the Holy Spirit. If it is the will of the heavenly Father for us to baptize persons who respond in faith to Jesus Christ, then we can do no other than to share with them the symbol of baptism. Why is this such an offense to you? The important thing is their conversion to Christ. Baptism is only a sign of that faith."

It was after four grueling hours that the council finally concluded the session. They issued a forceful order to the brethren of the Zollikon circle to stop their practice and to desist from their harmful separations. At the close of the trial, Conrad bid Felix and George a tearful farewell and left for his home. A crowd had gathered outside of the City Hall and Felix surveyed the faces. Suddenly, he saw Trini's eyes, red with tears; he paused and turned, wanting more than life to go to her, but the guard pulled on him. Felix and George were led the same way they had come, the road back to prison.

On March 25, the verdict of the Large Council was brought to Felix and George. The council claimed to have interacted with the brethren in prison at the Augustinian monastery and reported that the men and women had agreed to "desist their separation and their baptisms" and to cooperate with the church. With this agreement, they had been released.

Blaurock was taken from prison and a decree was read that he and his wife should be shipped by boat down the lake and back to Chur. The council requested a written pledge by the authorities in Chur to keep him in that region and to prevent his meddling in the Zurich community.

Several of the men and women from Zollikon were returned to prison as an example that the council was serious in their opposition to the free church movement. They were accused of going back on their commitment of February 8, at their previous arrest. One of their leaders, Rutsch Hottinger spoke for the group: "What we promised in the Augustinian prison, namely that we would stand still, we have kept. We stood still until God bade us to do otherwise."

Felix, as a Zurich citizen and a leader among the brethren, was not released. His heart sank as he was told that he was to remain confined to his cell on bread and water. During the week which followed, the sympathy of the guards who attended the prisoners became evident. On April 4, when the turnkey brought Felix his evening meal, he spoke to him briefly.

"It is reported," he told Felix," that Zwingli told the council that 'all the earlier battles with the Roman Church were child's play compared with this one with the Anabaptists.' "

When he left the cell, Felix noticed in amazement that he pushed the barred door closed but did not turn the key in the lock. Felix waited until it was quiet and then tried the door. It was not locked! Again he hesitated, wondering what this meant, what he should do. As the evening shadows darkened the recesses of the prison, he moved slowly down the hall to try the door which led to the wharf. It too was open! Almost without thinking, he slipped through the doorway and closed it behind himself.

A few quick steps and he was across the short bridge and on the street. Hurriedly, he passed the market bridge stretching across the Limmat and rushed down the street. He skirted the Grossmünster and, taking a shortcut through several narrow alleys, he arrived at his mother's house and rapped briefly on the door. It seemed like forever until his mother appeared. Her mouth formed his name but no sound came out and she pulled him inside. They embraced and she stood, weeping, in his arms. Knowing that he must hurry, he told her of the escape and that with a change of clothes and some of her good cooking he would be on his way under the cover of darkness.

Anna quickly pulled things from the cupboards while Felix bathed and changed his clothing. As they sat at the table and bowed their heads in thanks, Felix led in prayer for his mother and brother and for the renewal of the church according to the will of Christ. As he looked up from prayer Felix said, "Mother, we are about the work of Christ. Jesus said he would build his church, and the gates of hell shall not prevent him."

Chapter 10

The Itinerant Evangelist

It was early morning when Felix left his mother's home and stole through the streets of Zurich on his way to the Hottinger homestead. He made his way cautiously through the Neumarket gate, then hurried on. As he walked into Zollikon, a village of farmers, he smelled the smoke rising from the chimneys. How warm and pleasant it must be to be comfortably inside one's home, free. There were signs of the farmers already in their barns for the morning's chores and he hurried his steps so as not to be caught by the bright daylight.

As he walked up the path to Trini's door, he thought about what he must say to her about their relationship. He had meant to give it careful consideration on his way to Zollikon, but he was so caught up in the feeling of freedom and in all the sights he had missed, that he had put it off. He stepped up to the building to rap at the door, but it opened before his knock.

"Felix, you're free!" Trini exclaimed, throwing her arms around his neck, uninhibited.

"Shhh, only for the present, my love," he whispered, "I escaped last night."

"Escaped?" she breathed.

"The turnkey failed to lock the door and I was able to get out of prison. But I can't stay, Trini, I must get far away from Zurich." He stepped inside the door and held Trini, tightly and in silence, for some time. Finally, he said quietly, "I've missed you so."

136

"And not an hour has gone by that I didn't think of you," she said. Felix, knowing that he should be going, kissed her with the passion of unfulfilled love. Suddenly, he backed away while her eyes were still closed.

She looked up with a twinkle in her eyes. "You have whiskers; your face feels so different."

He chuckled ruefully. "There was no barber in the tower, and I haven't been able to shave."

"I like it," Trini commented. "You were handsome, now you are distinguished. And," she added, "you should keep the whiskers if you are on the run."

"I have no idea what the future has to offer," he said. There was pain in his voice. "I do know that there is much to be done for the church and that I must do it outside of the Zurich area."

"It is better that you are away and free than for you to be in prison." There were tears in the corners of her eyes. Just then, Trini's father, Conrad Hottinger, entered the room.

"Felix! I had no idea . . . ."

"Herr Hottinger, I must go immediately; I am a fugitive."

The man asked for no explanations. "Felix," he said, "you need a horse."

"Yes, but in some settings it would be a liability, not to mention the fact that you would be in danger for helping me."

Conrad seemed to ignore that latter part of Felix's statement and said, "If you are going far, you should have a horse."

"Well," Felix said, thinking for a moment, "I may go to Schaffhausen and perhaps to St. Gall."

"But you will be back," Trini's father said, putting his arm around her shoulder, "so take the horse and return it when God leads you to come this way. Trini, go with Felix and help him saddle one of our best."

As they walked together to the stable, the morning sun broke brightly in the early dawn. It illuminated their faces and showed their emotions more honestly than either of them could bear. Trini picked out the best tack and bridled and saddled a strong horse on which her beloved would leave her again. She led the gelding out of its stall and stood, holding the reins for Felix. Felix went to her and brushed back a strand of hair that had escaped the hold of her bun. She looked up at him through teary eyes and gasped lightly as if trying to keep from crying harder. He enfolded her in an embrace that felt so comforting, so right. Then, he let go, turned, and mounted the horse. With one last look at the woman he loved more than he ever thought possible, he rode off.

With the horse, he could travel faster and so he first headed east. He decided that if he was seen, it would be better that it not be known that he was going north toward Schaffhausen. Instead, he went to the area of Bäretswil and met with some of the brethren there who told him to go to the home of Hans Hotz, a carpenter in Grüningen. There, he was told he would meet Marx Bosshart, whom he knew from earlier association, and who had been one of those in prison in the Augustinian monastery.

He arrived at Hotz's carpenter shop in the early afternoon. Marx was there and was anxious to hear about his escape. Hotz and Marx told him enthusiastically that a meeting was planned for that very afternoon in a cave deep in a nearby forest. Before he knew it, Felix was tramping through undergrowth and peering around trees. The cave was quite large, a low ceiling but a broad and deep cut into the rocks, and several hundred people soon gathered for the meeting. Felix wondered how they had all gotten there. He had not seen another person as he and his two friends had made their way to the meeting place.

As he stood among them, secure in the density of the forest, he thanked God for the privilege of being among believers and not in the prison cell. When they invited him to speak, Felix shared with them his witness of personal faith and his understanding of the authority of Christ and of the Spirit's work in calling forth a free church.

"Only one who has faith in Christ can obey, and only one who obeys expresses genuine faith in Christ. We have been called into a new order of life, the community of discipleship in which we support one another in faith, in family life, in material needs, in love. This is the fruit of the Spirit of Christ."

Felix spent the night in Hirslanden, north of Zollikon, at the home of Felix Lehman. Early in the morning he was again on his way, traveling north, to stay in Embrack, that evening and minister the next day to the people there. Since it was only ten miles northeast of Zurich, he was anxious to leave.

Immediately after arriving in Winterthur, tired as he was, he found lodging at the Crown Inn. He bedded down the horse himself, trying to save as much as possible of the little bit of money that the brethren had given him. It was early evening but Felix crawled into bed and slept long and deeply.

Late the next morning, following a lead given him by Marx, he called on Bosshart's brother-in-law, Arbogast Finsterbach. The family and friends, as Marx had told him, were very interested in Bible readings and teaching. Felix had thought that his stay in Winterthur would be a brief one, but he spent the next several days meeting in homes with groups in Bible study. As he shared the meaning of personal faith in Christ and of the inner presence of the Holy Spirit, a number of persons made commitments to Jesus Christ and asked Felix for the sign of baptism.

Felix enjoyed his new friends but left them behind and rode on to Schaffhausen, anxious to be there by Palm Sunday. He hoped that Conrad Grebel might be there. His travel through the hills was pleasant but more difficult. Many times as he saw what a rough walk it would have been, he was grateful for Hottinger's loan of the horse. The animal never hesitated, never rebelled, only carried him along, and he patted its neck from time to time.

He enjoyed the rich green vineyards on the hills sloping to the Rhine. Renting passage on the ferry, he crossed the river and traveled first to the west to the village of Hallau. It was easy to obtain directions to the home of Johann Brötli, who was now the pastor of the city church. Brötli's wife greeted him warmly, having met him earlier in the Bible studies in Zurich and having heard much of him through her husband. She told him that Johann and Wilhelm Reublin had gone to Waldshut for conversation with Dr. Hubmaier, but she invited him into her house and gave him tea and bread.

Frau Brötli was a robust woman with unceasing energy. Felix decided that if she ate like she talked, it was no wonder that she was so chunky. He watched and listened as she bustled around the kitchen, barely letting Felix pose one question. Her enthusiasm was energizing and she was intensely excited about what was happening in the Schaffhausen district. In their community of Hallau, Felix quickly learned, nearly the whole population had been baptized and had become members of the movement for a free church. In fact, the rural subjects of the Schaffhausen district had organized a general assembly to protest the payment of their tithes to the church-state. This, she said, had created a problem for Dr. Sebastian Hofmeister in the city of Schaffhausen. The City Council had sent emissaries to arrest Wilhelm and Johann, but the neighboring peasants had learned of it and had warned them. They had even given the men armed protection! In fact, the community at Waldshut actually sent thirty men as a contingent to join the peasants and help protect the outlaws.

"This," she told Felix with a laugh in her voice, "was not especially consistent with our conviction on nonviolence, even though there had been no fighting." She shrugged her shoulders and grabbed the poker, stirring the flames with short impatient movements.

Felix took the moment of silence to ask about Conrad.

"He has gone to St. Gall," she told him. "He is now accompanied by a new brother, Wolfgang Ulliman who was converted to a faith commitment to Jesus Christ and was immersed in baptism by Conrad in the Rhine near Schaffhausen. Ulimann had been with the same monastery in Chur from which Blaurock had come, and," she stood with both hands on her wide hips, "he is like George, a son of thunder."

Frau Brötli moved to the table and began to peel an apple. The way in which she handled the knife, Felix almost feared for her life, or at least for a thumb! But before he knew it she had two apples peeled and had set one in front of him. He had already had enough but so as not to argue with her, he picked up the choppy slices and ate them as she continued.

"Ulimann's home is in St. Gall where he is known for the effective Bible readings on reform he has been conducting there. His strong leadership will be a tremendous asset to our movement and to Conrad himself. They have just recently left us, and going to St. Gall they plan to work together there." She plopped down in a chair across from him and ate her apple while resting her elbows on the table. "Another person you must meet," she told him between bites, "is Marty Lingg, who has also come to faith. He is a well-known weaver here in Schaffhausen and is having remarkable success in sharing the gospel. He is also a close friend of Ulrich Teck, the brother who is working with Michael Sattler in Oberglatt. Michael and Margarita had to leave Zurich, you know, and are living with Hans Küntzi in Klingnau, between here and Zurich."

"I have wondered about Sattler," Felix commented, "I did not know what he was doing."

"He is learning the weaver's trade from Küntzi and is a rather quiet, studious man," she said, as if being quiet were a character flaw. She added emphatically, "But he is one of us!"

Frau Brötli invited Felix to accept their hospitality that night as her husband would be back from Waldshut by evening. Johann planned to be present in Hallau for Palm Sunday services. Felix agreed, gratefully, and said that he would take a walk and would be back in time for the evening meal.

He left the house smiling over how informative and entertaining Frau Brötli had been. He started toward the Rhine, thinking of what his next move should be. He wanted to go to Schaffhausen to meet Dr. Hofmeister, but as he thought about his situation, it seemed wise to wait until Monday, lest word of his being in

141

the area get back to Zurich and his time here be interrupted.

He walked leisurely to the falls of the Rhine and spent an hour observing the majestic sight of the turbulent waters cascading down over the rocks, sending a cloud of mist high into the sky until it disappeared, melding with the atmosphere. As he viewed the scene, he was reminded of the words of Jesus, "Whoever believes in me, out of his inner being shall flow rivers of living water." Felix bowed his head and prayed that God would make their movement a mighty stream like that which was rolling past at his feet; a stream which, like the Rhine, would flow across Europe and refresh the lives of the populace.

When Felix returned later to the Brötli home, Johann had arrived from Waldshut. Their reunion was warm.

"I'm sure my wife has filled you in on all that has been happening here," he said, playfully putting his arms partway around her as she set the table. She eased them off and turned to pick up more dishes.

"You know me," she laughed.

"Well, I can tell you with great joy," Brötli said, clapping his hands together, "that Dr. Hubmaier is leading the city of Waldshut to an evangelical faith and a public stance on believer's baptism. Hubmaier's correspondence with Oecolampad of Basel, Bucer of Strasbourg, and even with Zwingli, has now made him a key figure in the new developments of reform."

"That is indeed cause to rejoice," Felix responded.

Before they retired for the night, Johann invited Felix to share in the morning service in the church of Hallau. It was expected that the pastor would bring the Word, but he wanted to introduce Felix to the congregation and to give him opportunity for a presentation.

"They all know of you and of your steadfast faith in prison. I've seen to that," he chuckled, "and now I want them to see how God has delivered you and has upheld your spirit."

On Sunday morning, Felix addressed the congregation, sharing his personal testimony. He spoke of what it meant to follow

Christ in faith, in open discipleship, and in holiness of life. He urged the believers in the Hallau congregation to walk in the will of Christ unashamedly. As he then listened to Johann exhort the people and observed their enthusiasm, Felix felt a new freedom in his own soul. The weeks of being in prison had given him a subtle feeling of despair, more deeply than he had admitted to himself. But in the service that morning, he felt a birth of new hope, an assurance that the free-church movement was alive and well.

The next day Johann accompanied Felix as they walked down the streets of the medieval town of Schaffhausen. They passed the cloister and made their way into the Abbey Church built of ochre-colored stone. Here they found Dr. Hofmeister in his study. They were given audience, although somewhat reluctantly. As they shared introductory comments, Dr. Hofmeister told of his conversations with Conrad Grebel earlier and of a particular interaction with the French nobleman, de Coct, who had so unfortunately been taken by sudden death. If earlier it had seemed that Dr. Hofmeister was tolerant toward the free-church emphasis and believer's baptism, his discussions with Zwingli had altered that. As they conversed further, Hofmeister revealed his current thought.

"As I have expressed to Conrad," he said, "it is important for the sake of the total movement that we stay by the reformed church movement of Zwingli. This is the necessary step for all of us if we are to be free from Rome."

Felix was emphatic. "Sebastian, we are not just breaking from Rome, we are building a New Testament church. You well know the meanings of the evangelical faith of which I speak and the importance of recognizing that Christ alone is head and Lord of the church."

"Yes, Felix, but he orders the earthly authorities to maintain order in society, and we need to be subject to them."

"But there is no authority except that which is given by God. Even the powers that be are named by God, which means that he does the ordaining; he is above the powers. And there are times in which earthly powers function contrary to the will of Christ, even the Council of Two Hundred! In such occasions, we must obey God rather than men."

"Yes, but it is our responsibility to call those powers including the council to allegiance to the Word of God," Hofmeister responded.

"When they stand opposed to Christ and to his church, we must also oppose them in the name of Christ. What I am calling for," Felix raised one finger in an insistent gesture, "is that persons commit themselves openly and aggressively to Jesus Christ, to create a church that is free of the state, not a church-state which gives false hope to persons who have never made a decision of their own for Jesus Christ. The church of which I speak will be made up of volunteers, people who choose for themselves to receive Jesus Christ as Lord, to live in obedience to the Scripture, and to walk in the will of Christ."

At the close of the conversation Sebastion said, "Felix, I have heard you, and I admire your sincerity, but I choose to remain with Zwingli and the reform which he is promoting in the church."

"Is there no interest in continuing our conversation then?" Felix wanted to know.

"So long as you are in Schaffhausen and are conducting yourself in good order, we can continue our conversation." And so for the next several days, Felix called at the Abbey and met with Sebastian. He was impressed that the man would at least listen to him, but by Wednesday it was clear that Hofmeister meant what he said; in spite of their study of Scripture, Sebastian would remain on the other side. Felix was also quite certain that word had now been sent to Zurich of his presence in Schaffhausen.

That evening Felix shared for the last time in the Brötli home, participating in the evening Bible study and the fellowship of the Lord's Supper. Again, he spoke of the community of the reconciled, that true fellowship in which Christ is expressed in fellowship with one another.

He planned to leave the next morning for St. Gall, anticipating that he would meet Conrad there, so he retired early. In the morning, Felix left Schaffhausen traveling east along the Rhine. He finally stopped for rest in the picturesque town of Stein am Rhein. The houses of studded woodwork built on foundations that dipped into the river were fascinating to him. The Benedictine monastery near the church offered lodging, which he accepted uneasily. He had heard that in 1524 pastor Schmid had been banished by the Roman church, an act which was followed by an uprising of Zwinglian confederates, who had then vandalized the monastery at Ittinger. He wondered if the volatile tension between the Catholic and the Reform churches had continued in this city.

Felix was able to engage several of the monks in conversation at the table. He first asked about the influence of the Lutheran voices in their community and then about the conflict between the forces of the Roman church and Zwingli's reform. The monks had few comments. He felt somehow free to talk of a third way of believing discipleship that was more than identification with either course. There was little reaction, but Felix felt that he had, at least, sown the seed.

During the next several days, Felix was on the road, traveling along the Untersea which joined Lake Constance to the town of Kreuzlingen, twin city to the adjoining town of Constance. The scenery refreshed him—north Switzerland's rolling hills, green forests, rock formations, rivers, and lakes. As he turned south, after the first day, he had a marvelous view of the Freudenberg mountain, which marked the region of St. Gall. The closer he got to the city, the more spectacular became the view of the rolling hills and fields which stretched along the alpine range that lay far beyond St. Gall. He paused frequently to rest and to enjoy the view. He wished Trini could have been there to enjoy it with him.

As he traveled the remaining distance to the city, he thought often of the vast difference between his position in life and that of

145

his friend Conrad. In St. Gall, Vadian, Conrad's brother-in-law, was an influential member of the City Council, town physician, noted scholar, and chief reformer. This apparently made it somewhat easier for Conrad to live and work in the region. Felix also knew that the lighter treatment given to Conrad in Zurich was most likely because of the presence of his father on the City Council. Even with this analysis, Felix was hardly prepared for what he found. Conrad and his associates in St. Gall were having remarkable successes.

Arriving in the city, Felix first set about to locate the home of his friend Lorenz Hochrütiner. Lorenz welcomed Felix with great excitement, elated to find that he was out of prison and free. Immediately, he began telling of the amazing things that were happening in St. Gall and in Appenzell. Lorenz related enthusiastically, "There are now eight hundred persons in this region who have accepted baptism. Gabriel Giger, who came here from Zurich, has been in St. Gall working effectively in the church. His partners in ministry are Marthy Linck of Schaffhausen, and Wolfgang Ulimann, son of Andres Ulimann here, of St. Gall, and master of the Large Council." Lorenz paused for breath, then added, "Ulimann is a distinguished scholar of a patrician family of the weaver guild and accepted baptism by Grebel in Schaffhausen. Grebel immersed him in the Rhine!"

"So I was told in Hallau," Felix commented.

"He has become one of the most outspoken leaders of the brethren here in the region of St. Gall. He is an exceptionally articulate speaker, and both winsome and forthright. Our brethren met in the Weaver's Hall at the market place to ask him to assist Dominik Zili, the schoolmaster, and conduct readings in the church of St. Lawrence. He declined, saying he was called to preach in freedom. The attendance at his sermons is extraordinary! Thousands of people flock to hear him. He often speaks to large groups in the Shooting Lodge. In fact, the movement has become so popular that the City Council is distressed over not being able to suppress it," Lorenz continued.

"That is wonderful!" Felix exclaimed. "It appears that many of our friends expelled from Zurich are here in St. Gall. This may be the center for the believers' church."

"Felix, you should have been here on Palm Sunday! We had a public baptismal service in the Sitter River." Lorenz's eyes twinkled with excitement as he relived the events. "Grebel had been here preaching for two weeks and hundreds of persons had responded to the gospel. A baptism was announced for Palm Sunday in the river and crowds of people streamed out of the city to its banks. True, many were spectators, but we actually baptized several hundred persons Sunday afternoon."

As Felix stared at Lorenz in amazement, Lorenz shook his head and said, "And that is not all. The same is happening in Appenzell. Bolt Eberli of Lachen, although a peasant farmer, is a fluent speaker and a good student of the Scripture. He has had great crowds thronging the Birlisberg hillside to hear his preaching and many in the town of Teufen have asked to be baptized by him. Hans Krüsi is a pastor there now. He was a teacher in Wil, twenty miles west of St. Gall, and he was taken to Grebel's meeting by two of his friends, Johann Ramsayer and Martin Baumgartner. He was converted to Christ under Conrad's teaching and accepted believer's baptism. His ministry is so effective and he has now baptized so many that he says he cannot keep count of them."

"And the Council of St. Gall is permitting this?" Felix asked.

"No, the City Council has moved to suppress Krüsi, but representatives of more than thirty hamlets in the area committed themselves to defend him; so the council backed away from an arrest. But they took his position from him; he is no longer teaching. He has learned to weave and is now supporting his family as a weaver. He is outspoken against the social oppression of the Catholic bailiwick of the Abbey of St. Gall, but he is not supporting any peasant uprising. His activity at present is in St. George."

Felix smoothed his hair with one hand, "This is almost unbelievable," he said.

"But they did arrest our brother Gabriel Giger. He became so distraught at the reading of Zwingli's booklet on baptism at the cathedral that he interrupted the reading, calling out from the balcony for equal time!"

"Your friend, George Blaurock, is in Appenzell the last I heard, working with a church there."

"George is free! And where is Conrad now?" Felix asked impatiently.

"He was so excited about the response on Palm Sunday, but criticism from the council was so intense that he left the next week and went back to Zurich. He would like to bring Barbara and the children to this area. Grebel, as you suggested, does see St. Gall as the center for the development of the free-church movement. He is hoping that Vadian will protect his family if they are in St. Gall."

"That may be a good move," Felix commented. "A little distance from Zwingli may be the best strategy at this point."

Felix and Lorenz prayed together as they discussed their work. Felix was certain that Lorenz had been very modest about the role he himself had been playing in the movement, the months of influence he'd had in St. Gall. He admired the spirit with which Lorenz complimented the others for their work.

"Felix, our brethren here in St. Gall must hear you. This evening we can attend several of the meetings, and you can share."

The enthusiasm was invigorating as Felix joined the crowd, first at the Shooting Lodge, where he called them to walk with Christ in faith and not just be dabblers in the matters of religion, to become truly disciples and accept the baptism of faith. The larger meeting was in the fencing hut under the linden trees by the Multergate. Here Felix preached late into the evening, speaking from Hebrews, chapter 6, emphasizing the need for full repentance and genuine faith, "lest they renege on Christ and sin against him again. A true Christian does not go back on Christ and live in sin."

Felix enjoyed the spirit and interchange with the brethren. But as they assumed that Vadian would soon hear from Zwingli about Felix's escape from prison, it was agreed that he should go to Appenzell and stay out of St. Gall. Hopefully, he could find his friend George and work with him. Felix was pleased to think about the two of them involved together in evangelistic proclamation. George would attract the crowd and Felix could concentrate on teaching.

Agreeing with their advice, he left St. Gall and journeyed to Appenzell. The short trip was uneventful except for the scenery and his horse's insistence on stopping for a bite every now and then. He could understand the animal's wish to roam from the path into the rolling pastureland. Felix looked at the Alpine heights beyond, gracing the rolling farmlands with a majestic range of erratic cliffs. He remembered that Zwingli had shared about his boyhood here in the mountains of the Toggenburg.

Having been given directions to the home of Hanz Krüsi, Felix found the city church and the adjoining parsonage with no difficulty and was told by a caretaker where he would find the former pastor. Soon, he had a friend in Krüsi, a very intelligent and dedicated man, and their fellowship soon gave Felix evidence that the Spirit of God was creating effective leaders for the free church. The movement was by no means limited to the few persons who had shared in the original calling in Zurich.

Felix was delighted to find one whose spirit and dedication was so much like his own. He encouraged Hans in his sharing the gospel and in calling persons to the obedience of Christ. Later in the evening Krüsi accompanied Felix to the home where the Blaurocks were staying. On the way he told of the remarkable hearing Blaurock had been receiving in Appenzell.

"He is being called a second Paul. He is as effective here as Ulimann is in St. Gall. The people gather to hear his preaching, amazed at his boldness and the clarity of his call to commitment."

Felix smiled. "That is George. He is bold and he spares no words. You can't hear him without knowing exactly what he is asking."

When they arrived at the chalet, Hans quickly introduced Felix to the host, who welcomed him warmly. Then Hans went to call George from another room, "to meet an old friend." When George came from behind the curtain in the doorway, he was speechless. He rushed to Felix and embraced him.

"So the angel of the Lord has brought you out of prison!" George exclaimed.

"Yes, but that angel had quite an earthly form," Felix chuckled. "I believe it was the turnkey himself who left the doors unlocked after his evening visit."

"Ah, ha! How interesting. I am so glad you have come here. There is freedom to preach the gospel. Together we can work from Appenzell south into the Oberland, all of the way to my home in Chur spreading the good news."

"That is just what I want to do," Felix said, "I am anxious to be involved more aggressively in a preaching ministry. For too long I've been cooped up in prison. My pattern has been systematic Bible teaching, but I would like to adjust that to sharing the heart of the gospel in evangelistic proclamation."

"And there are others with me that you will want to meet, Felix. I've been in Grüningen, as you may know. Among the disciples there, we have some excellent leaders. One very fluent spokesman is Hans Hotz. And there are several others, such as Jacob Falk and Heini Reimann, who have come with me and are holding teaching sessions here in Appenzell."

"I have met Hotz. In fact, I stayed in his home in my flight from Zurich. I want to meet these brothers, by all means, and share any way that I can."

The next several weeks in Appenzell were rewarding times for Felix. The larger team of workers was especially exciting, for they supported and stimulated each other. They found every occasion possible to share the gospel, standing in the park, on the corner of the street, or at intersections of the highways where people traveled. He learned to know Falk and Reimann well, and found them to be all that George had said. They told of the fruitful ministry of Conrad Grebel and Marx Bosshart in the Grüningen area. Falk had recently been baptized by Conrad at Hinwil. They were both able and dedicated persons, and they easily identified with the people of the countryside. During the next few weeks, scores of persons made commitments to Christ. George and Felix baptized them and directed them to establish Bible studies in homes to help one another to grow in their understanding of the Word.

Felix loved the work. He enjoyed the fellowship of new converts and his association with George and the other preachers. Appenzell itself was a refreshing contrast to the city of Zurich. He never tired of the beautiful, rolling hills and the well-kept farms where he often made visits. He evangelized all the way to the mountains to the south, to Ebenalp, its bold promontory jutting above the dark waters of the lake at its base.

But the freedom they enjoyed was short-lived. Late in the month of April, the City Council arrested a number of the brethren, including Falk and Reimann. Learning that these men were from Grüningen, they released them after a few days with strict orders to leave the region. Felix and George agreed that they would delay their trip to Chur and travel with these expelled brothers to Grüningen. Felix himself had a special interest in returning to the region near Zurich. How much he missed seeing Trini! He prayed and hoped for an opportunity to get back to Zollikon soon. Since they were now working in the western part of the Appenzeller region, in Urnäsch, they could readily travel on southwest to Grüningen. En route, they laid plans to spend some time there and then later to follow the river east to Chur, as Blaurock was anxious to continue their evangelistic work in his home area.

Travel west across the forested ridges took considerable time. But they relished their conversation together and the opportunities to meet people along the way. As they approached Grüningen they could see the beautiful waters of the lake to the south. Glistening in the spring sunlight, the scene seemed a refreshing gesture of peace. Seeing the mountains beyond, Felix began to quote, "I will lift up my eyes unto the hills. From whence comes my help? My help comes from the Lord who made the heaven and the earth."

A strange sense of at-home-ness came to Felix as he approached the town. Conrad had so often talked of his boyhood in this village that Felix felt that he already knew each street. He could see the castle at the end of the town and could imagine Conrad growing up in the halls and rooms of this impressive building. The contrast with his own life as a youth made Felix aware again of how Christ could unify such different persons in his one body, the church.

Soon after arriving, Felix went to the familiar home of Hans Hotz and the two renewed acquaintance. They spent the next days in Bible study, and Felix enjoyed teaching the Scripture. Hans himself was so anxious to learn the Scripture and so enthusiastic that the teaching session soon grew into a class as others joined them.

Reports from Zurich were disturbing, for the oppression of free church advocates was increasing. The community of Anabaptists in Zollikon appeared to be Zwingli's special target, for it was evident that he sought to crush the new church emerging there. In early May, Felix told George that he would like to slip into Zollikon to visit Trini. Possibly he could also see Conrad, who had risked going back to Zurich to get his family.

"Perhaps," he said. "Conrad will be ready to return with me. In any event, I need to see Trini before we travel to Chur. And you can teach the believers here in the Grüningen area while our brothers go on about their evangelizing."

From Grüningen the trip along the lake west to Zurich was not long. He traveled steadily, late into the evening, and early on the next day he was near Zollikon. He made his way with excitement to the Conrad Hottinger home and to the warm welcome of his beloved. He felt as much at home with Trini's family as with his own, and they gathered around to hear his news.

"I am returning your horse to you on this visit," he told Conrad Hottinger. "Otherwise I may commission the beast for evangelical service!" Everyone laughed. Felix told them of his travels, of what God was doing in eastern Switzerland, of how the free church was growing. But his mind was on Trini and his eyes kept wandering to hers.

"Where will you go next that you do not need a horse?" Hottinger asked.

"To Chur, and my trail will take me through rugged terrain— not so easy for a horse. I can't travel the main road."

Anxious to see his friend Conrad, it was agreed that he would slip into Zurich in late evening just before the gate closed, under the cover of darkness, and return in the morning to the Hottinger home. He was warned to be careful, for during recent days there had been repeated arrests. Andrew with the crutches, he was told, and Marx Bosshart had been in the city to see Conrad several times. They were quite certain that this had not gone without the notice of the Zurich authorities. They suspected that it was only with the influence of Conrad's father that he was able to stay at home. Perhaps this enabled Conrad to receive a number of the brethren for conversation, although their visits must have been observed. Unfortunately, many of the Zollikon families that had been rebaptized had now been so intimidated that they were practically silenced.

Felix sneaked into Zurich, passing through the Neumarket Gate with a group of farmers entering the city. He made his way to Grebel's house straightaway, next door to Thurm auf dem Bach, where Conrad's father lived, and knocked rapidly at the door. Barbara's familiar voice called through the door, asking who was there. Felix hesitated but quietly answered. Quickly she opened the door and Felix stepped into a warm, comfortable home. It was the reunion of close friends. Soon Conrad said, "Felix, I have some special news for you of your mother and brother Heinrich."

"They are well, I hope," Felix breathed.

153

"Never better," Conrad said and smiled. "My news is about their faith. They have both been baptized, Felix, here, in our home!"

Felix couldn't stop his eyes from filling with tears. Softly he said, wiping them, "Please tell me all about it."

Conrad related how Anna Manz and her son Heinrich had come to their home one afternoon and the two of them had shared their commitments to Christ and requested baptism.

"And you baptized them?"

"I did, right there where you are sitting."

Felix was silent a few moments, then he said, "I am so thankful. Now we are one in the family of Christ."

The evening lengthened into the late hours, as Conrad shared enthusiastically his perspective on the Palm Sunday events in St. Gall. He talked of the interchange the brethren were having with the council and told of writing to Vadian, but stopped when he learned that Felix had been there and had already heard the reports.

Conrad then asked him, "Have you heard of the happenings in Waldshut on the same Easter Sunday?"

"No, I've heard nothing from there since my visit to Schaffhausen. That was the week before Easter."

"Our brother Wilhelm spent considerable time with Dr. Hubmaier, and on the day before Easter Sunday he baptized Balthasar in the city church of Waldshut! And this was followed on Easter Sunday by about sixty other people accepting baptism, administered by Hubmaier and Reublin together in the city church!"

"Wonderful!" Felix exulted. "And is the City Council holding still for this?"

"Their bigger problem just now is the opposition of the Hapsburgs. The Austrian authorities are seeking to stop this movement and maintain the unity of the Catholic church. Ferdinand has ordered the Swabian league to arrest Dr. Hubmaier. But it appears," Conrad continued, "that the whole of Waldshut is about to join the free-church movement. Hubmaier talks about his 'war for the gospel.' This, along with the new sense of power among the peasants in their quest for freedom, has Ferdinand quite frustrated. This movement is going to change society! But," he leaned closer to Felix as if deeply troubled, "I don't agree with Hubmaier about his defense with the sword!" There was a silence. "However," he continued, "this is God's day for a free church to emerge."

"Conrad, I believe this," said Felix, "and it is one of the reasons that I have risked coming back into Zurich. We must encourage Hubmaier to be careful not to try the same 'power tactics' in Waldshut that Zwingli is carrying out in Zurich. That is not my understanding of Jesus' teachings."

"Yes, Felix, you are right. Someone will need to speak with Dr. Hubmaier about the way of peace and the rejection of the sword."

"In the last few days, Conrad, I have been having remarkable success in evangelism, working with George in your home town. As we see it, we now need to move on to other areas in our evangelism. We plan to move up the river to Chur. I came back to Zollikon today and have come this evening, by requests of the Grüningen brethren, to ask whether you would accompany me from Zurich to provide leadership in their developing church. Some fine leaders are emerging, as you know, such as Hans Hotz and Jacob Falk especially, but they need further teaching to help them to mature. You and Marx are the persons to help them. If you will come, George and I can then be free for evangelism."

Immediately Barbara reacted, "Felix, you do not understand. Conrad is a family man. You are free. He has been gone so much, leaving me and the children here alone. He must stay in Zurich."

Conrad only smiled and said, "Now, now, my Barbara, we must be free to discern what God is asking of us in this work."

"Yes," she said, "but he can scarcely be asking for you to leave your family and be gone all of the time. And beyond that, you are suffering. Your limp is so serious that you will soon be known as Conrad-with-the-crutches unless you take care of yourself."

Felix listened, trying not to be caught observing them. He understood her pain, the ache of separation. Still, the work so needed Conrad.

"It is important that I should support Felix and George in their ministry," said Conrad, "and Grüningen was my home, you know. And I've had such a good response there to the gospel." He had a far-off look. "I am impatient sitting here writing and not being in face-to-face involvement with the people."

His wife kneeled next to him, perhaps feeling that she was losing a battle. "I know that, Conrad, but there is much that you can do here. With your father on the council you have a measure of safety which the other men do not have. Don't forget that your trips to Zollikon and your friends coming here have served as a ministry to them."

"Yes, I know Barbara. But even another week in Grüningen could be an important ministry." Turning to Felix he said, "You will want to go to your home. I can meet you there and we will be on our way."

"Conrad," Barbara stood before him, her lips trembling, her arms folded tightly in front of her body, "You are not going." She turned to Felix. "Felix, I am sorry, but I must keep him here. If he leaves this house with you, I will go to the authorities and tell them that you are in Zurich and where they can find you in Zollikon."

Conrad's eyes were large with surprise. He was openly angry and yet, after some hesitation, responded to his wife with respect. "Barbara, you would do that?"

"Yes. I am truly sorry, but I must. I am not ready for you to leave."

Felix looked at Conrad with regret coupled with understanding. "So it must be, my friend, you belong here."

A long uncomfortable silence followed, but there was no change in Barbara's expression. Despite the disagreement, they all shared together in prayer and Conrad said, "Let's sleep over it." The Grebels retired for the night and Felix slipped down the street to his mother's house. It was a risk to go further into the city, but he felt he must.

Being with his mother and brother was different this time. They had adopted the same faith as he and he loved them all the more for it. They talked into the early hours and Felix slept only briefly. In the morning, before the sun was up, he drank some tea and ate too much of the cheese and bread that his mother had set out. After his days in prison, he felt that he could never get enough to fill his stomach. Once again, he said farewell to his family and went back to Conrad's house. When he rapped on the door, Conrad stepped out and spoke softly lest they awaken the children.

"Let's go," he said, "it will be all right." And they started toward the nearest gate out of the city. It was locked, and Lady Meis next door recognized Conrad from their family business dealings and called to them that no one was being allowed passage. They hurried to the Neumarket Gate, but it too was closed. Perplexed and concerned, they went back to Conrad's house to find that Barbara had slipped out another door as Conrad left and ran to his parent's home to enlist their help in preventing his going. She was returning as they came up to the house. Felix, she said, had not been reported, but he had best hide himself.

Felix quickly said farewell and headed for the market. There he found a farmer who was going to Zollikon for produce. He slumped in the back of the wagon and messed his hair. Scraping some dirt from the floorboards, he wiped it on his face and clothes. The farmer did not even look back at him as he drove the wagon through the streets toward the Neumarket Gate.

They were the first to leave Zurich that morning. Felix sighed with relief that he was not recognized. His untidy appearance had identified him well with the unkempt farmer, who had spent the night in his wagon at the market.

Felix had much to think over as he steadied himself in the

empty wagon. The road was not smooth and he was jostled and tossed. His mind reviewed the interchange between Conrad and Barbara the evening before. How desperate Barbara had been to keep her husband. How much Conrad felt the call to go to Grüningen. Conrad had even asked which was more important: one's marriage, or the work of the church, since in many cases, it came down to that. Felix decided that he would need to share with Trini that as much as he loved her, it would not be fair to either of them to think of marriage just now. His calling was in itinerant evangelism, inviting persons to commitment to Jesus Christ. With all of the risks and the travel involved, they should postpone any consideration of marriage to a more distant future. He would need to talk with her right away. It would not be kind to leave her wondering why he hesitated to marry.

Chapter 11

Arrest in Chur

It was late evening of the following day when Felix approached the town of Grüningen, the seat of government for the district. As he walked, the sound of the bells which hung from the cows' necks rang across the rolling pastureland. He lifted his eyes to the mountains in the distance. The evening sun was casting a pink glow on the snow-covered peaks. Hearing the melancholy notes of the alp horn sounding from the hills made him sad. His sadness caused him to think of Trini, and the inner summons, the longing, to be with her.

It had not been easy to say "Good-bye" to Trini, to explain to her that he must be on the move during the next months and perhaps years, until the believers' church had established its place and was recognized by the authorities as a valid entity. He should not have been surprised that she took his words so well. It was abundantly clear that she was committed to Christ. Now, he knew, she was committed to his ministry as well, and it was a source of inner strength to Felix.

An added source of courage was the open confession of faith and the support of his mother and brother. He had risked going into the city to see them, and the risk was well worth it. Felix warmed with the memory of his mother's words of her commitment to Christ and her joy in discipleship. Heinrich had embraced him saying, "Felix, I am your brother in a new way, not only by the first birth but by my rebirth."

159

When he arrived at the house where he and Blaurock had been staying, he found George anxious to get on the way to Chur. He was disappointed that Conrad was not with Felix.

"So Conrad couldn't come?" he said with his disappointment showing in his voice.

"Barbara was adamant. She would have exposed me to the authorities. We were even ready to risk that," Felix replied. Then he added, "Things aren't easy for Conrad in Zurich. Financially, he is in difficult straights. He is even negotiating to sell his books, and he had some very prized copies!" Felix paused. "And his feet are so bad he can hardly walk. He winces with every step."

"I can imagine his personal hurt," George sounded sympathetic, "but we do need him. The peasant revolts here in Grüningen during the last weeks have led many to defy the authorities by refusing to pay their tithe for the church in Rome. This has made it difficult for us and the new believers in Grüningen, to distinguish our course of action as different. The brethren want the community to know that we are advocates of peace and nonviolence."

"Conrad and I were just speaking of that in Zurich. The new converts must understand this as the way of the kingdom of Christ. The brethren here in Grüningen need to develop a clear and positive commitment of obedience to Jesus and not simply react against the authorities."

"Conrad would have been a great asset," George said wearily.

"Yes, but we can take an alternate approach. We can ordain Hotz, Falk, and Reimann for roles of leadership. They are strong persons and have grown so much in their knowledge of Scripture."

George was supportive of Felix's suggestion and, with Bosshart assisting, the men were commissioned in a special meeting with many of the new believers gathering to express their support. Feeling that they now left the work in Grüningen in good hands, Felix and George set out on their long trek to Chur. Felix had scarcely had time to rest. The journey became increasingly dif-

160

ficult as they left Lake Zurich and passed along Lake Walenstadt. The road was steep and they were both tired as finally they climbed the wooded terrace of the Kerenzerberg. As they gained the summit, the view was breathtaking. They sat together on a flat rock and gazed at the alluvial plain below them and then at the gigantic rock bastions of the Churfirsten.

"It is all that I said, isn't it?" George asked.

"Yes," Felix breathed. "A wonderful reward for a hard climb."

As they started across the summit, Felix stood in the Wessen Pass and gazed over the ridges to the valley below. He pushed back his hat and wiped his sweated brow. His shirt clung to his body, perspiration from the exertion of the long climb turning it black. The cool air made him shiver and he was soon ready to move on. They continued east, through the gap, down into the Rhine valley, a beautiful plain reaching to the south, toward the river's further sources high in the Alps.

The nearer they came to the city, the more aggressive George became in his talk of plans for their evangelism. He knew the region well, having ministered in Chur, and having publicly renounced the Roman church here two years earlier. He had departed from Chur at that time because the City Council was in full support of the traditional position of the church. But his time in Zurich and his identification with the brethren in a believers' church movement had convinced him that the message of Christ, calling people to freedom, to affirm their faith, and to accept baptism, would be received by many of the townspeople of Chur. When he and his wife had been expelled from Zurich, his return to Chur had been brief, sharing with only a few friends.

When Felix and George arrived, they found that the city was thoroughly involved in church reform. In the last two years, the church leaders had taken decisive steps to break with Rome. They had declared their identification with the evangelical movements of Luther and Zwingli. The Catholic dignitaries had been forced out and the church leadership was now working in basic agreement with Zwingli. This provided a setting in which they

161

might work with limited freedom, at least until they clashed with the voices of a church-state reform.

Felix and George began at once a proclamation of the gospel of Christ. They preached a freedom to affirm one's own faith, to take the rule of Christ personally, to open oneself to the presence of the Holy Spirit. They called people to follow a life of discipleship and to regard the love of Christ as their own lifestyle. They held Bible studies in homes, preached on the street corners, in the fields, wherever people gathered. Their message was the same as in other communities, but each person's response to Christ was a special joy. Scores of persons responded to their presentation of the gospel and were baptized. Many of them were older persons, well-known citizens of Chur, who in their break with Rome were now ready to espouse the position of *sola scriptura*. Their activity was soon known by the City Council. As their following grew, public pronouncements were made against those who were divisive and subversive in their attitude toward the official church.

Early in July they welcomed their old friend, Andreas Castelberger, on his return to Chur. This had been his home as well as George's, and they shared a happy meeting. But Andreas had a very sad report to give them. Bolt Eberli, their beloved Hypolytus, had died a martyr's death! Having continued Grebel's work with great success in Appenzell, Bolt had, by the end of April, been forced out of the city. He had gone south to work in the Canton of Schwyz. In May, he had been arrested in his home town of Lachen and on the twenty-ninth he and a priest with him had been burned at the stake by the Catholic authorities! Felix and George sat numb. George stared straight ahead, while Felix buried his face in his hands.

"This is another case of Catholic opposition to the Reformation," Castleberger continued. "Even though Bolt was an Anabaptist, this is of grave concern to Zwingli and his associates as also to Vadian of St. Gall. To them, this means that the Roman church intends to stamp out the evangelical reformation."

All three men had known and worked with Bolt as a brother. This was the first of their colleagues martyred for the believers' church. There was a long period of silence. Finally George stood and said, "I can still hear him preach in the Butcher's Hall in St. Gall, a pious and fearless person."

"Yes," exclaimed Felix, "and such preaching must go on. 'The blood of the martyrs is the seed of the church,' according to Tertullian."

"There are other things I have to share as well," Andreas said quietly. He had had time to deal with his grief. He knew that his brothers had not.

"The tensions in St. Gall have increased," he continued. "Vadian denounced the Anabaptists in a public hearing before the council the third week of May. The brethren read a letter from Conrad in response, to which Vadian gave a written reply, asking the brethren to respond. They asked for time, and were given two weeks. Immediately following Pentecost, they met in the Rathaus. Our brothers read another letter they had gotten from Grebel in Hinwil, and again Vadian responded. The council has now placed severe restraint upon these brothers. It ordered them to hear a reading of Zwingli's book on baptism at an evening reading in the church of St. Lawrence. The brothers were in the back, in the balcony, but Ulimann and Giger were clearly heard as they called out. Ulimann cried, 'You give us Zwingli's words, we want God's words.' "

"And what followed?" Felix asked.

"The believers' church lives," Andreas chuckled, "even though the council mobilized a squad of 200 in case of a revolt."

"Can you tell us more from Zurich or Zollikon?" Felix asked.

"Grebel has left Zurich and he and Marx Bosshart have been in the Grüningen area since July the second. Grebel has been preaching to large crowds in Hinwil and Bäretswyl. He left Zurich in June, and first he went north to visit Hubmaier in Waldshut. He has given up on Vadian, since their unhappy separation in St. Gall. On his return, he became fearful of going back into Zurich and so he went on south to Grüningen."

"You are right; that is good news," Felix affirmed.

Andreas continued, "During this same time, especially following Pentecost, the church in Zollikon has become missionary. They have sent out Bible teachers to various villages to the east." Andreas chuckled. "Zwingli has now written that these Anabaptists are running all over the countryside preaching! One of them is your old friend, Felix Kienast. Another is Rudolf Hottinger, Trini's brother." Andreas looked at Felix and Felix smiled his satisfaction.

He and George then began sharing reports with Andreas of what was happening in Chur. "Yes, we have had opposition all right," Felix said. "Jakob Salandronius, a teacher in the monastery in Chur, has let it be known that he has written both Vadian in St. Gall and Zwingli in Zurich of the stirrings in the city. He credits this upheaval to the teachings of George and myself."

George cut in, "And we have been covering the countryside. Last week we were in Maienfeld to the north and had a very good response from the people there. Conrad's sister lives there and we enjoyed her very special hospitality. We can expect more aggressive opposition, I am sure."

George's projection was right. Two days later, on July 13, both men were arrested. Felix was interrupted by several of the soldiers from the City Court. He was summarily taken to the City Hall, where the magistrate informed him that he was disturbing the peace, defying the church, and misleading many persons, thereby creating discord in the city. Since Felix was not a citizen of Chur, he was ordered to leave the city and was forbidden to return. He was given notice that if he should return, he would be arrested again and shown less tolerance. The soldiers escorted Felix down the street to the edge of the city and told him to be on his way. George was given a heavy fine and was released with a warning that, as a citizen of Chur, he was to conduct himself in harmony with the will of the council.

Now Felix was a man with no country. To leave Chur and go

back to Zurich meant facing the risk of arrest there. If he was without a home for the present, it might as well be in this region as in any other. He found his way into the forest area to the south and, after quite a lot of searching, to the home of one of the brethren. His host sent a young lad to the house where he and George had been staying. Late that evening George visited him and they talked and prayed over their plight. They agreed that Felix should work in the rural areas around Chur and George would find more secret ways of sharing with the people in the city.

Felix had been preaching only two days among the homes clustered in the mountains when he was surrounded and arrested again. Arriving at the prison, he found that George had also been apprehended. On this second arrest, the magistracy was much more severe. They denounced Felix for his violation of their wishes in staying in the district. They informed him that, since he had been warned previously, he would now be escorted back to his hometown. The Great Council of Zurich could deal with him. The magistrate drafted a letter to be sent along to the Zurich Council. It was read to Felix as the sentence of the Council of Chur.

> For a long time we have had among us one who calls himself Felix Manz. The same has created much trouble and discord among our people by baptizing old people and corner preaching, to such an extent that we ordered him to leave the city. After this, he returned and went on as before, disregarding the public proclamation in the church, which forbade adult baptism on penalty of death, loss of honor, and loss of property. Therefore, we arrested him and held him a few days, but because he is an obstinate, recalcitrant person, we released him from prison. And because he is one of yours, we have sent him to you, with the friendly request that you look after him and keep him in your territory, so that we may be rid of him and our people remain quiet; in case of his return, we shall be compelled to take severe measures against him.

Felix was deeply wounded. It is never pleasant to be so despised. He tried to remember that he was first a citizen of the kingdom of God and not primarily of the kingdoms of the earth, but it was difficult to know that he was an outcast among his neighbors. He dreaded the trip to Zurich and facing the council.

The small group of soldiers moved quickly out of Chur, with Felix walking between them. People stood along the street watching them go, some calling out to Felix a friendly word of encouragement, some calling out words that were not so friendly. As they began their climb to the Wessen Gap, the progress became more slow. Climbing along the wooded terraces above the Walensee, it was soon evident that Felix, from his travels, was more physically fit than the soldiers. They allowed him freedom to stroll along before them, unencumbered. It was a relief not to wear the heavy chains.

The trip was long. The men grew tired and then taunted Felix. They seemed to delight in prodding him with questions, "What do you think Zwingli will do with his errant scholar? What will he now do with his most rigorous opponent?" Felix made no answer to their sinister comments. Rather, he sought on every occasion possible to share with them the peace and meaning that he found in Jesus Christ.

"Zwingli and I were friends and colleagues," he told them, "but that relationship broke off when I continued to move farther in the direction which Zwingli had taught me. The free church will live. We are not building on the word of Zwingli, but on the Word of God."

The men chided him, saying, "We'll see whose word decides your fate, once we are in Zurich. You would have fared better as one of his storm troopers."

Felix thought over his situation. At his second arrest in Chur, George had been arrested as well, but his many friends in the city had negotiated his release. He and George had been taken from prison to the City Hall where the verdict was read stating that they were expelled from the city. George had quietly told Felix that he would go to Appenzell again, be with his wife, and work with the churches there. Assuring Felix of the prayers of the brotherhood that his time in prison would be short, they had been perfunctorily parted. Again, Felix had the dismal feeling of being very much alone.

The little troop finally moved into Zurich, traveling along the northern side of the Zurich Sea. Felix was extremely conscious of the familiar homes in Zollikon and of his proximity to Trini. However, he shared nothing with the soldiers with whom he walked. If the hostility and opposition increased, it was important not to implicate those who were close to him.

The familiar sight of the City Hall and the towers of the Grossmünster stirred Felix nearly to tears. In one way, it was wonderful to be home; in another, the circumstances could scarcely have been worse. How different it could be, he thought, if the freedom which he preached could be known in Zurich, and if the City Council would just permit the church to function in the freedom of Christ.

Felix was pushed hurriedly now along the street to the City Hall where he was presented to the magistrate. The soldiers were anxious to be free from their assignment. Felix knew the magistrate and watched his expression as he read the message from Chur. He turned to Felix and said gruffly, "I thought we had gotten you off our hands. You are not wanted in Zurich any more than you are wanted in Chur. You may be a citizen of this town, as far as your sordid history is concerned, but we have prisons for the likes of you and we will stop your influence by confining you there."

In what seemed like only a few moments, Felix found himself once again in the Wellenberg Tower. The door had the same squeak he had remembered as it closed behind him. The turnkey was not the same, however. This one locked the cell securely. Felix walked the three short steps across the cell and sat on the bench.

He now had to prepare himself for more discussions with Ulrich Zwingli. But to what end? he thought, for the defense which he had written nearly a year before had not been given adequate

167

attention. While he still held basically the same beliefs, the last months of preaching and of sharing with so many had enriched his thought. Guiding converts to a personal faith in Christ, sharing the joy of their baptism and of the Lord's Supper, teaching the meanings of discipleship, all had prepared him more adequately to represent the position of the free church, now generally known as the Anabaptists, or rebaptizers.

As he sat in the cell, he reflected on his past friendship with Zwingli. He knew him so well from their several years of work together. Somewhere within Zwingli's conscience, he believed, there must be a call to recognize the truth of Scripture and its full implications. If only Zwingli would recognize that they were simply carrying out in freedom much that he had earlier taught. If it was the authority of Scripture which had enabled Zwingli to break from the Roman church, then he should be able to see that the same authority of Scripture called them to a church that stood under the mandate of Christ. The true church must have the freedom to walk in the will of Christ, separate from the structures of power and violence which characterized the magistracy.

The weeks passed and the plans Felix made were not permitted to come to fruition. He was given only a brief trial. First, he was asked to account for his escape from prison early in the spring. He was then asked about his posture on infant baptism and was referred to Zwingli's recently published book, *Concerning Baptism, Rebaptism and Infant Baptism.* Felix said, "I wish to stand by the truth that infant baptism originated not with God but with men. True baptism takes place in voluntary confession to God, in response to the believer's commitment to a better life as a disciple of Christ. Whoever desires of me that water be applied in baptism, I will not deny it to him."

The clerk was not able to record all that Felix answered and so he invited Felix to write his own response in the official record of the trial. Without hesitancy, Felix wrote his response. To his satisfaction, he was able to express his interpretation of the Scriptures on baptism, as well as to add his assurance that Christ acknowledged him before the Father in heaven.

Felix's repeated requests to the City Council for an opportunity for further disputation were ignored. This treatment almost crushed his spirit. He was certain that Zwingli knew that he was being totally disregarded and how this kind of treatment could lead to a feeling of worthlessness. He did not understand how a pastor could allow such treatment, even of a former friend. To bolster his spirits, Felix purposely concentrated on God's accomplishments through him and on his mission as a leader in the cause of the believers' church. Perhaps Zwingli was jealous, trying to humiliate him. He would need to draw on the inner strength of the Holy Spirit. His faith would need to triumph over even this insult.

And so the hot summer passed from August to September and into October. He was able to obtain little information on his associates, for he was not permitted to have visitors. He wondered if Trini knew where he was. He did learn from a temporary prison mate that his friend Lorenz Hochrütiner had earlier gone to Basel to promote the free church in that setting, but that he had been expelled from the city by the end of August. Strangely, this note gave him a feeling of companionship. He was not alone in his persecution.

By early October Felix resigned himself to the fact that he was not going to be given the privilege of further disputation. In his last communications with the City Council, he had received the brief answer that his request was being considered, but he had no personal assurance that indeed it was.

On Saturday morning of October 7, a surprising change took place. The cell door was opened and the turnkey said, "Manz, you are free to go. The City Council has said that rather than to dispute with you, they would prefer to get rid of you. The order reads that you are to leave Zurich and desist from defying the church. If you are found again baptizing persons you will be arrested and dealt with in measures of severity corresponding to the seriousness of your offense." The turnkey read from the paper sent by the council, and then he looked up jeeringly at Felix and said, "I think that means that they will give you a final baptism!"

Felix looked into the man's eyes with a mix of distaste and sympathy. "My word to you," said the turnkey, "if I may give my advice, would be to heed this warning, to leave Zurich, and to find a quiet little valley where you can make your home and be at peace. Otherwise, they will execute you."

Felix smiled as he walked out of the cell. He said simply, "I have found my home in the family of God, and I am at peace, even in the valley of the shadow of death."

Chapter 12

The Public Trial of the Anabaptist Leaders

It was an odd feeling for Felix to walk down the streets of Zurich in broad daylight. His release had caught him by surprise and he moved with uncertainty. It seemed as though everyone were staring at him. He decided he was probably only imagining it. Still, he felt a stranger in his home city. For some reason, he was drawn to the less conspicuous streets and made his way to Neuenstadt and his mother's home.

Heinrich was at home and Felix marveled over the way he had changed. He now spoke like a man, even like one with a cause. When he had become accustomed to the shock of seeing his brother again, he told Felix all that had been happening to the believers' church movement around Zurich.

Felix washed himself from head to foot, many times, and found clean clothes to wear. He was just coming from Heinrich's bedroom when his mother walked in. She had her head down, watching the basket she carried so that it would not get caught in the door.

"Heinrich, we'll have turnips for supper and . . . ." She became aware of another presence in the room and it took a moment for her to believe that it was her son, Felix. The vegetables rolled across the floor as she dropped her basket and ran to her son.

"Felix!" she cried, "I was afraid I would never see you again!"

"The Lord has taken care of my body and my spirit," he said, cheerfully.

He told Heinrich and his mother, Anna, of his ministry across eastern Switzerland and of his arrest and imprisonment. He shared the joy of participating in the free-church movement, of seeing so many persons come to personal faith, and of having the privilege of baptizing them. Felix was thrilled that the expressions of his mother and brother showed that they understood completely, as only committed disciples could.

"You must leave the city immediately, you know," Anna Manz said, the pain of it in her voice.

"I know, mother. I have thought so little of where I will go now."

Anna grabbed her shawl and said, "We will walk with you as far as Zollikon; it may be safer."

Felix agreed and added, "I am so anxious to see Trini. How is she?"

"She is fine, son. A wonderful Christian woman, still very much in love with you."

Felix's heart missed a beat. "We would be married if my way of life permitted," he said.

"I hope things are soon different," she said, and he and Heinrich followed as they left the house.

The trip went quickly since there was so much to talk about. Before long, Felix was alone with Trini, in the garden. They spoke of personal things, of feelings and hopes, of pain and insecurity, and of their undying love for each other. At times in their conversation it was a though they had never been apart; at times, as though they barely knew each other.

Much too soon, Trini's father interrupted them. He wanted to know whether they might gather a few friends for fellowship before Felix would leave. With Felix's consent, Conrad sent word to some of the neighbors to meet at the Hottinger home for the evening. When they gathered, Felix taught them from the book of Hebrews, sharing his understandings of the work of Jesus Christ as their one mediator and Lord. He looked frequently to Trini, to see her warm response.

The joy in that home was shared by each person present. They sat around the table and broke bread together, sharing the emblems of the Lord's Supper. Heinrich looked at his older brother Felix with a smile and said, "You are a strange one, released from prison this morning, forbidden to promote a free church, and within a few hours you have led a service here in Zollikon."

Everyone laughed, but they all knew the danger which threatened him in this action. "Things are difficult for us here," Trini's father spoke. "We are being crushed as a group of believers, but the free church is still alive. Our influence is being felt beyond our village. Recently the community of Wassberg called for us to send them some Bible teachers. We chose Rudolf Rutschmann, my son Rudolf, and your friend Felix Kienast and sent them over to teach the Word."

"I'm so glad to hear that," Felix responded, remembering that Andreas had reported this. "The key to our future is simply in obedience to Christ and his Word. It is his church; he is Lord."

By early afternoon of the next day, Felix had bidden his friends farewell. Heinrich and Anna Manz left ahead of him to go back into Zurich. Felix was planning to head in the opposite direction, east toward the region north of Grüningen. Once again he embraced Trini. Both were aware of how deep their love had grown, in spite of their many separations, and yet they were reserved about plans for their future. They said few words, each aware that they had no choice but to part. Trini stood at the door watching him until he was completely out of sight. Felix stopped often as he walked down the road away from her, to look back. Several times he thought of running to her, but no, he had nothing to offer.

It was a monotonous walk and by evening he found himself scarcely half way to his destination. Securing lodging for the night in the home of Anabaptists whom he knew, he was up in the early hours of the clear Sunday morning and on his way to the village of Hinwil. He was quite certain that here he could locate Conrad Grebel, who, with Marx Bosshart, had been having a remarkable ministry in the region, especially in Hinwil. At least this was the report from several brethren in the village where he had slept. They told him enthusiastically of Conrad's debates with the pastors, his appeal for justice, and his offer to debate with Zwingli, saying that if Zwingli defeated him they should burn him, but if he defeated Zwingli not to burn Zwingli!

Walking through the pine forest he enjoyed the quiet of the morning. Arriving in Hinwil in the mid-afternoon, he found a tremendous stir in the town. A crowd was gathering in the marketplace and Felix joined them to discover what was happening. He soon recognized Jacob Gross, with whom he had shared in St. Gall, and pressed through the crowd to get to him. Gross was excited to see him and related to him the unusual events of the morning. George Blaurock had taken over the pulpit in the village church and had preached the morning message. Felix remembered another time when George had tried to do the same and wondered if his actions this time would have similar repercussions.

"He announced a Sunday afternoon meeting in the market-place here," Jacob related. Felix could hear George's strong voice in another part of the crowd. "Magistrate Berger was summoned," Jacob continued, "and he rode forthwith from the Grüningen castle, intending to arrest George. By the time he got here, this large crowd had gathered in strong support of Blaurock and the other free-church leaders. By surrounding George they have prevented Berger from making the arrest."

Felix shook his head in amazement. "Come," Jacob insisted, taking his arm, "let's join the other leaders."

Jacob led Felix to the center of the group. There was Conrad, George and Michael Sattler along with Martin Lingg and Ulrich Teck, of Waldshut. Conrad and George welcomed Felix as if they were blood brothers, and before any of them could speak—of the trials of their mission, of the sacrifices they were having to make, of the risks they were forced to take—George began to sing and Felix, with his clear, strong voice joined him, and then Conrad. They were together again, unified by their convictions, freed by their mutual understanding.

As they led the crowd in song, Felix was able to see Magistrate Berger on the outer edge of the circle of people. He was finding it difficult even to penetrate the edge of the crowd and so, suddenly, he turned and hurried away into the village. In his absence, the meeting progressed freely. First George, then Conrad, and finally Felix gave forceful presentations of the gospel of Christ and the freedom to be known in commitment to him. There was no disturbance and the meeting continued for an hour and a half.

In Felix's presentation, he emphasized the life of discipleship as a life which takes seriously Jesus' mandate to love God fully, and to love our neighbors, including our enemies.

" 'Love,' he quoted Paul, 'is the fulfilling of the law.' And again, 'The love of God is spread into our lives by the Holy Spirit.' We cannot live the life of Christ apart from the spirit of Christ." Lifting his voice to be heard by all, he called out, "If love was possible without Christ, we would not need Christ! If love is not possible with Christ, we have not fully known Christ. That love is possible through Christ is what Christian discipleship is all about!"

Suddenly, there was the sound of horses. Magistrate Berger had returned. Felix realized that he had probably secured horses from the neighboring village and had called additional officers to join him. He should have known that Berger would not give up so easily. Now the constables began riding through the crowd, forcing the people aside, making their way to the center of the circle. The people could not stop the horses, and they began falling back. Felix turned to Conrad and said, "I think I shall leave. I am not ready for another stint in prison just yet."

"Hurry, Felix," Conrad said, "I can't run with the shape my feet are in, but you can. Go!" And he stepped in front of Felix to shield him from the Magistrate's sight. Quickly, he ducked through the group opposite Berger and the horsemen. He looked back as he heard outcries and saw that they had already apprehended George, whose tall form was readily visible in the crowd. As he moved on he was certain that Conrad and the other leaders were being arrested as well. Felix ran without hesitating into the safety of the adjoining forest. Hurrying on through the trees, he made his escape. From the shouts between officers he could tell that the horsemen were circling by the tree line seeking to find others of the group.

For the next days, Felix remained in hiding, secure in territory that had already become quite familiar to him from his stay in the Grüningen area months earlier. He spent the first night in a cave in the hills and after that, in various homes of friends and fellow Anabaptists. From his hosts he learned that Conrad, George, Michael Sattler, Ulrich Teck, and Jacob Gross with Hans Hotz and Heini Reimann of the local brethren were confined in the prison at Grüningen. How strange, Felix thought, that Conrad was now in prison in his boyhood home. He wondered how his friend felt in the cell where his own father once held prisoners when he was Bailiff of Grüningen.

Jacob Falk was at large, Felix discovered, and they were soon able to meet. A number of the prominent citizens were urging Magistrate Berger to be considerate of the prisoners, Jacob told him, and to be careful in any agreements with Zurich. Magistrate Berger had notified the City Council at Zurich of the arrests and he was offering to hold a local disputation to gain clarity regarding the differences in doctrine. He was now awaiting word from Zurich as to the willingness of the City Council to send representatives from Zwingli for such a disputation in Grüningen. In view of this negotiation the local brethren were encouraged to think that Magistrate Berger was not going to turn this group over to Zurich.

Felix knew that Berger had scouts out looking for him. Early one morning as Felix was traveling to a neighboring farm, he saw a group of soldiers coming toward him. Placing his walking stick on his shoulder and acting as nonchalant as he could, he turned, into the forest which edged the road. They were so near that he stretched himself under some small pines by a large rock, face pressed to the ground, as he listened over his seemingly loud breathing. The men passed, their voices fading as the distance increased. He waited for a long while and then slowly rose from his hiding place and went on his way through the forest instead of the much-too-public road.

After this, he did not dare to show himself among the people, but the brethren with whom he met conveyed to him the strong sentiment among the populous against Berger's having arrested the group. In fact, they said, the people were asking the magistrate to release the prisoners. But Berger was firm; he would hold these men until there was clearance from Zurich.

The negotiation continued during the next several weeks and the brethren gained an increased sense of freedom about their ministry. Felix and Jacob Falk were working together, conducting Bible teaching in farm homes and even open preaching sessions in the forest areas. They visited a number of the small villages of the region to teach and encourage the brethren. Out of caution, Felix continued to stay on the move, going from one community to another so that if his ministry were noted he would not readily be found. His teaching now focused on the new people that Christ creates, a people of love and commonality, a people who share both in spirit and in mutual aid.

The day before All Hallows' Eve, October 30, Felix had spent the forenoon in the home of Karl Brennwald, using the quiet hours for study and prayer. Brennwald was often away, going into Zurich, meeting with people at the Widerkerin house, or at other times to Seeb near Bülach, where many met at the home of Hans Meiers. After lunch Felix was ready to leave for Meiers' home, when suddenly he heard voices at the door. The loud pounding was punctuated with sharp demands: "Open the door! We're here by the order of the magistrate!" In a moment the soldiers had burst into the house and it was too late for Felix to make an escape. He stood, looking boldly and calmly into the faces of his captors. Immediately, he was seized and with little explanation was led away. His arrest, when it came, was a shock, for his freedom from prison had been so brief that the memory of the cell now hit him with a depressing force.

When they arrived at the prison, Magistrate Berger was especially pleased. With this arrest, he now had the full contingent of the well-known leaders of the Anabaptists. This placed him in a unique position with the City Council of Zurich which, as the members said, "meant to stop this Anabaptism mischief in the Zurich Oberland." The Grüningen castle became his prison as he was taken to the room with the other Anabaptists.

The populace of Grüningen was continuing to express to Magistrate Berger their displeasure over the arrests. It appeared that a peasant revolt was developing. To quiet the excited population, Berger gave them a report on his negotiations with Zurich. He assured the people that there would be a disputation, and that these men would be given opportunity for a proper defense of their position. The blame for their long imprisonment he laid at the feet of the Zurich Council, which had yet to agree on the disputation.

The prisoners hoped that Berger would succeed in asking for a local trial; they much preferred that to a trial in Zwingli's Zurich. During the week following Felix's arrest the prisoners shared with one another their reports of experience in the work. At least, Felix thought, he was not in prison alone this time. The prisoners were able to talk freely and to write short letters, sending them by their brethren in the Grüningen region. Felix wrote a brief note to Trini telling her of his situation. One of the concerns the group had was to overcome the connotations of heresy that the term "Anabaptist" implied. They spoke of believer's baptism as the first actual baptism, since infant baptism had no meaning for salvation. Hans Hotz expressed himself for all of them: "Baptism is always the sign of the renewed person, buried in the death of Jesus Christ, and always a certain announcement or testimony of resurrection through the death of Jesus Christ."

The announcement they had awaited finally came. The Zurich council had been firm, and a disputation was scheduled to be convened in Zurich. The date was set, November 6-8. Magistrate Berger, having negotiated for an open disputation, now consented to move his prisoners to Zurich. Just two days before the date, Berger and a score of soldiers led the small group of brethren out of the prison for the journey to Zurich.

It was early morning, scarcely dawn, when they left Grüningen. Berger said he wanted to make the trip in one day. They were sure that he wanted to be ahead of any gathering of the citizens. This was a familiar trek to Felix by now. Yet, it was quite different to go in the presence of the brethren with whom he shared so much. Along the way he found opportunity for further discussion with Michael Sattler, Martin Lingg, and Ulrich Teck, for he had developed close ties with them during the week in the Grüningen prison. His admiration for each of them was high, for their integrity as well as for their faith. His conversations with Conrad and George along the way were free, even at times lighthearted—the interchanges of familiar friends.

Late that same afternoon the tired group passed through the edge of Zollikon. Felix's mind was on Trini as they crossed familiar streets, several which would have taken him to her. In the early evening they approached the city, passing through the Neumarket Gate, making their way to the City Hall. What conversation they were permitted was now given primarily to their anticipation of meeting Zwingli and his associates again in the disputation. Some of them were fearful that Zwingli would not keep his promise to Berger to give them opportunity to express themselves. The group had all agreed back in the Grüningen prison that Conrad and Felix should be the primary spokesmen for the interchange, with Michael and George supporting them and helping whenever possible.

As they were led along the streets of Zurich they saw that the news of their coming had preceded them. Once they had passed through Neumarket Gate they saw that many persons stood

179

along the streets. Some were close friends and were there to assure the brethren of their support. At the City Hall, Magistrate Berger presented the prisoners to the Zurich magistrates with a dramatic flourish, proud of having captured the troublemakers. He instructed his guard to stay with them until they were securely imprisoned in the Wellenberg Tower, and then they would be free for the evening. Two groups of soldiers now marched the prisoners along the Limmat River to the tower which seemed to rise like an ever-present warning out of the dark cold water.

The negotiations with Berger had set the date for the disputation. The council did not delay. In the early forenoon of November 6, the prisoners were escorted to the Grossmünster for the first session. The streets were crowded. The cathedral was already filled when they entered. Over eight hundred people were packed into the building. Conrad, Felix, and George were given prominent seats to the one side of the large cathedral hall. Their associates were seated behind them. On the other side sat Zwingli, Leo Jud, and Megander Grossman in the front row of seats and just behind them, Heinrich Bullinger, Heinrich Engelhart, and Oswald Miconius. The other city pastors occupied the seats in back of these. The scene was familiar to Felix, and he had a sinking feeling that things would be much as before.

Felix observed Grebel's facial interchange with Miconius, an old friend. The recognition lacked warmth. He saw Conrad's gaze move to his brother-in-law, Vadian. Their eyes held for a long moment before Conrad found his own father. Felix felt for his friend. What an inner struggle he must be having to be in such an adverse position to his family. The aging Jacob Grebel was seated with the council, his eyes fixed on his son. Felix could not detect any hostility in the expression; rather, his wrinkled brow conveyed genuine concern.

The first action was the announcement by the burgomaster that fellow presidents had been chosen to lead the discussion. Both of them were well known to the prisoners. The chairman was Dr. Sebastian Hofmeister of Schaffhausen, with whom both

Conrad and later Felix had shared extensive dialogue. He was assisted by Dr. Joachim von Watt from St. Gall, as cochairman, known to all as Vadian. The prisoners knew him as Conrad's brother-in-law.

Zwingli opened the dialogue with an introductory statement of accusations against the brethren for their rejection of the authority of the council. This, he said, was evidenced by their rejection of infant baptism and their insistence on an adult rebaptism. He interpreted this not as a biblical issue but as a position in defiance of the church-state. He said that the movement of the Anabaptists was spreading so rapidly that it was a threat to the security of the church-state. "The prisoners," he added, "have become revolutionary in their impatience with the more ordered movements of reform and are contributing to the peasant unrest."

Dr. Hofmeister, as chairman, outlined the procedure and designated other lords who would preside over the discussion: Lord of Cuppel, Herr Wolfgang Joner; the commander of Kassnacht, Herr Conrad Schmid; as well as the honorable Dr. Joachim von Watt of St. Gall. Hofmeister perfunctorily opened the session with a prayer. In his final comments he introduced the several theses for debate: "One, children of Christians are no less children of God than their elders, as was true in the Old Testament. If they are already God's, who is to prevent their baptism? Two, circumcision was to the ancients what baptism is to us. In as much as it is now given to infants, baptism should likewise be given to infants. And third, rebaptism has no mandate or example or proof in God's Word. Therefore, those who are baptized again, crucify Christ again, either by their own obstinacy or by inventing a new practice."

Following this brief presentation, Hofmeister recognized Conrad and Felix as spokesmen for the brethren. Conrad began his response by reminding the council of the meaningful associations he and his associates had enjoyed with Zwingli in the past, and of their common study of the Word of God. He affirmed that most of the leaders of their movement had come to personal faith in Christ through Zwingli's preaching. These words produced whispers of positive response throughout the audience, and Hofmeister rapped his gavel on the oak table from which he presided.

Felix picked up the deliberation at this point. He reminded everyone of Zwingli's teaching on the importance of faith in Jesus Christ alone for salvation, and his earlier teaching that the rite of baptism is only a sign of that inner faith. Zwingli too, he reminded them, had questioned the value of infant baptism. Noting Zwingli's discomfort, Felix appealed directly to the council, saying, "Noble lords, we ask only that you recognize this sign of baptism as properly following the believing commitment, a commitment which can be made only by a mature person who can understand the gospel of Christ. If the reformation of the church acts to remove the relics and the hope of saving merit in the mass, for, as we have heard, you have abolished the mass as of this Easter past; is it not consistent to recognize that in the sacrament of baptism there is no more saving merit than in the sacrament of the mass?

"We, too, believe," he continued, "that all children belong to God, that through the redemptive work of Christ they are safe until they come to an age of accountability. Once they are responsible for their decisions they too must come to faith in Christ, a faith that is their own, and then they should be baptized as a sign of that faith." After a moment's pause, he added, "Is it not possible that while you practice what you believe, you could grant us the freedom to practice as we believe?"

Zwingli and those around him were argumentative in their response. They were not of a mind to recognize the validity of the brethren's statements, nor to permit diversity of practice. The sessions closed in the late afternoon of the first day without any adjustments on the part of either side. The brethren were led out of the church by the guards and taken back to their prison cells. Their sparse meal and their proximity in the cells left them, tired though they were, with time and opportunity to review the proceedings. Michael Sattler and Ulrich Teck were especially helpful in the review, reminding them all of the relation of baptism, as a sign of the new life in Christ, to the nature of the church, to the new life in covenant, and to the need for disciplined holy living.

The next morning the guards came to their cells and brought them out again for a similar interchange. There were so many people present now that rails were installed in the sanctuary and the nave of the Grössmunster to contain the crowd. The prisoners were again led to chairs by the table opposite the one which stood before the presidents and preachers. The debate this second day was long and often heated.

The focus moved from baptism to the nature of the Christian life. The brethren emphasized the call to personal faith and discipleship for all who would be Christians. Their emphasis on a fully voluntary decision was so revolutionary that it received scarcely any serious review. This second day proved little better than the first, for their emphasis on discipleship was foreign to the understanding of the Christian faith known by the council.

The prisoners were awake before dawn on the third day and prepared themselves by prayer and reflection together. This session was much as the others and, after lengthy interaction, they were given opportunity to summarize their beliefs, before the council would arrive at its verdict. Conrad began the summation.

"Let everyone notice that we hold the Scripture to teach that baptism belongs to those believers who devote themselves to the Son of God and separate themselves from evil. The believers who bear the fruit of the Spirit which is love, peace, kindness, good will, trust, meekness, humility, patience, righteousness, and truth, and who walk therein, they are the church of Christ and the body of Christ in the Christian church. Now we hope and are assured that we are in the true church. We object to your intent to force us out of the Christian church into what would be a foreign church."

183

Felix followed with a direct address to Dr. Hofmeister, presiding chairman of the council. "Since various accusations have been made on specific aspects of my beliefs, I want it known that those who desire to accept Christ and be obedient to his Word and follow his example should be free to unite themselves by the sign of baptism and should leave the others with their own faith. As far as a community of goods is concerned, it should be understood that what I have meant is that a good Christian should share with his neighbor when he is in need. I do believe that no Christian should be a magistrate, nor can he use the sword to punish or to kill anyone, for there is no scriptural support for such a thing."

Hofmeister nodded and said in a matter-of-fact tone, "It is so recorded."

The disputation was formally closed and the Anabaptists were told that they would be given the council's verdict in due time. Hofmeister then announced to the public that all others who thought that Ulrich Zwingli was wrong should gather in Zurich on November 10 and he would give them answer. He smacked the gavel on the table, nodded to the guards, and they came forward to lead the brethren back to their prison cells in the tower. Locked in their small cubicles they could now only wait the verdict from the trial.

One bit of pleasure for Felix had been that in his seeing Conrad Hottinger in the crowd he was able to catch a brief sight of Trini beside him just as they were being moved down the street. How he longed for opportunity to talk with her, to sit by her side. Now, in his cell, he sat thinking of her, daydreaming of their times together, imagining their next meeting . . . if this was just over . . . if the council would just grant them the freedom to practice their faith as they understood it.

As days passed, and they heard nothing from the council, the prisoners supported one another with prayer and encouragement. Occasionally, Felix or George would lead a song, and the others would join in. Some of the songs had been composed in their group, but most often they sang praises from the Psalms. Even the guards became more friendly as they sensed the spirit of these peace-loving men. In a rare conversational moment, the soldiers told them the reason that their expectation of Dr. Balthasar Hubmaier being at the trial had not materialized. The agents of His Imperial Majesty had prevented Hubmaier's coming through the Hapsburg forces' occupation of the city of Waldshut.

Finally, after ten days, on November 18, the verdict was brought to the prisoners. It was read to them perfunctorily (SSA, p. 442):

> Conrad Grebel, Felix Manz, and George Blaurock are sentenced to remain in prison on bread and water and mush, and no one is to be permitted to visit them but the guards, who will keep them in prison as long as God should please and it seems good to the lords. The foreign brethren, Ulrich Tech of Waldshut, Marty Lingg of Schaffhausen, Michael Sattler of the Black Forest, and Jacob Gross from St. Gall are banished from Zurich, never to return, and if so they risk the same imprisonment.

The guards then proceeded to lead the four prisoners out of their cells. The men's emotions were mixed, relieved to be released even with banishment, but sorry to leave Felix, Conrad, and George. Conrad called out to them as cheerfully as he could, "The work is yours, while we are here. Be faithful and the Lord will give you his blessing."

Felix listened to the sounds of their feet shuffling down the hall. It left him fighting a sense of despair. Prison had robbed him of so much of his life in the past year and he knew well its torment. Once again he faced cold, damp days in a lonely cell, a prospect which, with his memories, was almost numbing to his mind. At least he was not completely alone.

"Be encouraged, brothers," George said to his cell mates, "The church is free—a work of the Spirit, not of our labors. We will trust God."

185

During the next weeks of winter cold that dragged by slowly, others of the Anabaptist community were arrested in Zollikon, Wytikon, and the northern environs of Zurich. They were imprisoned in the tower as well, thrown into the adjoining cells. Among them were Felix's friends, Hans Hotz, Jacob Fulk, Heini Reimann of Grüningen, men known for their effective leadership. In mid-December those of Grüningen were taken from Zurich back to the Grüningen prison to be held there. Christmas came and went, and there was no change in their situation. Jacob Grebel appealed to the council, asking leniency for his son Conrad on the basis of Conrad's poor health and the needs of his wife and children, but his arguments were disregarded by the council.

Early in January they learned that the Grüningen prisoners had escaped. Hans told them that the brethren reported that Reimann and Falk had gone to St. Gall, as had Gabriel Giger and Jacob Gross. Sattler, with Tech and Lingg, had earlier gone north to Zurich Unterland, probably to Klingnau.

In late January 1526, to their amazement, Dr. Hubmaier of Waldshut was arrested. He had fled to Zurich when the Austrian forces occupied his city. But in opposition to his influence, Zwingli had him seized and he was confined in the same tower prison as Felix, Conrad, and George. Although he was in a different section, the men could call greetings back and forth. Hubmaier recognized Conrad, but they could not actually converse.

Clearly the Zurich Council was trying to suppress all forms of the Anabaptist emphasis. Still, they had allowed the brethren their Bibles, and it was this that kept the men from total discouragement. They read the Scriptures and discussed various passages. They were able to convince one of the guards to carry a few notes between themselves and Dr. Hubmaier but their communications remained limited. They learned that he had been under such pressure when he had first arrived in Zurich that he had submitted to Zwingli's demand that he recant his free-church stand, but he then regained his composure and stayed by his conviction. Consequently, predictably, he was in prison. The final interchange with Zwingli had actually taken place at a public meeting at the Fraumünster, in which Zwingli had preached and then presented Hubmaier, who had been expected to give his recantation. He had surprised them all with his bold declarations.

Hans Hotz was placed next to the cells of Felix and George. This was especially good fortune, for with Hans' excellent leadership potential he needed encouragement and help in biblical understanding to clarify interpretations of his faith. And George especially offered affirmation to the prisoners. His spirit was undaunted, and he insisted repeatedly that they would be released and would soon be back at work. Felix well knew why people had nicknamed him "Strong George," and his respect and appreciation for the big man grew.

The winter months passed slowly, with many days of bitterly cold weather. The ice formed on the edge of the tower from the waters of the Limmat. It was February when they learned more about how their friend Balthasar Hubmaier had come to be imprisoned. He had been deported to Austria and had immediately fled to Augsburg. While still in prison, he had talked to a guard in hope that his own account would be conveyed to Felix, Conrad, and George. He had fled Waldshut and had come to Zurich to escape the Hapsburgs. But even after he arrived in Zurich the Austrian authorities had asked the City Council to turn Hubmaier over to them, to which the Great Council had responded that it intended to deal with him. Zwingli had then negotiated with Hubmaier for protection on the condition of a recantation to be held in three public services, including the Fraumünster, the Grossmünster, and the Gassau church in Grüningen. The latter was important, Zwingli had said, to discourage the growing Anabaptist movmment in that region. It was at the Fraumünster that Hubmaier had ruined Zwingli's plan by delivering a strong sermon reaffirming his commitment to the way of Christ as he understood the Scripture, calling for a believers' church. This had landed him in prison.

On the first of March word came that the council wanted to dispose of their case as well; a further trial had been set for March 5 and 6. This, Felix calculated, would be his tenth disputation with Zwingli and his associates. He, with the other prisoners, was concerned about whether the result might be banishment or a move toward a death sentence. When the trial came it was less publicized and more brief and formal than the previous one. There was little change in the argument; it was almost perfunctory. The City Council clearly sought an early verdict. Zwingli charged them with three points: that they taught there should be no magistracy, that they taught that all things should be held in common, and that they taught the security of the saints. He further confused the issue by saying, "They have also taught their group to be prepared to resist my lords in case you send a company of soldiers against them." It was evident to Felix and Conrad as well as to the other brethren that Zwingli was seeking a more severe sentence by charging them with sedition and revolution.

The witnesses called were actually Zwingli's associates. Each one reported on conversations with the prisoners in the tower. Felix listened with gratification as each man told of these conversations. "Hans Hotz," one told the council, "said in the Hexenturm, that Blaurock first taught him and also strengthened him, likewise Felix Manz. In this way they all encouraged one another in the tower. Hotz holds infant baptism to be an error and rebaptism right."

One of the witnesses muttered something about having the ability to change Hotz's tune on the rack. He said, "We've had Dr. Hubmaier stretched there three times, and it has a way of making a person talk differently!"

When Felix heard this he cried out involuntarily, "No!" He sat, his head in his hands, imagining the horrifying torture. Zwingli appeared somewhat embarrassed at this disclosure that he tortured Dr. Hubmaier, for it was well-known that within the last two years he and Hubmaier had amiably shared similar views before that very court. It was at this point that Felix realized how desperate Zwingli had become, how determined to have his will carried out. Felix looked up at him and saw someone he had not known before. Had Zwingli been looking at him, he would have known exactly what Felix was thinking.

Now, individually, each one in the group of prisoners was asked of his or her position. Felix sat listening to each expression of conviction and their knowledgeable use of the Scriptures. He was proud to be one of them. Uli Hottinger of Zollikon simply replied to the council that since the Scriptures do not expressly teach infant baptism it shouldn't be done. Ernst von Glatz of Silesia told of having been baptized by Karl Brennwald at the house of the furrier, Widerkerin, and that he would stand by his baptism. Guildmaster Huber turned to Brennwald for confirmation and he affirmed that he had also baptized Master Eich's servant and that he would stand by his belief even to testimony in blood. The guildmaster turned to Anna Widerkerin for her response and she told of Brennwald's baptizing Eich's servant and the servant of her brother, Master Bluntschli. She added that she would stay by her baptism as Christ and his apostles had commanded and so it seemed good and right to her. As she spoke, Felix thought, "How thorough is the reform of the believer's church, women and men both alike testifying of their faith and convictions."

The second guildmaster, Heinrich Trüben turned to Anthony Roggenacher of Schwyz, also a furrier, and asked of his belief. He responded, "Baptism is for those who forsake sin and diligently follow Christ, for God gives them much grace to walk in his will." Hans Hottinger, the watchman from Zollikon, was next, stating, "Had God the Father asked infant baptism I would support it, but what God has not planted needs to be uprooted." Rudolf Hottinger was next. He was Trini's brother and Felix listened with deep empathy. Rudolf had a family and was risking much by his words.

"I have done nothing wrong by being baptized, but I beg M'lords for the sake of brotherly love to let me return to my family." He paused and then said, "I will not oppose infant baptism." He could not face Felix but sat with his head bowed.

The guildmasters conferred and then the third of the lords, Hans Usteri, addressed Hans Ockenfuss, asking for his comments. He knew him well, having been with those who in Zwingli's presence had eaten sausages at Froschauer's print shop where the acts of reformation had actually begun. Ockenfuss said, "Since neither Old nor New Testament assert infant baptism I will stay on the side of truth and seal it with my blood as did my Lord Jesus Christ. In all other things I will be obedient to M'lords."

Huber, another of the lords, addressed Elizabeth Hottinger of Hirslanden asking whether she would not accept the decisions of the council. With clear conviction she declared that she would stay with her baptism to the death; that it was good and right as Christ had so practiced it. Margaret Hottinger, sister of Jacob, added her word, that in this baptism we are saved and that anyone not believing so in Christ and fighting against his baptism was a child of the devil!

The guildmasters now turned back to the other men, Fridli Ab-lberg of Schwyz and Hans Heingarter of St. Gall, and each testified that having recently come to Zurich and knowing Ockenfuss as a tailor, he had gone to his home and had identified with the Anabaptists. Having met Brennwald they were accompanying him in the city when they had been arrested. With a shrug, Huber turned to the last two prisoners: first, Winbrat Fanwilerin of St. Gall said she also regarded her baptism as God's teaching and accepted it as the righteousness of God. Then Huber addressed Anna Manz, Felix's mother. She told of her faith calmly but with unmistakable conviction. Felix had not seen her in the room before she had been addressed. Her small stature had kept her hidden behind the larger men. His eyes met his mother's, and the smiles they each wore showed their familial resemblance. They also showed peace and security. A warmth of love spread through Felix as he let his eyes move from one to the other of the prisoners; what a marvellous variety of people they were, reflecting the nature of a voluntary believer's church.

The hearings were now completed, and Zwingli turned to the leaders, Conrad, Felix, and George, and asked if there was anything he could do for them. George asked whether he could submit a brief confession by letter stating his position since he had not been heard adequately. Conrad requested that Zwingli have a writing which Conrad had prepared in prison be printed for better understanding of the beliefs of the brethren. Felix remained silent. He had asked for so much and had received so little from Zwingli and the council; he would not lower himself by begging. And Felix suspected that the gesture of grace was only a token, for the requests were denied. This second trial was quite obviously a way primarily of publicizing the council's new and more severe action.

The council wasted no time. The mandate was announced on March 7, the day following the conclusion of their trial. It concisely and sternly forbade the rebaptizing of any person. The council now established the death penalty by drowning as the punishment for all those who would be found performing such baptism. The mandate further pronounced that Felix, Conrad, and George, plus nine of the other Anabaptist men and six of the women should be placed on straw in the New Tower, and should be granted only water and bread until they should die and decay. No one would be permitted to visit them or have power to change their condition be they well or sick, "without the consent of my lords."

The group of prisoners were confined within the tower. The men in one section and the women in another. Each of them was forced to search for the inner disciplines of faith in a new way. Now, they were confined to the death! They tried to support one another with encouraging words, with prayer, and with quotation and interpretation of Scripture. At times, they would even sing together. But all felt the severity of the edict. That rebaptism was now punishable by drowning made adult conversion the ultimate issue in the life of the believers' church.

The guards informed them that copies of the public notice had been widely distributed by the City Council, announcing the severity of their sentence. The public was warned that no one, man, woman, or child should henceforth baptize another, and anyone doing so would be seized and drowned without mercy.

Held together in what they called the Murder Tower, they were told that anytime any one of them recanted, he or she would be released. The guards taunted them daily with this possibility, the chance to have this whole terrible thing ended. But it was clear that none of them would compromise their commitment to Christ. Day by day, their spirits actually became stronger for sharing together and close fellowship.

Two long weeks passed, when on Wednesday evening as they were eating their bread, they found that the cell doors where the men were held were not locked! Felix could hardly believe that this could happen twice to him but he and George wandered about through the prison, talking with the various prisoners and enjoying their opportunity to exercise. They had not considered seriously the opportunity of escape from the Tower since the main door to the cells was bolted tightly from the outside. Suddenly, Karl Brennwald ran to Felix's side and told him that he had discovered a window, high on the wall, and that the shutter appeared to be unlocked! Seeing another shutter low down, they broke it off and by setting it in the corner the servant of Master Eich climbed up and propped open the window. Excitedly they searched and in another small room found several pieces of rope, which they tied together. Master Eich's servant tied the rope securely to a bar and Felix climbed up, calling for the others to follow.

But as the group gathered before the window, the question was raised by Ockenfuss, "Is it right to disregard the orders of the magistracy and to escape from prison?" After a few moments of query, George declared in his robust way, "God in his providence has made this escape possible and we should do so in haste!"

Felix swung the rope to Karl and pulled him up, then Anthony, then one after another up the wall and through the open window to the ledge. Using the rope of the capstan for their descent, they each made their escape down the stone wall of the tower and into the moat below the drawbridge. The last to descend was Eich's servant, a tall, athletic young man who knotted the rope under his arms and dropped down beside them. Happily, the men congratulated each other, glancing around to be sure that no one was around to stop them. As they climbed the bank, Felix took one sad look up at the tower, knowing that his sisters in Christ were still imprisoned, then he turned and rushed across the bridge with the others. They ran into an alley and stopped to catch their breath and decide what to do. William and Fridli had been quite ill for several days, and their escape left them exhausted. They said that they would remain in Zurich since they were scarcely known in the area, and could hide themselves among the brethren. Ockenfuss said he wanted to go to Horgerberg to work.

"And where are you going?" several of them asked as they turned to Felix, Conrad, and George.

"That we will have trouble deciding. There are so many cities that want us!" Conrad joked, thinking of the authorities rather than the citizens,

"Perhaps we should go join the red Indians across the sea!" offered Felix.

"They might treat us better than what we are facing here," George growled.

The comedy was a welcome relief. They chuckled and then stood in silence pondering the seriousness of the situation.

"I'm going first to Barbara, of course," Conrad said softly.

"And I will go to find my wife. No doubt she is in Appenzell," said George.

"I," said Felix, "will go first to Zollikon and then wherever God may lead."

Chapter 13

Triumph Amid Persecution

Upon their escape, Felix quickly made plans to accompany Hans Hottinger, Jörg Schad, and several others from the Zollikon community. They would go in different ways for the rest of the night and meet in the morning at the Green Shield Inn. Conrad bid Felix farewell and said that he would be on the way to St. Gall, certain that he would find Barbara and their children with his sister and brother-in-law, Vadian. George planned to accompany Grebel and go on to the area of Apenzell.

"I think we will go north with Brennwald to Oberglatt," Conrad told Felix, "then on to Enbrach and east to St. Gall. Our friends will hide us along the way." His face changed and his expression showed concern and fondness. He placed his hands on Felix's shoulders. "Felix, you have been in and out of prison three times. You are the senior in years among us. In the movement you are regarded as the voice of distinction. In addition to the clarity of your preaching and the zeal with which you have evangelized, you have a reputation of integrity in your confrontations with Zwingli. We need you to travel across the country as much as possible to strengthen the church."

"But, be careful," George added, "for it is evident that Zwingli means to be especially severe with you. He needs to make an example of someone to show the firmness of his posture."

194

Felix nodded and said, "I will be careful. I will not invite unnecessary attention. However, the lines are now drawn, the issues are clear, and I intend to promote the gospel of Jesus Christ in all of its truth. If that involves me in actions which lead to further persecution so it must be. But I will keep moving from place to place and make it as difficult as I can for Zwingli to keep track of me."

They parted in the dark street and Felix along with the small group going to Zollikon agreed upon a time and place to meet. After leaving them he went to spend the rest of the night in quiet watchfulness at his mother's home, for she had not been sentenced to prison as some of the other women had been. Late that night they quietly talked of the dangers which now faced all of them.

"My son," she said, combing his hair with her fingers, "we will be well. You are not to worry about us and we will do the same for you. We are with God, and he is with us."

Long before the sun had risen, the men met at the Green Shield, and together they moved quickly through the city. They were among the first persons through the gate, sighing with relief when they passed the guard. It seemed but a short time until Felix knocked at the door of Conrad Hottinger's home.

"Who is there?" a man's voice responded. Felix answered and immediately the door opened. Conrad Hottinger could hardly believe his eyes and he insisted on hearing the whole story of how the men had gotten free. They sat around the ceramic-tile oven, the heat limbering their cold, sore muscles. The rest of the family was called and Trini rushed into the room. Felix rose and scooped her into his arms. For a moment, no one else was in the room and it was only the two of them, holding each other as if they would never let go. Felix was suddenly aware that he was free! He was free among his friends, free with the one he loved more dearly than any other.

When they realized that those behind them were making teasing comments, they separated and blushed at their impropriety.

There was no disapproval; everyone in the room had known of their love for years now.

"Felix," Jörg Schad said, "this is the first place the magistrates will look for you. You must not stay here." They all knew it was true, and Felix felt a short burst of anger that he could not really be free. To go out now in the cold, again to be alone and running was, for a moment, enough to make him give in. If he were caught, at least he would have a memorable day to help carry him through imprisonment.

"Jörg is right. You must go quickly." Trini grabbed his coat and held it for him. He looked at her, longing to stay, knowing that she did, indeed, care more for him than she did for herself. He slipped his arms into the sleeves and bid all farewell.

"I will go to the cave and wait there. A number of the brethren can gather tomorrow afternoon for fellowship and prayer. We can then discuss our next moves. Perhaps those coming from Zollikon could bring the elder, Jacob Hottinger." Felix paused a moment, then added, "I need the benefit of his counsel."

Trini stepped outside with him and again he took her in his arms. He lifted her chin with one finger, as he had the first time he kissed her.

"I love you," he said softly.

Jörg Schad came out of the house and insisted on accompanying him to the cave so that he would not be alone. Felix was weak from his time in prison and welcomed the company. They bade "auf Wiedersehen" to Trini and set off on their way. It was a hard walk, up and down hills, through the forest. Finally, in early evening, they crossed a rivulet of water that marked the nearness of the cave. It seemed warmer in the stone structure and Felix fell asleep immediately, wrapped in the heavy blanket Trini had given him. Schad sat in the mouth of the cave watching while Felix slept, later covering up in his own blanket to join him in sleep.

When Felix awakened he looked around the large cave with its low ceiling and mineral water dripping from the sides. It opened, like a mouth in the hillside. Jörg had already eaten his share of the cheese, bread, and wine they had carried. Felix savored each bite, looking out into the sunlit forest. A small cascade of water fell in silver sparkles across the opening. It made the only sound in the woods. *God's music,* Felix thought.

Late in the afternoon several dozen persons arrived, coming one and two across the fields and along separate paths. Felix began the meeting by simply sharing reports with them of his discussions with the other leaders of the believers' church. They talked about their dreams and hopes for the new church. Felix told them of his concern that the new communities of disciples find their direction from Christ and his Word. They should not simply react to the programs which they had renounced.

"If Christ is our authority, we need truly to hear his Word. And this means that we interpret it in harmony with his example, with his life. And," he paused for a moment, "with the recent edict we may also need to share with him in death."

He could tell that his words were an encouragement to a group of fearful people. Even he was renewed by sharing with them. The singing began softly, echoes filling the dark cavern. It brought out emotion, absorbing them in the meaning of the songs. It called forth dedication, firming their consecration to the one of whom they sang. Felix introduced several stanzas of a verse he had written in prison and helped the group to sing it to a well-known tune (*The Mennonite Hymnal,* Herald Press, No. 40):

> I sing with exultation,
> All my heart delights,
> In God, who brings salvation,
> Frees from death's dread might.
> I praise Thee, Christ of heaven,
> Who ever shall endure,
> Who takes away my sorrow,
> Keeps me safe and secure.

197

Whom God sent as example,
Light my feet to guide.
Before my end he bade me
In his realm abide.
That I might love and cherish
His righteousness divine;
That I with him forever
Bliss eternal might find.

Christ bids us, none compelling,
To his glorious throne.
He only who is willing
Christ as Lord to own,
He is assured of heaven
Who will right faith pursue
With heart made pure do penance,
Seal'd with baptism true.

After a long time of prayer, they discussed how best to share their enthusiasm and to encourage the communities of believers. The elder, Jacob Hottinger, led the discussion, making assignments for each person. It was agreed that Felix should go north, possibly meeting with the leaders in the region of Schaffhausen, but he was to stay clear of the city and of Hofmeister. From there he could journey east and seek to join up again with Conrad in St. Gall. A list was provided him of friends with whom he could stop and share hospitality in his travels. As the group left, one and two at a time, Felix suddenly realized how lonely his role of leadership could be.

Over the next several weeks, his pattern was to work his way north, moving almost furtively from one home of the brethren to another. Repeatedly he shared his faith and taught the small groups that gathered for fellowship. He was impressed with the spiritual hunger of the people, begging to be fed the Word of God. Although many had frequented the liturgical rituals of the church for years, they had not heard the gospel taught from the Scriptures.

Felix enjoyed teaching and his facility with the biblical lan-

198

guages enabled him to teach with both freedom and freshness. In most places to which he traveled community members would agree to perform the sign of baptism for persons who made their commitment to Christ. This relieved Felix from needing to perform baptisms, lest he defy the recent action of the Zurich Council. But, on April 7, Felix was ministering in Embrach, some distance north of Zurich. The wife of a man with whom he was in dialogue responded in a decisive act of faith. She affirmed her commitment to Jesus Christ and her desire to be baptized. With deep conviction she asked Felix to give her the forbidden sign of baptism.

Felix was fully aware of what it meant for him to perform this act. Still, he rose and took the dipper of water from the bucket of drinking water. She knelt before him, her husband standing by her side, and Felix baptized her "in the name of the Father, and the Son, and the Holy Spirit." Her true joy was his reward. As he left that home and went on toward Schaffhausen, he thought of what he would say should he be apprehended and questioned. His only word was that of the early apostles, "We ought to obey God rather than men."

As he moved among the *Taüfer* (Baptists), as they often referred to themselves, the next contact he made was with friends of Hans Küntzi of Klingnau. He learned from them that Conrad and Karl Brennwald had succeeded in getting to Oberglatt after their escape from prison. During their short time there the "learned Schoolmaster," Michael Wüst, a friend of Billinger, had become a believer and had accepted baptism. As a community leader, his conversion was already having a strong impact for the cause. Felix also inquired after his friends Michael and Margarita Sattler, hoping to see them, but he learned that they had gone into the Breisgau to the north. They were working in the city of Horb on the Neckar River. Felix was pleased, rejoicing in the word of Sattler's aggressive efforts in the believers' church movement.

Hearing of his friends was a boon to Felix's spirit. He regained his strength and his health now, and he pressed on unflaggingly.

The river which flowed west from Lake Constance to the east marked his way. He paused to watch once again the turbulent and foamy Rhine falls. It was a beautiful sight.

"Nothing can stop the force of that water," he said to himself, "just as nothing can stop the force of God's truth!"

Some distance below the falls, he found the ferry and crossed the river. The pilot was a friendly chap and the conversation made the trip to the other side seem short. He found lodging that night in Hallau at the home of a family he had come to know when he visited their congregation with Johann Brötli. They told him of how the church continued to grow around Hallau, in Schleitheim, and in Waldshut. However, the peasant uprisings and Hapsburg military suppression had made it much more difficult to gather in group meetings. The magisterial pressure was suppressing the believers' church. The greatest tensions were in Waldshut, where Dr. Hubmaier had been expelled from the city. It was evident that with the oppression by the Catholic Hapsburgs, Zwingli had indirectly won the second round in Waldshut.

The Anabaptists, as they were publicly called, although they preferred the term "Täufer," were suffering intense opposition from the Hapsburg authorities. Wilhelm Reublin had fled the area, going to Strasbourg. Reublin was hoping that with the more moderate position of the reformers, Martin Bucer and Wolfgang Capito, he could gain understanding and freedom for the Anabaptist community. Michael Sattler had been earlier living in Klingnau, north of Zurich, working as a weaver with Hans Küntzi, but he had recently traveled with Wilhelm to the north. Along with his wife, Margarita, Sattler had continued the work in Horb, on the Neckar River, while Reublin and his wife had gone west to Strasbourg. According to all reports, Sattler was having great success evangelizing and bringing people into a believers' church at Horb.

In Schaffhausen itself, Felix found that with Dr. Hofmeister's allegiance to Zwingli, the Anabaptist movement was literally being driven out of the city. Small groups were now meeting in the forests and in homes. For several days Felix joined them, preaching in small pastures, in forest clearings, or wherever they could meet in secrecy. He encouraged the believers in discipleship and spent many hours counseling the leaders who were chosen by the people of each group.

Felix left the region of Schaffhausen after only a few days of ministry, repeating his trip of a year earlier, traveling east toward St. Gall. He knew that either there or in the Appenzell district there was the possibility of meeting with Conrad and George again. He enjoyed the beauty of spring, the opening buds, the changing of light green leaves on the fruit trees and other trees as they stood out against the spruce and pine. After more than a week of rigorous travel he arrived in St. Gall. Once there he easily located Grebel by inquiring of the servants at Vadian's home. Although Conrad was no longer granted hospitality in Vadian's home, they knew Conrad and where he would be, and this they passed on to Felix. He found Conrad leading a Bible study, and he joined in the discussion. After the session, they enjoyed a brief reunion, having tea with Barbara. Agreeing to meet again in Appenzell, Felix left that night, not wanting to increase the danger for them by being in the same territory with Conrad.

Taking their advice, upon reaching the village he went to the home of Wolf Uliman. He had been in Chur but had fled in late March, the success of his preaching ministry having so threatened the officials there that he'd barely escaped arrest. Now, he and George Blaurock were again working as a team, evangelizing in the Appenzell community. Sure enough, George was at Uliman's home when Felix arrived.

"Felix, my brother and prison mate!" George laughed, throwing his big arms around him, "how did you find us?"

"I was just in St. Gall and met with Conrad."

"Ah, Conrad was with us earlier but now he is spending most of his time with Barbara and the children. It is difficult for Conrad to exercise much freedom, as family ties place him in such close association with his brother-in-law, Vadian."

201

"Yes," said Felix, "Conrad told me that he even confronted Vadian over the position he had taken at our trial in Zurich, and that he criticized Vadian for supporting Zwingli and the course the Reformation is taking in Zurich. Conrad said that Vadian was as courteous as his position permitted, but he warned Conrad that he could not protect him."

"It is a hard position in which to be," sighed George. "And the famous historian, Johann Kessler, is an agent for Vadian, seeking to turn our brother back to Zwingli!"

A few days later Conrad came to Apenzell to meet with the other Anabaptist leaders. He cautioned them about Kessler and his dialogues under the guise of historical research. When Felix and Conrad were alone, he shared the problems which he faced because of Barbara's deep concern for their family. She believed in the faith which Conrad was promoting, but felt so deeply insecure for herself and for their children. Vadian had suddenly changed his mind and had offered Conrad and his family a place in his home. Barbara was inclined to accept. Actually, she was being strongly encouraged by Conrad's sister to begin an association with the evangelical church in St. Gall and drop out of, what Vadian called, this new sectarian movement. Conrad was certain that Vadian's present tolerance toward him was with the hope that through Barbara he could be led to change.

As Felix listened to his friend's story, he was struck by how discouraging Conrad's problem must be. Conrad's family ties were difficult. His parents had succeeded in getting Dorothy's marriage to Ammann anulled and had married her to the prosperous Hans Escher, a strong man for pensions and soldering, even speaking against Zwingli, whom he called "God's fifth wonder in the council." Conrad, however, remained as positive as ever regarding the importance of the believers' church and the need to build a free church on the authority of the New Testament. The two of them, with this conviction, set off together to teach and preach in communities in the southern region of St. Gall. Most of their meetings were out in the hills, in forest gatherings, and in farmhouses and barns. Groups would gather, often in the parlor of a home, to hear their effective teaching.

Conrad shared with Felix his special concern for his father. There was increased stress in the situation in which the senator was caught. His father, Jacob, had grown to respect Conrad's conviction and mission. While he identified with Zwingli and the church, he continued to appeal to the council for more tolerance. Over the last months serious tension had developed between Jacob Grebel and Ulrich Zwingli. Jacob was now being charged with embezzling funds from the scholarship he had arranged for Conrad from the King of France as well as from the papal stipend.

Conrad said, "That is not easy to answer, as I wasted so much and cost my family so much that who can say how my father handled the funds as he held them back from my use. I did send word with Vadian asking father to avoid unnecessary defense of anything relating to me."

Felix thought of his impressions of Jacob, remembering how he looked at Conrad from his seat with the senate during their last trial.

In mid-May, Ulrich Bolt came to St. Gall after being in prison in Basel. He had been released with orders to leave the community. He reported the promising growth of an Anabaptist church in Basel, especially with the successful work of Lorenz Hochrütiner. Felix felt a new interest kindled to visit the city where he had studied and worked. He began now to consider the possibilities of how and when he might travel to Basel and support this new community of believers.

St. Gall was becoming a meeting place for exiles, for Felix's old friend Jörg Schad arrived in the city at the end of the month from Zollikon. He reported that the Zurich Council had now introduced a compulsory baptismal register. "Every Zurich family is now required to register the baptism of its infants," he told them. "And you should also know that Falk and Reimann are in prison again in Grüningen. They were sharing at a meeting in the Herrliberg forest, between Rubikon and Wetzikon, when Magistrate Berger arrested them. But the Grüningen Court countered the March 7 mandate of Zurich and refused to put them to death! Now the Grüningen Council is in difficulty, as the Zurich Great Council has appealed to Bern for a verdict. The three Cantons, Bern, Zurich, and St. Gall, have formed an alliance to crush this movement."

"Jacob Hottinger, the elder, of Zollikon, has been imprisoned again in Zurich," Schad told them. "He has been the most faithful person in Zollikon in the believers' church. Many of the group there have been intimidated. Jacob's numerous times in and out of prison have so weakened him physically that his friends are concerned about his life. They are all praying that he will be able to withstand the rigors of this prison sentence."

Jörg reported also on a disputation that was currently in progress at Baden. This confrontation was being held between the Catholic and the Reformer's position. "Zwingli himself has kept aloof, refusing to attend because of alleged threats on his life, and so Oecolampad of Basel is debating with Johann Eck. There is a lot of talk about the disputation. It began on May 18, with Berchtold Haller of Bern assisting Oecolampad, and Johann Faber and Thomas Murner assisting Eck. Scores of priests are attending the disputation. Reports have it that Oecolampad is a skillful match for Master Eck!"

"At least Zwingli now has another front on which to fight," Felix commented. "The Roman Church opposes his reformation, and in this I sympathize with him. What news have you to give us of Dr. Hubmaier?"

"After Dr. Hubmaier disappeared from Zurich, it was reported among the brethren that he had gone east into southern Bavaria. Some say that he is in Augsburg. Perhaps he is hoping for more freedom where he is less well-known. With so many of our leaders traveling, we're certain to hear of his work."

George commented, "He'll need our prayers, for he is a marked man, just as we are."

After a week of ministry in the hills south of St. Gall, Felix asked George whether they might go again into the Grüningen area and minister among the churches where they had previously worked. George expressed his concern that they might not be able to avoid Magistrate Berger, but said he would still like to go and especially to help the Zollikon believers. Even with the reports of recent arrests, evidence that Berger meant to prevent Grüningen from becoming an extension of what he saw as the Zurich problem, they continued to talk off and on about going.

Early in June, the question arose again. Felix said, "George, I've given this a lot of prayer and thought and I will go with you to Grüningen when you are ready. We can evangelize and teach among the believers for a few weeks. I can visit Trini. And then, perhaps, I can fulfill another dream. Ever since Ulrich Bolt came from Basel, I have had an inner calling to visit the believers there. It is a new area for our movement, and I want to add my encouragement to the churches in and around Basel, perhaps even on south to Bern."

They were agreed, George bade his wife farewell, and they were on their way. By the middle of the month they were again in the familiar farmlands of Grüningen, moving through the hills from home to home, meeting in the cave and in the forests. The next several weeks of ministry were rewarding, although exceedingly taxing, for they needed to make their ministry known in the region and yet avoid being arrested. The response was overwhelming, as though the people awaited their word, even though since November 30 the Grüningen Council had been penalizing adult baptism with a heavy fine. Felix met with one group after another, preaching and talking with people almost tirelessly. Hans Hotz worked with him and Hotz's clear thinking and dedicated spirit were an inspiration.

Felix was now teaching extensively from the Epistle to the Hebrews, emphasizing the "new covenant in Christ." In the Grüningen community dialogue between the Catholic priests and the evangelical voices had continued and the interaction resulted in stimulating inquiring minds. His message was of Christ as the one high priest, the one mediator, the one reconciliation with the Father. He stressed the immediacy of living in relationship with the risen Christ, sharing a new life in the power of his resurrection, and living that life in day-by-day Christian behavior. This was the word of faith for searching minds. Felix was hardly prepared for the amazing response. The believers brought many others to the meetings and scores of persons made commitments to Jesus Christ and accepted baptism.

Jacob Falk returned to Grüningen from Appenzell reporting to Felix on his experiences. He had moved north and east from St. Gall as well. He brought reports that Hubmaier had joined the scholar Hans Denk in Augsburg. The believers' church movement was seeing rapid growth in that region under their leadership. Already, it was reported, there were a thousand followers. Hans Hut, formerly with the revolutionary forces in the peasant wars, had been converted and baptized. A very popular speaker, he was now a most effective evangelist. "But," Falk told Felix, "Grebel is concerned about some of the more individualistic and spiritualistic emphases that some of these men carry. His word to you is to continue clear scriptural teaching. He has some caution about the spiritualism of both Denk and Hut, as well as your earlier concern about Hubmaier's willingness to use the sword."

"I am in agreement with Conrad," Felix exclaimed. "We build only on the Word of God, on the love and peace of Christ."

In late June, Felix had a strong inner prompting to move on. His safety was better if he kept on the move. Bidding George and his many friends farewell, he set out for Basel, some sixty miles to the west. But first, he headed for Zollikon. The risk was worth it to see Trini. The visit had to be brief, however. The two had only time for a long afternoon, which they spent walking in the hills and talking together. Felix told her everything he could remember of his travels and work and she too filled him in on her life. And then they talked of plans of their future, of marriage, and children. It was painful that their lives could not be one, but their love had not been diminished, even with so much distance between them.

Trini's father gave Felix the names of persons he could visit in Zofingen in the southwest of the Aargau, en route to Basel. With reluctance he forced himself to get back on the road. He spent the first days of his travel in the hills and valleys of the Jura. He went north to circle the city of Zurich, then he turned west and joined the Limmat river, following it for a number of miles. Leaving the dale he again hiked up the hills. He liked the climb of the rugged ridges, demanding extra from his muscles. His reward was the view of the valley, spread out like a quilt below him.

Stopping at numerous farms for a drink or snack, he was welcomed by several with the request that he teach them the gospel. Many were anxious to hear, but some, being rigorously Catholics, were not interested and he did not impose himself on them. Rather than travel northwest to Baden, on the more traveled road, he chose the southern road toward Aarau, feeling that it would be more safe.

Felix's experiences during his brief stop in Zofingen would remain some of the most pleasant in his memory. Already a significant free-church fellowship had developed in the town and they welcomed Felix enthusiastically. Ulrich Teck, his former cellmate in the Zurich Tower, had been there earlier sharing in Bible teaching. Perhaps through Teck's reports of what was happening in the free-church developments, the reputation of Felix Manz had a noticeable effect on the group when he was presented. They rejoiced in his presence, regarding him as one of their most prominent leaders. His conviction, his suffering and imprisonments, and the effectiveness of his teaching had already been introduced to them. He found this popularity somewhat difficult to accept and reminded the community of believers that he was one of them and his purpose was to strengthen their faith and call new believers into the life of Christ.

"Leadership," he said, "is not status, but a servant role. We have one leader, the Lord Jesus Christ, and under him we are all on a common plain, even with our different callings."

For the few days that he shared with them, the Zofingen group discussed and prayed with Felix over their strategy of mission. Their unique location enabled them to reach northwest to Basel and south and west to Bern. Felix saw this congregation as a nerve center for this region, encouraging them to a strong emphasis on discipleship as their highest mission. As much as he enjoyed Zofingen, he was anxious to move on to the region of Basel. Being rather well acquainted with the area, he was hopeful that the free church there might at least be tolerated. With the humanism of Erasmus, the attempts at mediation by Oecolampad and his friend Wolfgang Capito from Strasbourg, the Anabaptists might find a tolerance in Basel that was not being realized in Zurich. However, discussing this with the Zofingen brethren before leaving them, he was disillusioned. There was, he was told, much more conflict in that city than he knew about.

The effective work of Lorenz Hochrütiner had made a major impact on Basel. A disputation had been held already a year before in the home of Oecolampad. In that meeting the reformer had thoroughly rejected the Anabaptist movement. One of the Zofingen brethren had a printed copy of the proceedings of the debate which Felix read carefully. It was clear to Felix that Oecolampad had maintained a firm stance in his identification with Zwingli. He was also informed that as recently as June second, a mandate against the Anabaptists had been issued in Basel. It stated that "whoever has himself rebaptized is banned with his family from the radius of five miles around the city."

With this information and directions from the group, Felix made his way northwest to the home of Johann Hausmann. His house was located about five miles from the city of Basel, to the southeast, just east of the river Birs. It was early evening when he walked up to the house, and his host welcomed him warmly. Later in the evening Hausmann invited Lorenz Hochrütiner to his home. This was a joyous reunion, although they had limited time for personal sharing. Felix learned that Lorenz's family was with him in Basel, except his oldest son, Jacob, who had become a believers' church leader in Bern. "Further," Lorenz said, "you will want to meet with Simon Stumpf. He is here in Basel, but is working with Oecolampad, and with Capito from Strasbourg. We may have lost him."

Along with Lorenz, other persons had come to Hausmann's home, persons who were actively involved in the believers' church movement. Felix was introduced to Hans Seckler, Hans Romer, Volkman Fischer, and others who were ardent proponents of the free church. The evening of fellowship with persons of similar faith was refreshing, and Felix felt an inner renewal of spirit.

The next evening they went to the home of Michael Schurer, a brother whose house was frequently used for the gathering of Anabaptists. Felix was heartened by the gracious and free spirit of these people. A large group had gathered with many representatives of the more cultured men and women from the community. Matthias Graf, a printer, and his wife, Katrina, were one couple with whom Felix had immediate rapport. His experience from several years earlier, of having worked for Cratander the Basel printer, gave him facility in the conversation. Accepting their offer of hospitality, he agreed to spend some time with them. Meeting Ulrich Bolt, he was introduced to his friends. Elise Müller and Barbara Grüninger. His mind went to Trini, and he wished she were here in Basel with him.

For the several hours they were together, the group joined in singing praises to God, in studying the Scripture under Felix's direction, and in sharing together in prayer. Felix guided them through a careful reflection on the sixth chapter of Romans, emphasizing the character of the new life in Christ, a definite break from the conduct of the old life, and an active pursuit of righteousness and the fruit of holiness.

"The real issue," Felix said, "is following Christ in all of life, identifying with him as Lord. Baptism is a sign of this faith, and only a sign. It is to be administered to those who share the new life, who walk in his resurrection life." The meeting was concluded, but the more personal conversations lasted late into the night.

During the next week, Felix participated freely with the believers. He even came and went in the familiar streets of Basel, visiting St. Martin's church where he had heard Erasmus, and, of course, the university grounds. It was here that Felix met Capito, the reformer from Strasbourg.

"So you are Felix Manz! I've heard about your scholarship from Glarean. I'm sorry that you and Zwingli are antagonists, as you would have a lot to offer."

"My friend," Felix responded, "I'd like to work with him on the basis of Scripture, but it's not to be."

Capito nodded. "Zwingli has his mind made up. It is not easy for a man of power to keep open to truth. I've learned this from our mutual friend Simon."

After a few more words, Felix excused himself and hurried away. He should leave the city quickly lest others know of his presence. It might not be wise to contact Simon just yet, he thought, perhaps later. For now he would continue sharing the activities of the group in the region south and east of Basel. As he engaged them in the quest of faith he baptized those who, in their commitment to Christ, requested the sign. Felix enjoyed sharing, speaking often but also listening to others, especially to a brother known as Hans Pfistermeyer, a very effective and fluent evangelist. Hans accompanied Felix and Lorenz on several of their trips to the south where they ministered, usually in farmhouses in the rolling lands of the Jura.

But on July 24 the fellowship of believers had another jolt. The Basel Council issued a second mandate. Felix was quite sure that the increased activity of the brethren had become known. This mandate now forbade Anabaptist meetings beyond the previously set five-mile radius, anywhere in the vicinity of the city! It specifically singled out Lorenz Hochrütiner and Hans Pfistermeyer and issued them each official notice that they were banished from the city. Both men were summarily told to discontinue their propagation of the Anabaptist doctrine in Basel. While a different strategy than arrest and imprisonment, this was a major blow to the fledgling congregation. These brethren were their most effective leaders.

As he was leaving Basel with his family Lorenz came to the Graf home to find Felix. He strongly urged Felix to go with him lest he be discovered. "With the intense opposition to your ministry, with the continuing tensions with Zwingli and your recent experiences in Zurich," he said, "if they find you, Felix, you will be imprisoned here in Basel." Others of the brethren also encouraged Felix to go with Lorenz. "Both of you," Grof hastily added, "are of more value when free and itinerant among the new congregations." They urged them to go south, suggesting that they move into the Biel region of Canton Bern.

And so, as now frequently happened, Felix had his knapsack packed within the hour. They would find hospitality in familiar homes in the Jura. Lorenz's son, Jacob, was working in Bern, and so Lorenz would send his family there. He also knew a few followers of the free church who were already ministering in the area of Biel and they would find them. He had heard that they met by the "Great Stone," and he was sure that he could readily find it. With tearful farewells, they were off into the hills.

As they carefully made their way through the Jura, they occasionally met with small groups in farmhouses. By the Sonnenberg they were directed to a small cave high on the ridge for shelter. A few persons to whom they witnessed while getting supplies from the small village later came to the little cave for a session of teaching. They nicknamed it "the little goat church," because they had to climb like goats, through the rocks, to get to it. Felix was inspired by how these earnest people would take such effort to hear the gospel.

Several men from Solothurn urged them to take several days to accompany them of their city for the sake of their families, who should hear their words. They cautiously went along with them. It was worth the risk, Felix was sure. A number of persons made commitments and he and Lorenz baptized several men and women who came to faith in Christ.

After a few days they were again on their way. To keep off the main roads they returned to their earlier path, high in the hills. On that afternoon, south of the Sonnenberg, they met with a group of brethren at a stone bridge. It was a relatively safe meeting place, for if someone on the road detected the meeting they could slip away up or down the ravine. Here, beneath the bridge, they worshiped together. Quietly and reverently, they closed their time together by breaking bread and passing it as the emblem of the Lord's death, then by sharing their wine as a symbol of his covenant.

Felix and Lorenz finally arrived in Biel, by the lake. Tired and in need of lodging, they went immediately to the shop of a tailor. They hoped he would tell them of activities in the city while fixing a tear in the sleeve of Felix's coat. They inquired with caution of the location of the Great Stone, and the tailor was quite able to tell them where it was. As the conversation continued, by a few well-chosen words, to their delight they discovered that he too was an Anabaptist. Through his acquaintance they were soon introduced to a number of other persons who frequently gathered to worship by this landmark. Their names were soon passed from one to another of the church adherents, telling of Felix's presence in the area. Consequently, on the second afternoon many came to the Great Stone to hear Felix and Lorenz, receiving their ministry with open appreciation.

Felix spoke from Matthew's account of Jesus' Sermon on the Mount, emphasizing both the attitudes and the actions of true disciples of Christ. That afternoon, there in the shadow of the Great Stone, Felix and Lorenz baptized eight persons. They each committed themselves to Christ in faith and promised to follow the way of discipleship. "This," Felix exclaimed, "is the one foundation for a believers' church in Biel."

Felix and Lorenz spent the remaining days of the July summer in the region around the city. They were continually busy teaching and encouraging the growing congregation. By early August their work had taken them farther east, in the canton of Bern. They were now very conscious of the extensive power of Canton Bern and its large annexations as they talked with the people of the region. Earlier, Jörg Schad had told Felix and Lorenz how the Zurich Council had appealed to Bern for a death verdict for the imprisoned brethren at Grüningen. Knowing that Bern, Zurich, and St. Gall were united in opposition to the Anabaptists made them especially cautious about any publicity for their gatherings. Yet they knew that they had been led of God to come here to share their faith. They slipped into the city of Bern, finding it to be one of the more beautiful in Switzerland. Cradled in the bend of the river Aare, it was a capital of charming Swiss architecture, a breadbasket of plenty, and a center of continental culture.

Felix and Lorenz worked diligently in Bern but for only a week, teaching and baptizing new believers. Assured that the church in Bern was on its way, feeling their mission accomplished, they traveled further east, stopping in the village of Langnau. Here they were graciously welcomed by a small but animated group of Anabaptists living on farms around the picturesque little town. The community had been stirred earlier by the evangelical preaching of Hans Pfistermyer from Basel. Many persons had responded, seeking a meaning of faith beyond what they had known in their Catholic experience. The people here had known little of Zwingli's reform, but as traditional Catholics they were hungry for the reality of saving faith.

Felix and Lorenz felt privileged to assist the congregations, freely calling persons to faith in Christ, baptizing many and teaching them. Felix effectively guided the assembly in calling to roles of leadership those who were gifted for such service. He was pleased to have a hand in helping to structure the future of the church in that area.

The climate had been hot in August in Bern, but here in the

rolling lands at the rise of the Bern Oberland it was less warm and humid. Felix delighted in the breeze through the pines as he walked the paths from one farm to another. His thoughts were often of Trini, of their love and plans. He would dream of their marriage. They belonged to each other, and so they belonged together. Perhaps he was wrong, he mused, to wait for some measure of peace. They really were in this together. What a price to pay for their convictions. Sharing with Lorenz, he would long remember his words, "Some of us are expendable for Christ and his kingdom."

Frequently, Felix and Lorenz would discuss what their next course of action should be. As they talked and prayed, they each felt a growing conviction to return to the east, to Lorenz's home area of St. Gall. Felix felt that they were not needed longer in Canton Bern and that for their safety they should keep on the move. His concern for Conrad and his relation to Vadian also gave him a sense of urgency to go back to the community of Appenzell, hoping he would still find both Conrad and George there.

While Felix was anxious to know what was happening in the eastern regions of Switzerland, he also wanted to be in touch with his close friends. They now needed to plan a strategy to unite the scattered free churches for the future well-being of the movement. With the danger to him in Zurich, perhaps, Felix thought, he should work in southern Bavaria or Austria. Trini might join him and they could move east into the Tyrol of Austria, preaching and spreading the movement there. He smiled as he thought of it.

Since they were so far south, and it was late summer with no danger of snow in the mountains, Felix and Lorenz made their way east through the scenic Oberland. Their route took them to the beautiful Catholic city of Luzern. They enjoyed majestic Mount Pilatus, as they camped at its base. Felix recalled Conrad telling of climbing it with Vadian and Myconius. He also reflected on what had happened in the few years since he had traveled through this city to and from Rome.

Moving north and east they came to the southern shore of Lake Zurich, where they hired a boat. Crossing, they could see the river that led east to Chur, and Felix told Lorenz of the travels which had led him to Chur a free man and had brought him back a prisoner. They paid their fee and made their way north through the hills and forests of the Toggenburg, on into the rolling fields of the region of Appenzell. They were now able to more frequently find lodging with people who had a listening ear for their teaching.

When they finally arrived in Appenzell it was early September. Autumn had arrived in all its radiance. The brightly colored leaves and cooler air enlivened and invigorated Felix. It was as if the earth had opened and orange and golden light had burst out, caught by the trees and the cloud-filled skies. But when the news was told, suddenly it was as if all the world were nothing but decaying foliage, a facade covering ugliness.

Felix and Lorenz met Uliman soon after their arrival and received a warm welcome.

"It is so good to see you, Felix, and to have you here, especially now that Conrad is gone," Uliman said.

"Gone?" Felix asked. "Where?"

"Oh, you have not heard," Wolfgang responded. "Conrad Grebel has died of the plague." He said it with gravity.

Felix slumped into the nearest chair, tears immediately coming to his eyes. "The disease was spreading in Canton Appenzell and Conrad fled to Maienfeld to his sister's home, hoping to avoid it. He knew that he would not have the strength to fight the plague. But it caught up with him, and in a few days he died of it."

Felix was wrenched with grief. His good friend was gone, the colleague with whom he had been involved from the very beginning of the movement. For Felix, it was as though a part of him had died. In his sorrow, the fellowship of believers in Appenzell was a tremendous support, assuring him that although he remained as the only one of the original founders of the movement, he was now surrounded by many competent new leaders. From his inquiries he learned that Conrad's wife, Barbara, and their children had finally accepted the hospitality of Vadian. To his surprise, he also learned that upon Conrad's passing, Vadian had spoken out quite clearly regarding his brother-in-law's integrity and had appealed to Zwingli for more cautious treatment of the Anabaptist movement. In a similar way, Conrad's father had addressed the City Council, reminding them that the death of his son and the plight of his orphaned children was due in a large measure to the persecutions that were so rigorously carried out by the council in their oppression of the free-church movement. Jacob Grebel himself was now under increased attack by Zwingli and his colleagues. Perhaps largely in retaliation for his statements, he was now accused of being a sympathizer with the heretical Anabaptist movement.

The passing of Conrad brought to Felix an increased sense of his own responsibility. George had left for Grüningen, and Wilhelm was in Strasbourg. Felix realized that they were the leaders who were recognized as having had a primary influence in the development of the free church. With his teaching gifts and his reputation, Felix was acknowledged by the brothers and sisters as their leader. He was pleased, but he reminded them of the strong leadership developing in such persons as Lorenz, Michael Sattler, Jacob Falk, Hans Hotz, and many others.

While increasing his caution, Felix maintained his activity in preaching and teaching. His emphasis on the voluntary nature of church membership helped people to realize their own responsibility to Christ and his church. As the movement continued to grow, he knew that he was risking the opposition of the magistracy all the more. The recognition of his leadership increased the possibility of his arrest, even here in St. Gall.

In his work the real joy for Felix was the persons who came to Christ and asked for baptism. Among the recent converts was Martin Baumgartner, a man who was already providing significant leadership in the area of Wil. Felix spent only a short time there, discipling him; the successes which he and George had earlier known in this village tended to make Felix a marked man. People had not forgotten the stories which George had told without hesitancy, if not embellishment, of how God answered prayers for them in miraculous ways; of how they had been released from prison by the angel of the Lord! Felix had chuckled and said, "The angel was quite earthly, a guard who failed to lock the doors. But we did indeed accept it as from God." The populace, however, remembered those stories and told them in a manner that made them sound more unusual, as claims of a special, miraculous activity of God.

At the end of September Felix was encouraged by the arrival of a brother from Grüningen, Jacob Schopfelberg. He had accepted the gospel and had been baptized when Felix and George were working in the region months previously. He had now fled from Grüningen, to gain distance from Magistrate Berger. For his own growth in faith, he wanted to work with Felix in the region of Appenzell. Felix had adjusted to working with so many new persons, as they converted and came into the church, that he welcomed this new partnership.

On October 12, the two of them were in St. Gall, teaching and proclaiming the gospel in one of the larger homes of patrician circles. Suddenly, without warning, the magistrates were at the door and Felix and Jacob were arrested. As they were led to the prison, Felix said, "This is really no surprise. We have penetrated social circles of this city in a way which could not long go unnoticed. My one prayer is that they don't surrender us to Zurich."

Their imprisonment in St. Gall was fortunately short. To Felix's surprise, Vadian came to the prison and arranged their release. He actually paid a fine to the magistrate himself! Felix entertained the thought that Barbara may have pressed her brother-in-law to be lenient for Conrad's sake. While he and Jacob were deeply grateful, they had no opportunity of expressing this to Vadian. They were simply ushered out of the cell and told by the magistrates that they were free to leave. They were to get out of the territory, for they were banished from St. Gall. As they walked down the hall from the prison, Felix observed Vadian, standing at a distance. Felix was sure that in some way this act was an attempt on Vadian's part to express a token of gracious remembrance of Conrad. They were not able to speak with him, but Felix's expression communicated his gratitude and understanding.

After saying "Good-bye" to Lorenz, he and Jacob left St. Gall. The question was, where to turn now? They headed south, and Jacob assured Felix that there were many homes in the Grüningen region where they could find hospitality and keep out of sight of the magistrate. "It is also probable," he said, "that George is back in evangelistic work in the Grüningen forest region."

In early November they were in the forest in the eastern region of Grüningen when they learned of the fate of Conrad's father. Zwingli and the council had so deeply resented the elder Grebel's request of tolerance for the Anabaptists, that they had built up accusations against him which called for a trial. Jacob Grebel had been tried on what may have been trumped-up charges. The council claimed that money which had been secured through the King of France, years before, as a scholarship for Conrad's study, had been used for Jacob's own business ventures and for family expenses. Under condemnation for dishonest appropriation of funds, the council sentenced Jacob Grebel to death. On October 30, Jacob Grebel had summarily been beheaded in Zurich. Rumor had it that many people thought that Zwingli had instigated the trial because Jacob had favored dealing more mildly with the Anabaptists.

George and his wife were in the northern region of Grüningen, staying in a home in the forest northeast of the city. Felix was able to visit the Blaurocks frequently. He and George now pondered the news from Zurich, having no illusions regarding the firmness of the position of the Zurich Council. They both remembered, too well, that on March 7 the Council had said that anyone rebaptizing persons would receive the ultimate baptism! They were sure now that this death sentence would be carried out.

Felix began to weigh with care the risk of a visit to Zollikon to see Trini. It was already the end of November, and Felix and George had a circle of ministry in several dozen places of meeting in and around the Herrliberg forests. In each gathering, the Scriptures were taught, the Lord's Supper was observed, and new believers were often baptized. Through their teaching, there was now a clear distinction between the violent peasant reactions to the church-state and its demands, and the nonviolent position of the followers of Christ as interpreted by Felix and George. The Anabaptists were generally committed to the way of peace and nonviolence. It was well-known that they opposed Christians holding office in the magistracy, with its use of the sword, that they were committed to peace, to love, and to nonviolence. Their teaching from the Sermon on the Mount, about turning the other cheek and going the second mile, was known all over the area. In fact, Magistrate Berger himself acknowledged, "Were it not that this movement in its break from the Council defies the power of the church, the lifestyle of the people and their practice of faith would be quite acceptable, if not to be commended!" But for political reasons, Magistrate Berger was not about to allow any course of action in Grüningen other than that which was supported in Zurich.

Felix and George were sharing with brothers and sisters on December 3, in a small village a few kilometers from Grüningen. Magistrate Berger had learned in some way of the meeting and he, with his troop, surrounded the house in which the Anabaptists were assembled. Felix resented the arrest deeply, although he was not at all surprised. He had become prepared for this, accustomed to it. He had been captured so often by now, that it was not like the first time: the panging of his heart, the sick feeling in his stomach. It was more, a bother, a source of irritation and of discouragement.

The arrest was quick and orderly, even polite. Berger ordered

Felix and George to accompany him and escorted them hurriedly back to Grüningen to prison. They were led into town and down the one short street of Grüningen to the now familiar prison. Many of their friends in the fields and then along the street called to them words of encouragement. Berger ignored the shouts as he marched his prisoners to their cells.

During the next several days the brothers and sisters brought food to the prison and sought to strengthen them in words and in assurance of prayer. But they were not to stay long in the lenient Grüningen prison. Magistrate Berger acted promptly to get them to Zurich and to be free from the responsibility to hold them. Felix and George concluded that Berger did not want to be in a position in which the council could again ask him to execute prisoners.

Felix felt an overwhelming sense of despair as they marched through the edge of Zollikon and on into Zurich, along the Limmat to the tower. As they crossed the drawbridge, he looked into the moat where once he and his colleagues had made their escape. And once again, the two prominent church leaders were placed in the dark, damp cells of the Wellenberg Tower. It was cold, bitterly cold, for it was early December. Sitting on a small pile of straw, they shared the only comfort permitted them. Together they prayed and inspired each other to keep up their faith. Felix thought back over the last eight months—eight months of freedom, of opportunity to work in many different communities among many different peoples. Now, Felix thought, his work was most likely finished. He and George were realists, and they took seriously what might lie before them. Felix knew that he could be facing that final baptism.

Chapter 14

The Final Baptism

The sound of the cell door brought Felix immediately to life. Wrapped in his one lone blanket, stretched out on the scant pile of straw, he had tried to get some sleep. The guard stood in the cell doorway, but behind him were the faces of the women Felix loved the most, Trini and his mother, Anna. They had gained entrance by bringing food to the prisoners. The turnkey had helped himself to many of the fresh rolls and cheese, but there was still a goodly amount for Felix and George. The turnkey stood aside, permitting Felix to embrace Trini, and then his mother. The women wept. The guard walked back to his room and they were left alone. None of them could speak for some time. Felix held Trini's hand and stroked it gently. Finally, his mother wiped her eyes and spoke.

"You are the primary leader, Felix, of a movement which Zwingli means to crush. I am afraid there will be no relenting on his part. He needs to break you, to make an example of you, if he is to stop the spread of the movement."

Trini's eyes filled with new tears. "Felix," she said, "whatever happens, I am with you, in my love and in prayer and faith." She paused and gained her composure. "God has called you to a special service, and together we must rest in the assurance that it is his calling."

Felix looked from one to the other. His heart was warmed by their faith and their love. He put an arm around each of them

221

and stood between them with his head bowed. "I am so grateful for each of you." He turned to his mother. "For you, mother, the one who brought me into the world and helped to shape my life for this hour. And Trini," his voice had all the tenderness of his feeling, his eyes all the emotion of the moment, "you have taught me the meaning of love for one beyond myself. You are the one with whom I would have shared life. It is for your understanding and your love that I am ever grateful. Now all that I can ask is your confidence and your prayers. You can inspire our brothers and sisters to stand with George and me in this time of testing.

"There has been no trial," he continued, "and no date set for a trial. We are not certain what that means. It may even mean that we will not be given a trial, that the previous sentence will simply be carried out. I am praying that we be given at least an opportunity in some form again to share our faith from the Holy Scriptures. We can only remind Zwingli and his associates that they also answer to the Scriptures and ultimately to the Lord of the Scripture, our Master."

"We will pray for that," said his mother. The turnkey had returned and opened the door.

"Time is up," he said. Felix gave his mother a firm embrace and turned to Trini. He kissed her warmly and held her closely. When they parted he still held her hand and felt it slip slowly away as she left the cell.

The weeks were like years. Felix and George were kept in separate cells, confined in the cold prison. They knew that Christmas was approaching, and they listened to the sounds of activity in the city. When the wind was blowing in their direction, the sound of joyful voices could be clearly heard from the street, a painful contrast to the stark emptiness of the cell. Still, it cheered them and they were reminded of the joy within them—the joy of their relationship with Christ.

On the afternoon of Christmas Eve, Trini and Anna along with Felix's brother Heinrich came to the tower. They brought with them gifts of food and messages of support from many of their friends in the Zollikon community. In spite of the circumstances, they had a festive spirit, bringing a celebration of the special holiday to the prison cell. Felix tried to be as cheerful as possible, but, and he told no one of this, he felt that it would be the last time he would see his loved ones. He purposely kept the conversation lighthearted, wanting them to remember a pleasant time. All too soon it was time for them to go. There were smiles through tears, well wishes through pain, holding on and letting go.

Two days after Christmas, Zwingli came to the prison. As Ulrich and Felix met, there was a momentary return to those early days when they had enjoyed working together. They greeted each other with the familiar "shalom" they had so often used in their study of Hebrew. But the distance between them now made the word of peace merely a facade.

Zwingli expressed his regrets, "Felix, you and I were once great colleagues. We are of similar age. Your gift of theology and languages was a stimulus and a challenge to me. It is too bad that our ways have parted."

"The change, Ulrich, is not of my choosing. We were together as disciples of Christ, together on the path of *sola scriptura*. Our basic difference now is whether his word is authority or whether the City Council is to give direction to the church."

"Don't go over that again." Zwingli was quickly irritated. "You well know how important it is for the church to have the power of the City Council to carry through our reformation. Without their power we would be ground under the heel of Rome."

"But the church is not identical with society. There is no way that you can think biblically of the total social system as Christian. And persons must make their own step of faith to come into the fellowship of Christ."

Their conversation continued for over an hour. Felix finally said, "Ulrich, it is imperative that the church be truly his church, that it order its life by the mandate of Christ. We of the church should let the state be the state, even though functioning outside of the will of Christ. If, as you hold, there are Christians in the magistracy, they should call it to responsible action which will make possible the freedom for the church to function by the will of God. With such a separation and mutual respect the total society will be the better."

Ulrich looked at Felix with near disgust in his eyes. "You are an idealist!" he spat. "Now I must bid you farewell. May your faith grant you the satisfaction that you need for your fulfillment." With that, he strode out of the prison cell.

Felix was able, by trading some of his gifts, to secure writing paper from the turnkey. He would at least write an admonition to this fellow brethren. If there were no further opportunity of interchange with them he would at least send a written message, his last words. With only a brief introduction, he began to pour out his heart.

"My heart rejoices in God who gives me much knowledge and wisdom that I may escape the eternal and never-ending death," he wrote. "Therefore, I praise thee, O Lord Christ from heaven, that thou dost turn away my sorrow and sadness; thou whom God has sent me as a Savior and for an example and a light, and who has called me into his heaven, already before my end has come, that I should have eternal joy with him, and should love him and all his righteousness, which exists here, and which shall endure forever hereafter, and without which nothing avails or subsists; hence so many who do not have this in truth, are deceived by a vain opinion.

"But alas! How many are found at the present who boast of the gospel and speak, teach, and preach much about it, but are full of hatred and envy, and who have not the love of God in them, whose deceit is known to all the world, as we have experienced in these latter days, that those who have come to us in sheep's clothing are ravening wolves, who hate the pious on the earth and obstruct the way to life and to the true sheepfold. Thus do the false prophets and hypocrites of this world, who curse and pray with the same mouth but whose life is disorderly. They call upon the authorities to kill us, by which they destroy the very essence of Christianity.

"But I will praise the Lord Christ, who exercises all patience toward us; for he instructs us with his divine grace and shows love to all men, according to the nature of God his heavenly Father, which none of the false prophets are able to do.

"Here we must observe this difference, that the sheep of Christ seek the praise of God; this is their choice, and they do not suffer themselves to be hindered either by possessions or temporal good, for they are in the keeping of Christ. The Lord Christ compels no one to come to his glory; only those that are willing and prepared attain unto it by true faith and baptism."

Felix put down his pen and walked around the small cell, thinking. There was so much that he wanted to say. He continued writing.

"Whenever a person brings forth genuine fruits of repentance, the heaven of eternal joy is, through grace, purchased and obtained for him by Christ, through the shedding of his innocent blood, which he so willingly poured out; thereby showing us his love, and enduing us with the power of his Spirit, and whoever receives and uses it grows and is made perfect in God.

"Only love to God through Christ shall stand and prevail; not boasting, denouncing, or threatening. It is love alone that is pleasing to God; he that cannot show love shall not stand in the sight of God. With the true love of Christ we make friends of the enemy; he that would be an heir with Christ is taught that he must be merciful, as the Father in heaven is merciful.

"Christ never accused anyone, as do the false teachers of the present day; from which it is evident that they do not have the love of Christ, nor understand his Word; and still they would be shepherds and teachers; but at least they will have to despair, when they shall find that everlasting pain shall be their recompense, if they do not reform.

"Christ also never hated anyone; neither did his true servants, but they continued to follow Christ in the true way, as he went before them. The light of life they have before them and are glad

225

to walk in it; but those who are hateful and envious and do thus wickedly betray, accuse, smite, and quarrel; they cannot be Christians. There are those who run before Christ as thieves and murderers and under a false pretense shed innocent blood. By this we may know them that are not on the side of Christ; for they, as children of Belial, prompted by envy, destroy the ordinances of Jesus Christ; even as Cain slew his brother Abel, when God accepted the offerings of Abel.

"With this I will finish my discourse, desiring that all the pious be mindful of the fall of Adam, who when he accepted the advice of the serpent and became disobedient to God, the punishment of death came upon him. Thus it shall also happen to those who do not accept Christ, but resist him, love this world, and have not the love of God. And thus I close with this, that I will firmly adhere to Christ and trust in him, who is acquainted with all my needs and can deliver me. Amen."

Felix closed his letter with a notation of various Scriptures such as: 1 Peter 5:1; John 16:20; Galatians 5:21; John 5:42; Matthew 7:15; 2 Thessalonians 3:7; John 10:3; Acts 2:38; Luke 6:36; John 8:12; John 10:1; Genesis 4:8, 3:6; 1 John 2:15; and John 5:42. Having completed his writing, he shared it with George and George in turn showed Felix what he had written.

The Murder Tower was quiet during the next few days. But midafternoon on January 5, they had just finished their lunch of a bowl of soup when their cell doors were opened. Felix and George were brought out to stand before several members of the council and officers of the magistrates. A crier entoned that they were to hear the decision of "my lords" of the Zurich City Council. A judgment was read which condemned them both for being advocates of the Anabaptist heresy contrary to the will of the church and of the council of the city of Zurich.

The sentence for George Blaurock was read next. He was to be publicly lashed and expelled from the city, never again to return on pain of death. Felix breathed a sigh of joyful relief. George could continue the work.

The magistrate now turned to Felix and began to read.

Because contrary to Christian order and custom Felix Manz has become involved in Anabaptism, has accepted it, taught others, and become a leader and beginner of these things; because he has confessed having said that he wanted to gather those who desired to accept Christ and follow him, to unite himself with them through baptism, and to let the rest live according to their faith; because he and his followers have separated themselves from the Christian church and are about to raise up and prepare a sect of their own under the guise of a Christian meeting and church; because he has condemned capital punishment, and in order to increase his following has boasted of certain revelations from the Pauline epistles; and because such doctrine is harmful to the unified usage of all Christendom and leads to offense, insurrection, and sedition against the government, to the shattering of the common peace, brotherly love, and civil cooperation, and to all evil; therefore Felix Manz shall be delivered to the executioner, who shall tie his hands, put him into a boat, take him to the lower hut, there strip his bound hands down over his knees, place a stick between his knees and arms, and thus push him into the water and let him perish in the water; thereby he shall have atoned to the law and justice . . . . His property shall also be confiscated by my lords.

George and Felix stood for a moment in silence. Felix had no thoughts, only resignation, almost relief that it was finished. He felt George's arms surrounding him and the big man's tears on his face.

"God will be with you," George said.

"And God be with you."

There was time for no more. The officers led George away for the beating to which he was sentenced. Two of the officers stepped up, one on each side of Felix. One of them had a rope and the other placed Felix's hands together before him. Quickly they bound his hands at the wrists. For a moment, Felix felt near panic, but he closed his eyes and breathed in deeply, praying for strength and comfort.

The members of the council turned their backs and started out of the door. The officers followed, leading Felix out of the prison.

From the Wellenberg Tower they led him down the street to the Fish Market. The afternoon sun bounced golden reflections off the dark waters of the Limmat. It illuminated the narrow city streets, and although Felix's eyes were still not accustomed to the light and he could scarcely see faces, he could tell that many people had lined the path, watching the dismal procession. Suddenly, Felix threw back his head and began to sing, praising God with his strong, clear voice. As they passed small groups of people, he called out his testimony, telling them that he was about to die for the truth.

When they crossed the bridge at the Fish Market to the other side of the Limmat River, the officers finished binding Felix's hands and ankles. One of Zwingli's preachers came to his side and spoke sympathetically to him. He urged him to be converted to the acceptable church and to give up his Anabaptism. But another voice overtook that of the preacher. It was Felix's mother crying out to him at a distance. He searched for her and found her with his brother Heinrich, standing by the bank of the Limmat. She was calling to him to be faithful, to be steadfast to Jesus!

Felix turned to the religious man beside him and said, "Jesus asked his disciples, 'Are you able to be baptized with the baptism that I am baptized with?' Today I share that baptism of death as a disciple of my Master."

Once again, hearing his brother's voice joining his mother's in their call of encouragement, he responded in full voice. Loudly and clearly he sang out, "I offer my life as a sacrifice unto the Lord. In manus tuas, Domine, commendo spiritum meum. Into your hands, Lord, I commit my spirit."

Joyfully Felix sang the praise of God as they placed him in the boat. They stripped his arms over his knees, placed a stick through so that he could not struggle, and dropped him over the side of the boat into the ice-cold, swirling waters of the Limmat River.

His body was removed, to be buried in the Saint Jakob's Cemetery in Zurich. His spirit had gone home. He waits with the redeemed for the completion of the Master's work, calling a people for his name out of the world.

The Author

Myron S. Augsburger was born at Delphos, Ohio, in 1929. Educated at Eastern Mennonite College and Seminary and at Goshen Biblical Seminary, he served as a pastor in several congregations in the Mennonite Church in Florida and Virginia. As a young man he began an evangelistic ministry in interchurch meetings, which he continues. In the early 1960s he completed Th.M. and Th.D. programs at Union Theological Seminary, Richmond, Va.

Myron served as president of Eastern Mennonite College and Seminary, Harrisonburg, Va., 1965-80. Following a year as a scholar-in-residence at Princeton Theological Seminary, he and his wife, Esther (Kniss), went to Washington, D.C., under several Mennonite mission boards and planted a Mennonite church on Capitol Hill. In 1988 he began as president of the Christian College Coalition while continuing service in the Washington congregation as Minister of the Word.

Augsburger has written a number of books on inspirational and theological themes, commentaries on several New Testament books, and several historical novels published by Herald Press. One of them, *Pilgrim Aflame,* has been produced as a film by Sisters and Brothers, a young film production association in the Mennonite Church.